"Sprinkled with real recipes and hints of magic realism throughout, this tale of homecoming makes for a light bite to satiate yourself with."
—*Vogue* (HK)

"Lim serves up love, loss, heritage, and hints of the supernatural on a silver platter in this magical and mouthwatering debut. . . . This eminently filmable tale of finding one's own path while honoring one's history is delicious and spellbinding."
—*Publishers Weekly* (starred review)

"Exquisitely written, [this book by] Roselle Lim sifts through the complicated relationships between mothers and daughters, the freedom in unraveling family secrets, and the power of resilience."
—Amy E. Reichert, author of *The Coincidence of Coconut Cake*
and *The Optimist's Guide to Letting Go*

"Roselle Lim serves up a feast for the senses and the heart with this magical tale of love, loss, and redemption in San Francisco's Chinatown. . . . *Natalie Tan's Book of Luck & Fortune* explores the hidden ties of family, mental illness, and desires lost and found, through the delectably transformative power of food."
—Yangsze Choo, *New York Times* bestselling author of
The Ghost Bride and *The Night Tiger*

"Heaped with heart and topped with the sweetest sprinkle of magic, creating a literary and culinary feast. Infused with ancient traditions and tantalizing recipes, [this book by] Roselle Lim cooks up a mouthwatering tale that's sure to delight!"

—Lori Nelson Spielman, *New York Times* bestselling author of *The Life List*

. . . . .

Titles by Roselle Lim

. . . . .

Natalie Tan's Book of Luck & Fortune
Vanessa Yu's Magical Paris Tea Shop
Sophie Go's Lonely Hearts Club
Night for Day

Night

for

Day

ROSELLE LIM

ACE
NEW YORK

ACE
Published by Berkley
An imprint of Penguin Random House LLC
penguinrandomhouse.com

Library of Congress Cataloging-in-Publication Data

Names: Lim, Roselle, author.
Title: Night for day / Roselle Lim.
Description: First edition. | New York: Ace, 2024.
Identifiers: LCCN 2023022025 (print) | LCCN 2023022026 (ebook) |
ISBN 9780593335642 (trade paperback) | ISBN 9780593335659 (ebook)
Subjects: LCGFT: Romance fiction. | Fantasy fiction. | Novels.
Classification: LCC PR9199.4.L5545 N54 2024 (print) |
LCC PR9199.4.L5545 (ebook) | DDC 813/.6—dc23/eng/20230605
LC record available at https://lccn.loc.gov/2023022025
LC ebook record available at https://lccn.loc.gov/2023022026

First Edition: February 2024

Printed in the United States of America
1st Printing

Book design by Alison Cnockaert

To Andria Bancheri-Lewis
And those who love to escape impossible situations

Night

for

Day

Prologue

***

AT 4:00 A.M. on a Sunday, the stumbling souls inside the nightclub poured out from the Hippodrome's exits. They bypassed the empty bar and didn't notice the two patrons sitting four barstools apart. She cradled an old-fashioned while he swished a half-empty golden Tripel in a chalice. Smooth jazz filtered through the speakers, which had blared EDM an hour earlier, vibrating every particle in the building.

She made a vague gesture with her wrist. "I miss the smoke. It used to blanket the entire city until it filled their lungs and desiccated their fragile bodies. Insignificant specks. The only difference between them and the other animals is their ability to speak. Even then, it might be more of a curse than a redeeming quality."

"I think they have potential. It may take a few more millennia to see the evidence."

"For once, I won't disagree." She lifted her glass and took a healthy sip. "Your side should concede. This war has gone on long enough. Your losses are far greater than ours. How many more useless cease-fires do we have to negotiate? It doesn't work."

He snapped his fingers and refilled the beer in his chalice, complete with a thick, foaming head. "Round and round. Always in this endless cycle." His deep voice took on an undulating tone. "It's the boredom of it all. Don't you want an end to this? For one faction to be declared the victor."

"I suppose that could be a refreshing change. Of course, my side will win." She raised her glass and let out a deep-throated laugh. "The war has kept us all busy. There isn't anything more invigorating than conflict."

"How about power?" He snapped his fingers, and the room hushed to silence. Every living being aside from the two froze, yet the analog clock behind the bar and the screens kept broadcasting. The demonstration elicited a slight uptick in her left brow. She countered with a pointing gesture that sent the blank-eyed bartender sailing into the air, rattled vigorously like the martini shaker in his left hand.

Within one minute, everything had been restored to its place, including the bartender, who continued making his cocktail. Humanity resumed, as it had, since the beginning. Short lives moved about fulfilling these base needs until Death harvested them and they crumbled into dust.

"Imagine being able to do what we want with this world. What better prize is there for the victors?" He tilted his head. "The freedom. No more curfews in our interactions with these mortals. I suppose in your case, you can burn it all down and remake a new world—an endless, bloody battlefield."

She rubbed her hands together.

"The winning faction gets to draw up the terms. It'll put an end to our squabbling and brawling—"

"Then we should propose something together. It'll be received better by *them*." She pulled a cocktail napkin from underneath her drink and withdrew a sleek black fountain pen from the air. "How should we decide this?"

"*We* shouldn't, because *they*'ll never agree to it."

"This is our war. Why should we allow outside interference?"

"Because it's the only thing we haven't tried. We need something interesting to break this stalemate."

A drunken couple tottered toward the stretch of counter between them. The mortal woman giggled as she tossed her enormous rainbow-sequined reticule over her shoulder. Mascara dripped down the corners of her brown eyes and smeared across the tops of her cheeks. Her short hair puffed out on the right side. Her male companion's face matched the shade of his green tracksuit. Swaying, he had a hand over his mouth and his other arm wrapped around her waist for support.

"Them?"

"Why not? It's the most dangerous wager we can make. Of course, it doesn't have to be *these* particular smelly mortals. We can choose anyone we want."

"Then make them fight to the death in an outdoor arena. It'll be glorious. Perhaps we can also add other animals to make it fun. Big ones with sharp teeth and claws." She noted the disapproving expression on his face and rolled her eyes. "Tell me your objections."

"Violence is what we know and what we practice. It's how

we got here in the first place. *They*'ll never approve. However, I agree with the two mortal participants. Better if they're unaware of their task."

She scribbled down the accepted proviso. "Then they'd be charged with choosing a side. To make it harder, both should choose the same side. This eliminates any doubt of the results."

"That sounds good. Add that. We'll also need to confine these two. No mortal in their right mind would want to participate of their own free will." He stretched out his arms and cracked his knuckles. "They'll need to be engaged in some sort of menial work while they decide. Separating them should eliminate the possibility of collusion."

The two continued to make plans. This marked the first time not a drop of immortal blood was shed in the presence of two opposing members of warring factions. Perhaps, there was a smidgen of hope for change.

1

Camille

· · · · ·

Present day

· · · · ·

MISTAKES WERE MEANT to be in the rearview mirror—not walking, breathing, and able to cup your cheek to stoke every single smoldering memory long buried for self-preservation.

He shouldn't whisper my name as if he never stopped doing so for the past two years.

Even now, my fingers itched to reacquaint myself with the beauty of his face, then to trace the slight cleft in his chin down his smooth throat, and ever farther down, to where our once shared intimacy implied permission and invitation.

"Camille, I never thought I'd see you again, let alone in London." The way my name rolled off his tongue and slid through his lips always elicited the same response—it felt like a hot kiss at the nape of my neck.

Ward Dunbar. The mistake I'd commit again and again even knowing that the result would always be heartbreak.

"Job interview. If I get it, I'll be moving here." I adjusted the neckline of my buttoned dress shirt, expanding the view of bronzed skin below my collarbones. My traitorous body always reacted to him when he was in physical proximity. Easier to shut down my hormones through the sterility of a black glass screen.

He brushed an errant dark blond strand off his forehead. "I'm here for the same. Though I've passed the interview part."

The skies overhead darkened—clusters of gray clouds huddling together in conference. It had been sunny five minutes ago. Late-spring weather in London changed on a whim with wicked fickleness, and we were sliding into the heat of summer. I packed an umbrella and a cardigan in my lavender vegan leather tote, but I didn't account for him. My purse didn't contain what I'd need to cope with the nuclear fallout of a failed relationship.

Avoidance therapy was the only method that worked. Putting thousands of miles between us and preventing myself from checking his social media accounts fueled a comfortable sense of forgetfulness—the kind that allowed me to function on a daily basis, but didn't prevent an occasional damaging slipup. It didn't hurt that he hadn't had any long-term relationships since then. Moving to Manhattan helped, and London should have cured me completely.

I was wrong.

Two days ago, I slipped and checked his Instagram. The selfie at an outdoor bookstall on the South Bank caused me to stop breathing for a few seconds. He was here and in the same city. I wasn't thinking when I sent him a direct message asking to meet at this bookshop. It was pure instinct—I turned off my brain and my heart took over, grabbing the wheel and changing the direction of my life.

"I never thought you'd leave LA." I resisted the urge to straighten the bent corner of his collar. No tie. I'd been the one responsible for those. His long, elegant fingers had other talents.

"I needed a change. This opportunity was as good a time as any." He tipped his head toward the bookshop. "It's going to rain. Can we duck in and chat?"

I followed him into one of the most beautiful little shops in Westminster. These buildings reminded me of an eclectic bookshelf—the windows and architectural details were charming, decorated spines of antique leather. Weathered stone, traditional painted wooden signs mixed with flashy modern ones and clean-line aesthetics. The mix of old and new fitting together in seamless coexistence.

To me, the past and present were constantly at war when I thought about Ward.

As if on cue, the curtain of rain began as he stepped into the shop. I caught a bit of it at the ends of my long hair and the back of my shirt. Again, I was reminded of what I'd be getting into if I decided to have another round in his bed—because that was where it always began.

He headed for the science fiction and fantasy section. He plucked the newest N. K. Jemisin novel from the shelf, tucked it under his arm, and continued to browse the titles, tracing his finger downward on the ones that perked his interest.

"So how does this affect your job in LA?" I took a step forward but maintained a safe distance. The scent of his subtle cologne along with the aroma of Irish cream coffee would undo my crumbling defenses. "Are you on sabbatical?"

Ward's cushy position at a very exclusive and trendy art

gallery in LA was everything he ever wished for—flexible hours, the heavy array of movie stars and wealthy client meetings, and the perfect conduit to maximize his appeal. No one was impervious. He disarmed you with his good looks and gentle tone, then went in for the kill with the way he could make you feel. Empathy combined with charm was lethal.

"I quit."

I almost fell against a nearby bookcase. "You did what?"

"It's . . . I needed a change." He reached for my elbow to help me regain my balance. The heat of his touch distracted me. "I accepted a job yesterday and I start tomorrow. Now knowing that you're here, I'd say it's a great move."

Ward didn't let go yet. The worst part was that I didn't want him to. Instead, his fingertips grazed the inside of my forearm, tracing lazy circles with his thumb. I placed my hand on his.

"Do you ever think that—"

I didn't let him finish.

I covered his mouth with mine, devouring his words—my hands pressed against his hard chest, fingertips clinging against the thin silk fabric yearning for the lean muscle lying underneath. He kissed me back as if the present never existed, as if the past two years were a hazy dream and that the truth was that we were never apart.

It was a lie, but we both wanted to believe it. My mistake to repeat and, yes, it was his as well.

Everything rushed back. The flood of every single reason why we were so good together: the Sunday picnics and walks in Humboldt Park to visit the ducks, the easy late-night conversations curled up on the couch dissecting what we watched

on movie night, merienda at my parents' house on the weekends, and those spontaneous escape room dates.

I never forgot how we met—he helped calm my nerves
heading into my exams. I had one of my usual panic attacks
before finals in college. It didn't matter how much I'd studied,
I always panicked. He recognized the signs right away. He led
me into a quiet, unused workroom and talked me through
breathing exercises while holding my hand. He told me that
his younger brother had them and he could understand.

Before this, I chalked him up as one of those pretty white
boys who had no substance. This was the first time I came to
realize that he was one of those origami magic balls with infinite
folds. Every time I peeled back a piece of paper, I found another
reason why I liked him, and in due time, it turned into love.

Even now, I still loved him.

THE MARATHON BETWEEN the bedsheets was always
the easiest part of our relationship. The language of skin
against skin silenced any objections. The complications began
as soon as the scorching kisses ended.

As I lay in bed with him, I didn't want to acknowledge the
time; instead, I dragged my fingertips across the smooth mus-
cles of his abdomen. When it came to this, I was the child who
didn't want to leave a party because it was too much of a good
time. Didn't want to deal with any consequences after the fun
was over.

Through the slight part in the blackout curtains, the
capsules in the London Eye hung static with the rising sun,
marking the transition from dim blue to radiant pinks, violets,

and eventually golds and oranges. If he'd been awake, he'd wax poetic about the contrasting palettes of sunrises and sunsets. His fascination with them fueled his need to highlight passages in his beloved books whenever they were mentioned.

"That internal alarm clock of yours is uncanny." Sleep still coated his voice. He drew lazy circles on my naked shoulder with his thumb. "Your interview isn't until closer to noon."

"I still need to prepare."

The wrong parts of him stiffened.

And there it was. Being with him didn't change me.

"Let's compromise. One more hour in bed and I can help quiz you after our shower."

The mention of the promised help melted the last of my resistance. The morning ritual of communal showers started off every day on the best note—precious time spent without words—and he gave the best massages.

He chuckled, noticing the dreamy smile on my lips.

His left hand dipped under the sheets, and again, I'd forgotten every thought in my head except us, and how well we fit together.

MY JOB INTERVIEW was later that morning. My rationality returned as soon as we left the hotel room and parted ways. Ward hopped into a black cab headed to Carnaby Street to pick up a last-minute item before his shift.

Lethe's Curiosities was an antique shop in the shadow of Westminster Abbey and a convenient short walk from my location. I planned the entire trip to provide for any contingencies, and one of them involved transportation failures.

The job was lucrative and paid well over six figures without even factoring in the conversion rate. I'd be in charge of acquisitions and running the shop on my own after a probationary period. The quiet, posh neighborhood felt safe for the night shift, which probably accounted for the high pay grade. My first impression of the building was that it was upscale— implying a top-line security system and all the amenities.

I stood before the midnight-black facade featuring gold-painted, serif capital letters. The tall windows showed two vignettes on either side of the door. A trace of camphor sprinkled the air. The heavy occult aesthetic prickled the skin at the back of my neck. It was subtle and tasteful, in line with the type of establishment I'd researched. No skulls, creepy porcelain dolls, or spooky clown figures in sight so far.

I couldn't shake the odd feeling that something very old was here—far older than Londinium itself. The last time I had this feeling was when I held a Babylonian fertility idol in my gloved hands during my stint at the Field Museum in Chicago. It was the palpable sensation of being an insignificant speck in the river of time.

The left was an arrangement showcasing a Napoléon III Gothic writing desk paired with a matching high-backed chair with raven-black brocade upholstery. Various ornate, gilded mirrors hung around the desk, hovering in the air, probably anchored by invisible industrial fishing lines or wires. My reflection in each mirror was different—almost as if I were aging in each one, a decade here, three decades there, all eerie enough that I had to avert my eyes.

Might not be a true mirror but some sort of high-end plasma screen with a rapid aging filter from Instagram or Snapchat.

Even when dealing with antiquity, technology intruded like an unwanted visitor.

The other window was draped with a black velvet background with a Gothic Victorian double-door curio cabinet as the centerpiece. The top followed a pointed design reminiscent of church steps and roofs. The paned glass duplicated the motif—the design of leaded glass mimicked the wrought iron fencing surrounding grounds and graveyards.

Again my reflection splashed against many gilded mirrors floating against the velvet background. This time, I was aging backward, seeing my face as a teenager, a tween, a six-year-old, a toddler, and a baby. The results were fairly accurate.

The company must have contracted a tech firm for the display.

I checked my watch. Ten minutes before and the right time to make my entrance. I tugged on the polished brass handles and stepped into the shop.

"Ah, Ms. Buhay. You're early." My interviewer and potential supervisor greeted me at the door. "Welcome."

Mr. Samson was a septuagenarian expat with a soothing voice well suited for narrating nature documentaries. He was handsome in his old age and made me wonder what he looked like in his prime. Perhaps I could ask him to stand in front of those mirrors outside.

He pronounced my last name perfectly. Boo-hai. My Filipino last name often tripped up American tongues and created a mangled auditory mess. I could have gone as some of my relatives have, ignoring the mistake in order to conform. I was born and raised in Morton Grove, a suburb of Chicago, and the most American trait I could think of was to stubbornly correct people until they get it right, no matter how exhausting or tedious. My last name in Tagalog meant "life," and I refused to hear anything but its true pronunciation.

The minimalism of the window display contrasted with the cluttered interior, embodying the Victorian hoarder aesthetic. Every shelf, cabinet, and leveled surface housed a priceless antique in perfect condition free of dust. Thankfully, the polished wooden-paneled floor was clear, and the set paths throughout were wide enough to alleviate any anxiety of breakage or accidents from an errant limb.

Instead of an expected musty smell, the shop had the sterility of a museum, yet there was a faint trace of sandalwood incense lingering in the air. The soft hum of the air-conditioning vents kept the temperature comfortable, unlike some of the stores I'd been to. Taking the tube wilted me. Give me months of frigid winter and I'd be fine, but sweltering summer heat without air-conditioning was a deal-breaker.

Mr. Samson pulled out my printed résumé and tapped the sheet. "Your credentials are impressive. If it were up to me, I'd be ready to hire you, but I've been told to conduct the formal interview first." He gestured toward two Queen Anne chairs with golden brocade upholstery to the left of the cash register.

We took our seats.

I crossed my legs at the ankles and kept my hands stacked on my lap.

"This is by no means a rigorous inquiry. The owner of the shop insisted on only three questions." He withdrew his reading glasses along with a folded piece of paper from his inside jacket pocket.

My shoulders lowered. This was better than a multiday

battery of pointless interviews with different department heads. One of the reasons I wanted this position was the appeal of dealing with fewer people, because the night shift meant minimal clients, and appraisals and acquisitions were the bulk of my responsibilities.

"How well do you adapt to change?" He squinted at the paper and then at me.

"I can manage it with ease. I tend to prepare for any scenario to be able to handle anything thrown at me."

He flattened the paper's folds with his palm on his lap. "In addition to the pay, what else do you require for this job?"

Better to ask and be turned down than never to have the courage to bring it up. "A flat or rental and possibly grocery delivery service." The nearest supermarket wasn't within walking distance, and the thought of using transit didn't appeal to me. I used a similar service in Manhattan and loved it too much to give it up.

"I doubt that will be an issue. My employer is quite generous." Mr. Samson cleared his throat. "Time for the last question. Are you a believer?"

I narrowed my eyes. "Can you clarify?"

My interviewer shook his head.

Strange. This could be a religious inquiry, in which case, because I was a Roman Catholic, it would be a yes. My family was devout, and I tried to make it to mass on Sundays in New York. I'd been lapsing with my work schedule and often changed the subject when my parents asked. My relationship with God was personal and not communal.

"Yes, I am."

Mr. Samson grinned and rose to his feet. "Excellent. You are officially hired. Can you start tomorrow?"

"Yes, I'd love to."

Moving to London would be a refreshing change from Manhattan. I could start new here, and then applying to Sotheby's or Christie's would be a viable option for my future. This was a great first step toward my career goals.

"Bring your luggage. You'll be able to see the flat after your shift is done." His weary smile radiated kindness. "It'll be nice to have company. I've been running this place on my own for quite a long time. Look at me ramble on. Should I go over your duties?"

"Yes, please."

"Your responsibilities are simple. You are to deal with clients as they walk in, no matter how unusual. Process the acquisition, and you'll be done."

"Do you have a catalog of all the stock?" I glanced around at the overfilled shelves. "If not, I can build one."

His nod of approval was promising. "That is a wonderful idea. I can tell that you'll be a great fit here. I can answer all of your questions when you start tomorrow night."

I'd been told countless times that I was far too judgmental for my own good. But it had served me too well over the years to shed the habit. In this case, Mr. Samson hadn't set off any internal alarms. Instead, he gave off a warmth and familiarity I'd never encountered from a stranger before. My gut was at ease, and though it was rare and strange, I trusted my instincts.

After a brief goodbye, I exited Lethe's Curiosities and ducked into the nearest Pret A Manger to grab an iced latte and a chocolate croissant. I took a counter seat near the window while I nibbled on the flaky pastry and waited for the adrenaline from the interview to wear off.

The city in the two days I'd seen it was as charming as I expected after the copious amount of research I'd done. The various regional accents almost didn't sound like English. I supposed the same could be said about Americans and our verbal quirks. I'd love to listen in on a Brooklynite and Geordie conversation.

After finishing up at the café, I walked into a clothing store and browsed through potential additions to my wardrobe. As I picked a pencil skirt and a printed collared shirt, my phone rang with Ward's new London number. "You got the job, right?"

"I did." I let out a rare squeal. "I guess I'm staying here."

"We'll be seeing a lot of each other . . . that is, if that's what you want."

It had never been about the lack of love on both sides. It was everything else. The thought of living in this city with him in it fit into my plans. Perhaps this would be the fresh start we needed to make it work this time.

"Yes. I want to. Let's try again."

2

Ward

. . . . .

DAY ONE

. . . . .

TO WARD DUNBAR, Camille was his sun.

His wish was granted when she returned to his life. The searing kiss at the bookshop reminded him why he never stopped thinking of her and what could have been in the last two years. He suspected—rightfully so—that it was his fault, yet he didn't possess the wisdom or enlightenment to understand why. Shorter life spans weren't conducive to grand epiphanies in general.

Ward believed anything could be salvaged or wiped clean with a fresh start. What he should have done was have a postmortem discussion with Camille, but of course, he wouldn't do such a thing. He dreaded that doing so would break them apart again.

Mortal fear was a powerful motivator.

After Camille's job interview, the former couple met outside the Pret A Manger in the afternoon.

"You're serious." He took her hands in his. "We can do this?"

She nodded. "Unless you don't feel . . ."

He lifted her fingertips to his lips. "I want this more than you can ever know. We have a brand-new start. This is a gift. The past is far behind us."

A shadow fell over Camille's perfect face. "Is it though?"

Most of the breakups Ward witnessed were acrimonious—the kind that left both parties raw with so much vitriol that seeing the other person again would result in nothing less than a brawl. Emotions became an accelerant to searing combustion where all sense, good and common, was incinerated. Such were the ashes of romantic love.

It'd been two years, three months, and four days since the breakup.

He had offered to follow her to New York when she wanted him to move to LA. He couldn't live with the discomfort of a long-distance relationship. Ward often rationalized his allergy to adversity as justification for taking the easier path—that it wasn't a matter of the lack of love, but the question of why it had to be done. By his logic, the rat should bypass the maze to get to the cheese because the point of the experiment was feeding.

"We can't move forward until we talk about the past." She pressed her free hand against his chest. "Shouldn't we talk about this? Sort out everything before we even start again."

He wanted the past to stay buried. What he did next was out of survival—he leaned in and kissed her as if the simple act would smash every rearview mirror in the vicinity. She melted against him and moaned, arousing him.

Languages could be spoken or performed through touch.

In the case of this couple, physical chemistry was their preferred method of communication. The way their hands and lips found the right places in each other was biological as much as it was romantic. Mating rituals in the animal kingdom follow this pattern.

"I know what you're doing." She whispered in his ear and tapped his chin. "You're only putting off the inevitable."

"I know, because I don't want to lose you again."

She pulled away. Her dark brows knitted together and when paired with her full lips, swollen from his kisses, she appeared as conflicted as he was. "I get that. We have to do it though. I don't . . . can't go through *it* again."

"I promise we'll talk about it." He swallowed his honest lie with a subtle gulp.

"All right." She tucked a strand of dark hair behind her ear. "Sooner rather than later though."

"Why don't we figure out dinner first and go from there? There's a fantastic Japanese curry house close to your hotel."

"The sleepover is at my place again? I guess we can switch later to your place until we find more permanent accommodations."

Ward adjusted his shirt collar. He took her hand in his and she didn't pull away. He inhaled and allowed hope to fuel his steps as they walked from the tube station to her hotel. The rush of bodies and general foot traffic made it difficult to hold a conversation. Camille bristled at the heat. She always preferred a chilling blizzard to a heat wave—something about the ability to pile on more clothes being more versatile than stripping down to the skin. He was comfortable with higher temperatures. It might stem from spending his childhood running around wearing nothing but shorts in the summers at his aunt's farm.

He led the way to the restaurant, where they shimmied into a small booth by the front windows. London had such a different appeal from Chicago to him—the age of these buildings, the way the modern additions of glass and steel seamlessly blended into stone and mortar. He yearned to walk the city and explore every street and alleyway. The scale of time fascinated him as if being reminded of the existence of the world before his own short life became a source of wonder. It was the product of centering one's existence in the grand scheme of the universe.

Camille sipped her cup of hot matcha. "When do you start your job?"

"Tomorrow," he replied. "It'll be new to me, working at a high-end jewelry store. It's still art pieces with a unique provenance. Antiques, from what Madam Selene tells me. Six pieces were on display when I had my interview. The place is decked out in shimmering gold with a minimalist eye."

"Not sure if I'd be comfortable around all that opulence." Her fingers slipped the first two buttons of her blouse into place. The oppressive heat had caused her to undo them earlier. "The antique shop I'll be working at is nice, cozy, and elegant. They have these art installations in the front windows. I can't wait to hear what you think when you see them."

He widened his eyes. "Wait, you're going to be working with clients? Front facing and dealing with customers?"

"Yes. Don't act so shocked. Change can be a good thing. The benefits and pay tempted me enough to try it. It's supposed to be a low-traffic situation, and it's also the night shift."

He reeled from the revelation. Camille would normally want something more private and behind the scenes. She loved research and cataloging, thriving and getting lost in the nitty-gritty of the details. When they were in college, she'd be in the library when she wasn't in class or out with him. She'd told him it was her happy place: "Books are uncomplicated. You don't get into arguments with them, and if you do, it means you haven't found the right one."

"You'll be safe?" he asked.

"I've been told the security system is top-notch. It's also in a nice neighborhood—nothing dodgy. It's under the shadow of Parliament and Westminster Abbey. There's this amazing Japanese bistro at the courthouses across the bridge that I can walk to for an early dinner before my shift. Where's your work?"

"A few blocks away from the Globe Theatre. Can you believe it?" He rubbed his palms together. "We're within walking distance! I can't wait to take you there for a date night. You can pick the play."

He already knew the answer before she said it. "It has to be *A Midsummer Night's Dream* or *The Tempest*."

"I'll check the schedule and see what's coming up."

Camille leaned back, and her attention wandered to the people walking by outside. "I can't believe we're here. Together even. Of all the massive surprises and coincidences . . ."

Ward reached across the table and grasped her fingertips. "It's fate to me. Has to be."

"It might be." She lowered her eyes. "I'm trying my best to focus on the here and now and not to jump too far ahead."

Fate excused and rationalized all sorts of happenstances,

from picking up a penny off the ground to, in the case of these former lovers, their raison d'être. To clarify, Ward justified kismet as the invisible force that brought them together in the beginning and again now. He also hoped the four rounds of sex last night could only help their cause for reuniting.

Yet a frisson of fear traveled down his spine. In his mind, he rebuilt this relationship and how they'd be navigating London together for the next year at least. Losing her again would be devastating.

Camille tapped his arm. "You're lost in your own little world again, aren't you?"

"Yeah, sort of." He handed her the menu, and they both perused the items. "I suppose we better eat so we'll have energy later."

Ward gave her a not-so-subtle wink, and she laughed. Then everything was all right once more.

SEX WAS A means to an end—it depended on what ends you were trying to achieve. In Ward and Camille's case, the act served as a pleasurable truce to a mounting argument. She chased him about the past, and he hounded her about the future. All of this was conducted in a game of political verbiage— saying what they thought the other wanted to hear without committing to anything. Adding politics into the mix tended to sour all situations.

Words between them that morning were sparse. They agreed to meet after her shift. Ward kissed her goodbye before setting out for his first day of work, taking a brief stop at Carnaby Street to pick up something he spotted in a shop window two days ago. He bought Camille a small token to celebrate her new position.

Ward craned his neck to get a better look at the white-and-gold sign of Lethe's above. The high-end antiquities and jewelry shop had all of the features of any rival luxury chain. Through the glass windows, shimmering gold covered every surface, and it was the shade of warm, liquid honey gold that radiated and magnified every beam of light.

He opened the white-framed wooden doors with full glass inserts and stepped inside. The faint citrus scent of satsuma complemented the interior. Unlike traditional shops dominated by glass box counters, this one displayed its rare, prized pieces in shadowbox display cases mounted on the walls. Camille would have appreciated the modern, minimalist aesthetic with museum gallery sensibilities in mind—emphasizing quality over quantity.

Madam Selene stood by the lone counter in the space with the register. Her knuckles gleamed as white as her teeth as she pored through her leather-bound book, index finger tracing back and forth on the ledger. She was a tiny Asian woman in her midseventies with the elegance and regal bearing of a monarch. No doubt she must have been a beauty in her prime, for she still was now. She'd have fit in well at one of his mother's charity galas back home in Chicago.

She acknowledged the wrapped parcel under his arm. "A gift for your sweetheart?"

"Yes." He let a wistful murmur escape. "I hope to give it to her after my shift."

His supervisor arched a long, drawn brow. The heavy gemstone rings on her fingers caught the overhead lights as she rubbed her hands together. The weight of those stones contrasted with her delicate fingers. Each ring represented a birthstone. The last two missing months were in her pendant earrings—citrine and diamond.

Ornamentation suitable for a purveyor of jewelry was the best advertisement. Ward Dunbar in his current attire and lack of frippery had missed the memo.

"The shop works by appointment. We have a very exclusive clientele. You'll soon see that there are only four." Madam Selene regarded her new hire with a shrewd eye. "I understand this may sound unusual to you—to have such an elaborate setup to cater to so few."

"This has to be for a short or trial period of time? It's hard to move this kind of inventory to a small pool."

"I've been told that it was open to a bigger group. I haven't been able to corroborate this. I know it seems like this is a lot of work, but I assure you that our work is *essential* and worth the effort."

Ward dismissed the way she emphasized the word. *Essential*, to him, was defined as frontline workers like paramedics, nurses, and grocery employees. He wasn't responsible for lives—far from it, he was selling baubles.

His boss gestured to the lone, golden-mirrored desk and the two matching chairs on either side. Her fingertips glided along the smooth, dust-free surface. "All transactions and negotiations must be made here. Remember, you are always being watched, Mr. Dunbar."

There was one visible security camera—a telltale black bubble of glass. If there were other surveillance cameras, the interior designer of this establishment must have seamlessly incorporated them. Ward never doubted their presence. This was a jewelry shop after all.

"All inventory is listed in this book, along with its value and price. If anyone tries to haggle, under no circumstances will you accommodate them. Negotiations are forbidden." She narrowed her eyes, the corners pressing into hard lines. "I hired you because of your charm and your ability to close a deal. This is about quality and quantity. I want you to sell the item to the right buyer and clear out these display cases."

Ward's impressive track record of sales in LA was the key to his hiring. Quantity had always been emphasized, and he delivered. "So there is a quota?"

"Yes. I want all six pieces sold. Our clientele is very wealthy and quite particular. They'll need careful guidance and maneuvering. Apparently, you can be frugal while having the deepest of pockets." She snapped the leather book closed and then slid it toward him. "Study and memorize this."

He flipped through the pages, and as expected, everything was meticulous and precise—almost like a pristine blueprint. "You mentioned earlier that we had an appointment system. This would be the VIPs, yes?"

Madam Selene arched a brow. The expression was further deepened when he flashed his trademark disarming grin. If anything, the wrinkles around the corners of her eyes multiplied, as did the grooves of her thin-lined mouth. "Anyone who walks into this establishment is an important guest. The ones who make appointments run a tighter schedule."

"And they take precedence over walk-ins?"

"We don't entertain those. If they want to get into this shop, they need to make an appointment. From what I've heard, it does take quite a bit of effort to get here."

"You're saying they're from out of town."

"Something like that. Remember, privacy is valued here, Mr. Dunbar. The appointments are in the drawer." She handed him the portfolio and turned to a section near the back. "Check this every morning."

He confirmed the page with today's date: Mr. King at 1:00 p.m. Underneath, the tight, small cursive script detailed his profile: weapons expert, Eastern Faction.

A wealthy arms dealer. Ward was accustomed to all sorts of rich folks—those who expected to be catered to, at first sight, to be known without an introduction, those who acted like their eccentricities were justified by their bank accounts, those who refused to pay even a single cent in tips, or those who did none of these. One of Camille's sayings was "Being rich magnifies all your traits, especially the rotten ones. It doesn't change who you are but rather exposes your true self. A gold-plated asshole is still very much an asshole."

Ward was the type who fed off the energy of others while in their presence, and his love was the opposite. She was an introvert to the core, though she camouflaged herself well as an extrovert in social settings. In the aftermath of a work party, he used to ensure she was undisturbed in the bedroom for at least half a day before ordering her favorite maki rolls at their beloved sushi joint.

Camille didn't need anyone to take care of her. He did it because he wanted to—anything to ease the anxiety that constantly plagued her. He loved her, after all, but clearly, there were limits. Otherwise, they'd still be together somewhere in America, breeding children and fattening their 401(k)s.

The chime above the doors marked the entrance of Mr. King.

A tall Asian man, sharply dressed in a black fitted jacket over a crimson silk dress shirt and slacks, stood at the entrance. His dark hair spiked in the front into prickly towers and highlighted dark brown eyes sparking with energy—not the manic kind fueled by chemicals. The way he shifted his shoulders was like a cage fighter right before a match was to start. His angular face was balanced by a straight nose and a slight cleft in his chin. He appeared to be in his early thirties, close to Ward's age.

"Ah, Mr. King, welcome, welcome!" Madam Selene pasted an unnatural expression on her face, which Ward guessed was a congenial sales tactic. The display of the gums-versus-teeth ratio, when paired with the ultra-widened eyes, was alarming.

Mr. King turned his attention toward Ward and bypassed the older woman with a subtle nod. "I see Madam Selene has been busy." He offered his left hand.

Ward walked over to greet him. "Mr. King, I presume."

The handshake electrified him. Ward twitched from the jolt of energy streaking through his nervous system. The static shock zap wasn't from a childish game of scuttling across a carpet, for there was no conductive material nearby. Before he had a chance to even contemplate the scientific ramifications, Mr. King gave his hand another firm squeeze.

Ward jumped this time. His heart thundered in his chest, almost leaping up to his throat. The coils of electricity zapped the tips of his wheat-blond hair. His brain skipped over the obvious blip in rationality like an intrepid scooter over a speed bump. It could have been static electricity, for all he knew. He pulled his hand away with a forced smile before noting the sparkle in Mr. King's brown eyes. "Quite a grip you have there."

"The handshake is a revealing gesture. Historically, it shows that you are unarmed." Mr. King tipped his chin up, revealing a cleanly shaven square jaw. "It shows your true nature. Your mettle, if you will."

Ward hadn't realized this would be a dick-measuring contest—not that he had ever participated in such an activity, figuratively or literally. Some men beat their chests, some buy the fanciest vehicle on the market, and others ditch their spouse for a younger make and model.

"Is there anything in particular that you're interested in?" Ward cleared his throat and steered his client toward the mounted glass boxes lining the walls.

"Yes, yes, time to stop browsing! You need to buy something." Madam Selene glared at Mr. King and pointed to the items. "These are quality pieces at reasonable prices."

She dragged the arms dealer toward the glass cases. There were six pieces on display: a Tang dynasty headdress and jewelry set, a jade Mayan necklace, a pair of gold Hellenistic earrings, an elaborate Nubian crown, a ruby pendant necklace, and a gold Greek ring. The leather portfolio contained all the details.

Madam Selene possessed the subtlety of a sledgehammer in the way she clucked over her client and berated him for his inability to buy anything. It might have been a high-pressure tactic if not for the desperate and frustrated nagging that followed. Berating a potential client was unprofessional at best and ineffective at worst.

Ward cleared his throat and made a vague gesture toward her.

She squinted and frowned, waving her hand as if swatting away a fly. He changed his strategy and feigned cluelessness by the desk—searching through the drawers and allowing the leather book to drop to the floor.

It worked. He caught the teacher's attention.

Her annoyance at his supposed incompetence was enough to wrench her away from Mr. King's side. She picked up the book and placed it on the desk. "You have to be more careful, Mr. Dunbar. This is your first day."

"Yes, it is. Shouldn't I try to figure some of this out by myself? Isn't it your goal for me to be independent and run the place on my own without constant supervision?"

She narrowed her eyes and let out a tentative yes.

"And I can see how frustrated you are that there hasn't been a sale. A great leader delegates. Allow me to handle what you've hired me for."

She crossed her arms. The flat line of her mouth almost eliminated any hint of the mauve lipstick she wore. "I suppose. I'll be in my office for most of the day and locking the door. With your background, I'm certain you should be selling something soon. Good luck on your first day and don't disappoint me."

Madam Selene walked to the back of the shop and disappeared behind one of the two doors. The audible click of the lock indicated it was the heavier door of the room marked Private.

Granted his newfound autonomy, Ward rubbed his palms together and walked toward Mr. King, who peered into the pristine glass boxes, leaning forward while keeping his hands clasped behind his back. Ward held his breath and waited. No alarms were triggered with Mr. King's proximity to the glass. When Mr. King pulled away, there were no halos of moisture on the smooth surface.

Again, the growing idea that all was not what it seemed persisted in Ward's mind. This pesky mosquito of a notion flitted around in his head, buzzing for attention. He could choose to question the parameters of reality, or he could plod on and perform his job. Of course, he decided on the easier task—the latter.

Mr. King repeated the examination before every piece until he stood before the Tang dynasty set.

"Do you want to see that one?" Ward checked the portfolio for the section on opening cases. "I can bring it out for viewing if you wish."

The arms dealer bowed and made a sweeping gesture with his arm. "Please do."

Ward had his share of unusual clients. Mr. King's behavior so far struck him as an eccentricity, not from entitlement or a proclivity of strange habits, but from something else he couldn't quite figure out yet—and he considered himself a good student of people.

Following the handwritten instructions, Ward pressed his palm against an unmarked spot to the left of the display case. The golden wall under his hand pulsed with a radiating warmth. He rationalized that it had to be cutting-edge technology and made a note to ask Madam Selene about it.

The front panel of glass receded into a secret compartment. The open case revealed the antique jewelry set showcased in two stands—one pedestal for the elaborate headdress and a slanted display tray for the earrings and brooch.

He moved the headdress first onto the desk, then to the tray as Mr. King settled into the chair on the other side of the table. Turquoise stones interwoven with fine strands and golden webbing created the illusion of clouds and rain. The blue-green marbled gemstones with gold veins were carved into circles, forming the bulk of the crown as long strands dangled down with turquoise teardrops like a veil. The moving parts of the headwear tinkled, playing an unknown wistful melody.

Mr. King hummed an accompanying harmony. Still sipping the tea of denial, Ward filed this under the growing list of unusual curiosities of the day. He put on the gloves in the drawer and withdrew a separate pair. "Would you like a closer examination?"

His client kept his hands folded on his lap. "I don't need to, I know this set well. I had it made especially for *her*."

"Oh, a replica." Ward removed the gloves and tucked both pairs back into the drawer. Madam Selene had envelopes shoved in the back of the leather portfolio containing the provenance papers of each piece. "Because this is from the Tang dynasty."

"No." Mr. King pointed to a broken piece around one of the stones near the apex of the headdress. "That happened when she missed playing for the emperor's spring banquet because she chose to stay in bed with me. She left the bauble at the corner of the mattress." His wolfish grin displayed a set of pointed canines. "It fell after one enthusiastic thrust."

As those words wound their way into Ward's ears, he

considered the possibility that the raunchy tall tale could be true—which would mean Mr. King was many hundreds of years old. True to his nature, Ward swept this bit of cognitive dissonance under the proverbial rug. It wasn't that he believed the man, it was more that he could have misheard and didn't have the urge to get clarification at the moment. Everyone stumbled on their words now and then.

"Are you interested in buying it, Mr. King?" he asked.

"Not today." Mr. King tapped his chin. "It wasn't really the reason why I came."

"And that is . . . ?"

"You tell me."

Ward blurted out his answer without hesitation. "To see me and get a feel of what I'm like."

"There might be hope for you after all, Mr. Dunbar." Mr. King pressed his index finger to his lips and winked. While whistling the haunting melody, he sauntered out the door, the bell chime ringing to signal his exit.

Ward returned the jewelry set back to its place in the glass box.

Madam Selene left him a series of housekeeping tasks to do—learning the current catalog, memorizing the short client list, and adding his own observations, and by the time he was on the last pages of the notes, it was time to clock out.

With Camille's gift in hand, he headed for the double doors. He'd already picked a charming pub three blocks away that would be perfect for fish and chips and the Islay whiskey on the cocktail menu. He was so focused on the future that the thought of the present had completely escaped him.

The door handles rattled as he pulled on them. Locked. He

dismissed it as an automatic security measure before making his way to the back to knock on Madam Selene's office door. Silence. Polite raps with his knuckles escalated to loud slaps of his palms against the wooden door. The theatrics yielded no answers.

"Madam Selene!" He kicked the solid door and winced when his toes rebounded against heavy steel. "I can't get out!"

He pressed his ear against the metal and didn't hear a sound. Where had she gone? In his search for a separate exit, he rushed into the bathroom to confirm that it had no windows or emergency exits. Ward pulled his phone from his pocket, and the screen was black as if the battery were dead. It had been fully charged when he left the hotel room with Camille this morning. It had been at most only seven hours since he started his shift.

The mosquitoes in his mind had now grown to critical mass. Still, he clung to the last shred of flimsy denial with the stubbornness of a lone man trying to hold back the tide with a piece of bent cardboard. Such was the human impulse's tenacity for mental preservation.

The front of the shop was full of windows— even the front doors had panels of glass. The city street with its passersby and traffic continued on as Ward stood in his fishbowl prison. He could see them, yet he doubted they could see him. Anyone else would stop and gawk at his desperate flailing.

He banged on the doors, fists pounding against the transparent surface, and again, nothing budged. He pressed his forehead against the glass and exhaled. No condensation or smudges, not even a trace of the lingering heat of his breath.

"Where the hell am I?" he asked himself aloud.

It was then that panic flooded every fiber of his being. Instinct took over—that of a trapped animal when it realizes its predicament. Though he was never one for violence or breaking the rules, it seemed to be the only option.

Ward grabbed one of the two chairs by the consultation table. He lifted it by the legs and hurled it toward one of the large windows. The glass shattered on impact, then reconstituted as if time rewound—each piece stitching back together as the chair itself traveled backward, catapulting toward him. He dove down, pressing his body flat against the floor to avoid it as the intact chair sailed over his head.

It smashed against the far wall.

No alarms went off.

The broken furniture reassembled, pieces of golden Lucite floating to find their spot in the missing whole. The chair even skittered across the floor to its rightful place, mirroring its partner across the desk.

Sinking down, Ward clutched his head between his hands, fingers threading through his hair and clutching his scalp.

What the hell had he gotten himself into now?

3

Camille

. . . . .

DAY ONE

. . . . .

AFTER MY SHIFT, I'd have a second chance.

It couldn't have been a coincidence that Ward and I ended up here in London together.

It had to have been a sign.

It must have been.

The antique store's window display had changed since yesterday—starry, pointed crystals and golden skulls hung like stars on invisible threads in a diamond pattern to showcase a trio of identical, full-length, gilded baroque oval mirrors. The reflection in the first one showed a whirling galaxy, spinning at an accelerated rate, blinking stars teetering in swirling speed. The second featured rotating portraits, all contorted in a scream. The third was shattered—jagged pieces scattered along the black carpet on the floor with the blade of a scythe striking the heart of the mirror, its long, oiled wooden handle extended out like a suspended horizon line.

The hypnotic quality of the first mirror transitioned into the discomfort of the second to culminate in the violence of the last. Without reading the artist's statement, I'd hazard a guess that this was time and its effects.

In the evening, the storefront was well lit, as were its neighbors—a lively pub with blooming baskets of pink flowers and a hipster coffeehouse with a buzzing neon sign on the other side.

Ward promised some sort of early-morning date. It could be a sumptuous brunch or high tea somewhere. Romance was always his strong suit and never an afterthought. His thought-fulness was an even more attractive quality than his beautiful face and body. I still remembered when he scoured all the sta-tionery and pen shops of downtown Chicago because I had issues finding the right cartridge for my lucky Japanese foun-tain pen in time to defend my dissertation. I needed to have the pen functioning and with me before I headed into any im-portant event for my ritual of writing positive affirmations. The same pen was in my purse now, tucked against my worn leather planner.

I tugged my rolling suitcase alongside me as I opened the front door of Lethe's Curiosities.

The black bell above the doorframe tinkled.

Mr. Samson stood by the counter, poring over a thick, opened ledger, fingers dragging down the leftmost column. Time had tempered his height, sloping and rounding his shoul-ders forward—at one point, he must have been as tall as Ward. My supervisor wore a traditional white linen cravat above his black buttoned jacket.

I gently cleared my throat.

He glanced up and greeted me. "Ah, Ms. Buhay. I hope you're ready to start your shift. The evening is young. Clients might be coming in shortly." He waved me forward before spinning the ledger so I could read it from across the counter. "All the inventory is listed here. It's not comprehensive at all. I started the task years ago, and as you can see, it's far from complete."

I leaned over to scan the few filled pages. Vintage jewelry, keepsakes, books, and some paintings were listed. The more interesting items must be in older entries. I had my work cut out for me. This entire shop was crammed with oddities— which was why I'd been drawn to this job in the first place. Even now, a black pillar candle with an unusual, macabre carving in the wax held my attention and begged for a closer inspection.

He added, "You'll be in charge of acquisitions. Be stringent and careful about what you choose to procure."

"Is there anything I should look out for in particular?" I asked.

Mr. Samson closed the ledger. "It must be of sufficient value. I trust your judgment. It's why I hired you in the first place."

"And that value is . . . ?"

"Use the scale behind the counter. Remember to attend to every client. You must treat them with care and with respect, no matter what condition they're in."

His vague implications worried me. This was an unspoken rule of conduct, and to make it this explicit, I had to assume the clients walking in would be strange, to say the least. "I thought the foot traffic was minimal at best."

"True that it's never been crowded in here. In the last little while, there have been fewer visitors. It's to be expected. We have plenty of inventory, and yet . . ." He scratched his temple. "I haven't been able to make a sale."

Unusual but not unheard of. "Perhaps this shop feeds into a private collection then?"

"Yes, that must be it. Ah, you are as clever as I expected." Mr. Samson picked up a nearby silver-stamped locket. The simple chain wound around his fingers as he dangled it before me.

"What can you tell me about this? This isn't a test, more like you're humoring an old man."

I lowered my shoulders and accepted the piece of jewelry from him. The tarnished silver had become a motley of coppery tones from oxidization. The engraving on the front was a set of three letters—*L*, *L*, and *H*. The two Ls looped together with a flourish. I used my fingernail to pry the locket open. Instead of photographs, inside was a snippet of dark curly hair.

My field of study proved that items had a voice—that they had their own stories and came to life in their own way. This was why I didn't need company and was perfectly content spending hours by myself in research. I had my own internal conversations with whatever object I was examining.

"My best guess is that this is a Victorian mourning locket. Lacking any gemstones or other ornate details, the style is too simple for a member of peerage or even a wealthy merchant. Given the mode and material, it's more likely that it was commissioned by someone of means—a banker or a solicitor."

"The mistress of a barrister. Luella had her own lover on the side. This locket was hers, and it's Lorraine's hair in there." He took the locket from my cupped hands and tucked it back into its spot on the shelf. "Luella and Lorraine went to the same finishing school. Lorraine worked at the milliner's while Luella was an actress."

"They must have loved each other very much."

"Yes, it was one of those great love affairs. Luella and Lorraine were ready to move on, so the locket was sold to book their passage. But I digress, you were quite astute in your assessment." He clapped his hands. "I need to get something from my office. Can you keep an eye on the counter while I'm away?"

"Of course."

He strode to the back of the shop and disappeared behind one of the two doors.

The shop was deserted, and what he explained seemed simple enough.

I checked the shelves under the counter for a scale. It would've been more helpful if it were a chart or a manual. I lived for documentation, and the more thorough, the better. Nothing on the lower shelves but an expansive collection of first edition books—novels and natural science field guides complete with illustrations.

The cash register on the counter was an ancient monstrosity with an impressive greenish patina. It had to be ornamental. The real point-of-sale machine must be hidden somewhere around here. I'd seen micro-terminals, and it could be one of those.

The upper shelves behind the counter housed a variety of carriage clocks, and hidden among them in plain sight was a balance scale painted obsidian. This had to have been it. I picked it up and transferred it to the counter.

A swirling, monochromatic, geometric design made of

interlocking triangles decorated the faces of two plates. I placed my thumb down on the left plate and waited for the right plate to rise. The scale didn't react. It must need a heavier weight or something else to activate it.

I had no evidence that anything was amiss, but I couldn't ignore the tingling feeling at the base of my neck.

The black bell above the front door tinkled. A beautiful woman with dark-lined emerald eyes and upswept, raven-black hair made her entrance. A thick-corded lariat necklace dripping with diamonds spilled from the base of her throat downward between her full breasts. The black lace corset top accented her curvy figure, as did the glossy latex pants. Her patent leather pumps clicked against the checkered marble floor with each staccato step.

She walked toward me, lips red and pursed. "Fresh blood, and a pretty one at that." She licked her lower lip. Eastern European accent, not British. "I was hoping you'd be starting tonight."

"Can I help you with something?" I asked.

"Eryna." She presented her hand, black-painted nails facing out. A platinum skull ring with ruby eyes adorned her index finger. "You can call me Eryna."

Was I supposed to kiss her ring? I stiffened my spine and placed my palms down on the counter. "Can I help you, Eryna?"

She leaned over and placed her hands over mine. Under her hooded eyes and a thick set of lashes, her deep green gaze studied my face. "You're such a pretty girl. How did you end up here among these boring old knickknacks?"

I pulled my hands back, trying to shake them loose, yet

they were stuck. She tightened her grip and squeezed. Eryna
lifted her palms to cup my cheeks. My hands were frozen in
position, glued in place by an immovable force. None of this
made sense.

The stunning woman before me rubbed my lower lip with
her thumb. Everything about her was perfect, right down to
her invisible pores. "This is a long way from New York. What
makes you think that things will end up different this time?
People don't change. Even now you're looking at me and wondering why you can't move."

I jerked my elbows out and almost crashed backward into
the shelving behind me.

"See, everything is perfectly fine." Eryna giggled. "All normal.
Yes, it's all as it should be."

Her bubbly laughter had an edge—like a hidden switch-
blade in a birthday cake sent to prison, the glint of steel popping through the foamy buttercream icing. Everything she had
said she could have gleaned from a quick conversation with
Mr. Samson, and anyone could be googled these days because
of their digital footprint.

Nothing about her was natural. None of this . . .

The store, London, even the polished counter under my
hands adhered to the laws of nature, gravity, and physics.
My body was mine, and she had no authority over it. I clung to
my professionalism as a marker of my sanity. "Is there anything I can help you with, Eryna?"

"So unflappable." She clapped her hands. "Let's see how
well you do when you see things for what they really are."

My shoulders tensed up as my spine straightened. I didn't
like the sound of that.

Eryna stared at the baroque wall clock over my shoulder. Her pupils dilated in time to the ticking. I weaved my trembling fingers together in an effort to steady them as my heartbeat skipped and accelerated, making me dizzy.

"Yes, light the candle behind you when I leave. Mr. Samson always likes this place to have ambience." She closed her eyes and hummed an unfamiliar melody. "I'll be back soon. I don't want you to forget me, Camille."

She winked and sauntered out with a provocative shimmy of her hips.

When the door closed, I grabbed the black pillar candle on the shelf and placed it on a brass stand by the cash register. A matchbook with the emblem of an hourglass lay nearby. I struck a match and lit the wick.

Incense, camphor, eucalyptus, and a bite of singed cedar. It wasn't something out of a swinging thurible during mass, but the combination was close. The flame burned in shades of the aurora borealis—pinks, greens, blues, purples.

After the act, I regained control of my own body as if the puppet's strings were cut. I leaned against the counter and slammed my eyelids shut.

None of this was real.

Ward. Chicago. Inay's tray of pandesal fresh from the oven at 5:00 a.m. on the day of my flight to London. The faded Royal Pine tree air freshener hanging from the rearview mirror of my Uber ride to the airport. The takeaway of creamy lamb korma for lunch at a Pakistani restaurant near the hotel. These were *real*.

The multicolored flame danced before my eyes, burning

brighter than before. I leaned over, puffing my cheeks, and exhaled to extinguish it. The light didn't even flicker or waver. This . . . this . . .

The bell above the door tinkled again and a customer walked in—a middle-aged Korean woman with a greenish-blue tinge to her skin. Her black hair dripped over her shoulders as her soaked loafers squelched against the marble floor. Her sad, dark eyes dominated her pale face. She headed straight for the counter and placed her damp hands on it.

"I'm looking for Mr. Samson."

Her lips didn't move, yet her voice rang clear in my head.

She pulled out a locket from her chest. The piece of silver gleamed almost white. "You have to buy this from me. I need to move on."

Her high cheekbones glowed against her pallid skin. The radiant light spread across her face, revealing the outlines of her skull until all that was evident were bones and the delicate shape of her jaw and teeth.

"This isn't real." I gripped the edge of the counter. "No, this is all in my imagination."

"You have to help me," she pleaded with unmoving lips. "Help, help, help me."

She reached out to grab the front of my blouse. Her cold, damp fingers tugged at the fabric while I pulled her hands away. The touch of her skin chilled me down to the core, as if I'd been plunged into an icy lake.

My field of vision grew blurry as stars littered the edges, framing the darkness that consumed everything else. When I was six, I closed my eyes and pressed my forehead against the flat end of a baseball bat while running around in a tight circle. When I opened them and stood up, the entire world was topsy-turvy while my stomach threatened to heave everything I ate.

I dove behind the counter, hugging my knees while rocking back and forth.

None of this was happening.

There had to be a logical explanation.

With every ragged breath, I feared there wasn't one.

4

Ward

HE TRIED EVERYTHING.

He still couldn't get out.

The process of logical elimination yielded no favorable results because this wasn't a normal circumstance. He was now maneuvered into a position in an elaborate chess match. Being a pawn, he knew nothing of the board, the other players, or whose hands were moving him into place.

Ward Dunbar was in a pickle, and not the brined vegetable kind he loved in his hamburgers. Physics, logic, and science of any kind no longer applied here. He was trapped, against his will, held hostage by some unknown force he'd yet to meet. In the depths of his despair and self-pity, he could think only of Camille—how she was out there and that he could never see her again.

Through the windows, London continued to move on. Sunset painted everything in oranges, golds, and yellows before ushering in the cool hues of night. With nothing better to do, he watched the transition of day into night, wondering if this was a bad trip from an edible or some waking nightmare. The storefronts kept their lights on overnight, and after the last of the pub crawlers staggered out, he turned away from the windows. He could join them soon if he could get out the next day.

His empty stomach gurgled. Ward was starving, probably dehydrated, and definitely at some level of delirium. There was no coffee machine or kitchenette in the back—only a bathroom and Madam Selene's locked office. If there was another exit, it could have been through her room. He hadn't seen her since this morning at the start of his shift. No amount of screaming, pounding on the door, or even the two times he attempted to break it down had amounted to anything.

He rubbed his sore left shoulder and settled in on the cold marble floor for a long night.

Sleep might restore order. Ward Dunbar could wake up and find himself in his beloved's arms as if his first day at the job had never happened at all. Wishes were well and good for children, and though he was curled up in the fetal position, he was a grown adult.

Most likely, morning would bring much of the same mayhem.

A LIGHT SMACK across his cheeks woke him up. "Mr. Dunbar!"

Madam Selene loomed over him. She had a different pashmina shawl on today along with a new pair of pearl stud earrings. She appeared refreshed, collected, and everything he wasn't at the moment.

He pushed himself up on his elbows and rubbed his eyes. "You seemed to have locked me in last night."

"I did no such thing." She crossed her arms. "Though I admit, if I could have, I would have disclosed the more controversial terms of the work agreement. I'm not at liberty to say more than I'm allowed to."

"And other than being stuck here against my will, what else could there possibly be?" Ward's deep voice pitched higher as he raised his hands in the air.

She tapped her lips with her fingers, poppy-red nails gleaming under the store lights. Her gaze moved from him to the windows outside, where sunlight streamed in and the rest of the world went about their morning. "I'm truly sorry. I'm not at liberty to say. You'll discover them soon enough, as I have."

He bounded to his feet. "Wait, are you stuck here as much as I am?"

Her lips pressed shut.

When she all but confirmed that she wasn't responsible and was as much a victim as he was, Ward's righteous indignation died with a whimper.

Madam Selene wandered toward the desk and withdrew the ledger, scanning for today's appointments. "Make yourself presentable, Mr. Dunbar. You have one appointment with two clients coming in today."

"So in addition to being held hostage, I'm also still expected to work? I want to get out of here. I quit." He crossed his arms over his chest.

"You can't. It's not an option for you or me." She snapped the ledger closed and handed it to him. "We don't have that choice. You have a single appointment. Make it count."

He refused to accept the book. "What part of 'I quit' didn't you hear?"

Her dark-lined eyes narrowed. The hiss escaping her lips was accompanied by a shake of the head. Madam Selene's proud shoulders sagged, causing the shawl to slip down. Her voice softened as she spoke. "You don't trust me, and that's understandable. You and I can't quit or leave. You've probably tried it yourself. The shop doesn't allow us to leave. Nothing you can do will change that. The sooner you accept this, the better your mental state will be."

"Have you tried to get out?"

"It doesn't matter." She closed her eyes. "Our job is all we have. We must do it to the best of our abilities."

"You're saying that it's our only chance of getting out? Did they tell you this, or have you agreed to it?" he ventured. "I don't understand any of this. Then you are as much a prisoner as I am."

She gave him the slightest of nods before placing a finger to her lips, then gestured to the bubble security camera on the wall. "We are always being watched and judged. Never forget this, Mr. Dunbar."

If the cameras worked as the windows did, there was no doubt in his mind that whoever was the owner of this place kept surveillance that went beyond what those cameras were supposed to record. Ward took a small step toward the slow acceptance that this wasn't his version of reality anymore and any hope in hell of escaping this place rested on the job—a perfect example of prison labor in the form of retail. His captors must be capitalists.

Madam Selene turned to head toward the locked room in

the back. "If you don't have any further questions, I will be in my office."

"Wait, I have a few. How long have you been stuck here?"

She pursed her lips. She touched her left temple and grumbled. "Far too long. I don't even remember anymore. It's as if the time outside never happened."

"Have you tried to leave? Do you have any ideas on how to—"

"The sooner you accept your circumstance, the better you'll adjust. There is no way out." She punctuated every word with a sharp hiss. "We're here for the time being. I hired you for your ability to adapt. Start *adapting*. I'll see you tomorrow."

Before he could even ask her about food or lodgings or anything practical, she escaped to her office. Unlike him, she seemed to show no signs of being starved or tormented. He had never been in her office, and he suspected there was a kingdom of comfort and food in there. His healthy imagination conjured up a lavish, medium-rare T-bone steak with a side of truffle fries and gravy.

His stomach gurgled, growling from its missed meals.

The bell chimed and a couple walked in. The woman, the more striking of the two, had long, wavy auburn hair with golden highlights and piercing blue-gray eyes. She stood at least half a head taller than her companion and was dressed in ripped denim and a loose oatmeal cable-knit sweater that hung down to her thighs. Her small pixie nose was upturned as she walked directly toward the wall installations.

Her male counterpart made his way toward Ward. His short, light brown curly hair hovered over his wide, pale forehead. His hazel eyes were inquisitive—the lone remarkable feature in his average face. Pleasant, unassuming, and almost too ordinary in his dark jeans and plain black hoodie sweater.

"Don't mind Din. She's been dying to get in here." He held out his hand. His high voice had a Midwestern accent, and the cadence was quick, as if the words were tumbling from his lips faster than he wanted. "I'm Theo."

Theo's grip was firm as Ward completed the handshake. "Ward, Ward Dunbar."

"I don't mean to be rude, but you're looking pretty rough. This is supposed to be a classy establishment. Are they treating you well?"

"Uhh . . ." Ward stammered. "As good as can be, I guess?"

Theo withdrew something from his hoodie pocket. "Picked this up in Southgate. Looks like you need this more than I do." He handed him a candy bar with Greek writing on gold foil. "Greek chocolate. Tastes like a Butterfinger but less of the annoying toffee bits that get stuck in your teeth."

Ward's stomach rumbled before he thanked him. "I appreciate it."

Theo lowered his voice and cupped the side of his mouth. "I don't think they'll fault you for eating on the job. You sound like you missed a few meals. Can't work under those conditions, am I right?"

The small candy bar in Ward's palm crinkled when he squeezed it. He shouldn't be eating during office hours, yet he was also trapped against his will. One little trespass shouldn't tip the scales when he wasn't even provided with any kind of food. While his brain contemplated the ethics of the situation, his empty stomach decided for him. Animal instinct overrode logic in this instance.

Ward ripped the top open and glanced at the chocolate-covered treat before taking a healthy bite—milk chocolate with honey in between layers of wafers. His hunger was suddenly satiated as if he had eaten an entire meal or two. The throbbing headache he'd had also disappeared. All the aches and stress from sleeping on the floor and from digesting the hostage state he was in vanished.

"Good, huh? It's also an energy bar." Theo nudged Ward's arm. "By now you're thinking, what is it exactly you just ate? Don't worry, I didn't poison you. It's the exact opposite. I gave you a little bit of something magical—ambrosia."

"Like the Greek gods' ambrosia?"

"Yeah, but it's in better packaging." He held his palms out and wriggled his fingers in a hypnotic pattern, speed increasing until his hands were a blur, lighting up at the tips like a makeshift holiday sparkler. "I'm sure by now you know what you're dealing with."

Finally, the foundations of Ward's skepticism came crashing down. While he was a natural believer in magic, gods, and fairy tales, it was quite the leap from reality to fantasy—yet he made it, standing firmly on the other side.

Camille had always called him a dreamer. She couldn't understand or even begin to entertain that there were some things in this world that couldn't be explained away with science or logic, while he always believed in the intangible, and this was definitely of that variety. The way she had said it wasn't an insult, unlike the other times he'd heard it in his life—not like the indulgent twinkle in his parents' eyes whenever he spoke from the heart, and over time, his siblings learned to treat him how one would speak to a young child when they said they wanted to be an astronaut or the next president. The nod of the head paired with a sincere smile and the words "That's nice, dear."

"Your brain isn't broken. Perhaps you're not as fragile as your kind is purported to be." Theo rubbed his hands together. "Mortals can be unpredictable at times. Though I was confident your brain wouldn't explode with my honesty. Folks don't handle the truth well in general—gods and mortals alike."

Din hovered over a large ruby pendant on display. She kept her hands behind her back as her eyes focused on the jewelry. She had been examining each case in silence.

"Does she want to see anything for a closer look?" Ward asked Theo.

He shook his head. "Not yet. I don't want her to get too attached to anything I can't afford. Once she gets the idea that she wants something, it's like trying to stop an immovable force."

Ward nodded. "I get it. Camille would have been the same. Laser focus."

"Ah, a girl. Did you leave her behind out there?"

"I did. I don't even know when or if I'll ever see her again."

Theo held up a finger, and a mischievous grin teased his thin lips. "If you'll indulge me . . . I think I can help you."

"You've helped enough with the ambrosia. I don't—"

He shushed Ward and produced a small, silver compact mirror. He'd seen something similar in Camille's purse. "Watch and learn." Theo opened it, and the top mirror showed Camille as Ward last saw her—radiant, glowing with happiness at the promise of their date. The bottom was a sleeping Camille. Her dark lashes fluttered as she dreamed. She was safe.

Ward reached out to touch the lower mirror. His fingertips smudged the glass as Theo handed the compact to him. "This is real, isn't it? This has to be."

He proved to be a resilient creature. One minute, he was consumed with finding out how anything worked, like the psychology behind a failed relationship, and the next, he accepted ambrosia and the existence of Greek gods without question. All without causing a cranial leakage or a psychotic breakdown, at least in Ward's particular case.

"I mean, yeah. By the way, your girl's hot!" Theo wagged his thick eyebrows. "I can see why you want to get out of here."

After a few more glances, Ward reluctantly returned the magical compact to Theo. "Where exactly is here? Thank you for letting me see her."

"It's everywhere and nowhere. You've managed to get yourself into a really terrible sitch. You've been chosen for some purpose, and I don't think they'll let you out until you've fulfilled that. And as for your girl . . ."

"What about Camille?"

"She's stuck like you."

"Like stuck as in imprisoned like me?"

"Yes, she might actually have it worse. I don't know, but I can find out."

Ward covered his face with his hands and muffled a groan.

"Hey, it's not all that bad. I'm pretty confident you and your girl will walk out of here sooner than you think. Don't lose hope." Theo handed Ward a notebook and a pen from his bottomless pockets. "Why don't you write something down for Camille? Once I find her, I'll deliver the note."

"This is all really nice, but why are you helping me?"

Theo leaned forward to watch Din. She rubbed her lower lip with her fingertips as she studied a jade necklace set. A strand of hair fell over her forehead, showcasing her flawless profile. She had an otherworldly beauty that was unmatched. After all, she was a goddess. Theo worshipped her.

"I've been in love with her since the beginning of time. It was only in the last millennium that she realized I existed." Theo shoved his hands in his pockets and shuffled his feet. "Never ever thought I could walk in here, and with *her.* Anyway, when I first saw you, I knew you were missing your other half. Yeah, that proverb about humans being split in two is true—at least for me. Din calls me a softie, and I always have been with mortals."

Ward needed a friend right about now, for any gesture of kindness was welcome in his predicament. The act penetrated through the bleakness of his imprisonment and fed him the one thing more precious than magical chocolate—hope.

"Thank you. I didn't mean to sound ungrateful—"

"Yeah, I get it. I mean, if I was mortal and stuck here, I wouldn't trust anyone. Hell, I'd be going batshit nuts from what's going on. I don't know how I'd handle having my worldview shaken and turned upside down." Theo rubbed the side of his neck. "Do you know what you want to write yet?"

Ward stared at the notebook and pen in his grasp. He decided that explaining the situation at hand first would be ideal before wading into his feelings and how he still wanted to be with her if they ever survived this bloody mess in one piece. It would have been easier with a phone or video call, but letter writing possessed its own romantic charm.

Theo wandered off to join Din's side to afford Ward some

time and privacy in writing the letter. He took a seat at the desk and scratched out a short note. He had to find a balance between sounding concise and coherent while explaining their current circumstance, magic and all.

By the time he cobbled together a note, Theo and Din were arguing. The language was unfamiliar, but Ward suspected it to be ancient Greek. Din pressed her index finger against Theo's chest as she gestured toward one of the displays on the wall. Her generous mouth was curved into a grimace as the sharpness of her words cut the air. Theo held his palms out as he kept his tone even and diplomatic.

For everything Theo had done on his behalf so far, Ward ventured into something he never would have otherwise—a lovers' quarrel. "Is there anything I can help you both with? There's plenty of time to view something for your appointment."

Din froze. Her pleasant, curious expression returned, as did her twinkle. Her voice was musical and resonant. "I would love to see two pieces today—the ruby pendant and the jade collection."

The pleading expression on Theo's face combined with his palms pressed together against his lips broke down any of Ward's objections. If nothing else, kindness must be reciprocated.

5

Camille

. . . . .

DAY ONE AND DAY TWO

. . . . .

I CRADLED MY head in my hands, rocking back and forth.
My cheeks were soaked with salty tears. Ghosts, walking specters, and weird women holding me against my will. Nothing
made sense, and I could barely keep it together.

Above me, Mr. Samson talked to the ghost and attended to
her needs while I remained in a fetal position on the floor. I
couldn't move. Everything swirled around me still, no matter
how I tried to gain my bearings.

This was too much.

I'd thought nothing else would break me the way it did
when I walked away from Ward. I'd left the most vulnerable
parts of myself exposed to the elements. Contrary to what
everyone around us believed, he didn't walk away with the
best part of me. I was the one who cut those pieces out and
deemed them unnecessary.

And now, these were the only pieces I had left.

"What are you doing?" Mr. Samson roughly pulled me up
by the shoulders. "You're supposed to attend to any customer

that comes through the door. You can't shirk your duties. You leave me no choice."

His strength surprised me as he dragged me shocked and trembling down the hallway in the back of the shop. He opened an unmarked door and pushed me inside. "I deeply regret this. You'll be allowed out when the door unlocks on its own."

And with that, the door shut behind me—a complex lock audibly clicking into place.

The pendant lamp dangled overhead. A wide, white shade covered a steady humming iridescent bulb. I didn't have any rage in me to pound my fists against the exit. My life had been under my control to some extent up until now, and all I'd known had been debunked.

I found a bare patch of the wall without shelving in this small storage room and sat against it, hugging my knees to my chest. I could be out of here in fifteen minutes, an hour, the end of my shift, and even possibly a year or more.

Why bother worrying about it?

After a few minutes of wallowing, I got up. Fighting about my situation with physicality would be futile. No, I wasn't giving in. The way out of this was through planning and quick thinking.

I examined the shelves and sorted through them. The nine-by-eleven-foot room had perimeter shelving and one column of steel racks containing oversized relics. No trace of dust anywhere.

Out of habit, I pulled out my gloves before examining an amphora. The scenes painted on the surface were . . . I let out a hysterical giggle. The subject matter was definitely one of the more saucy topics of ancient Greece—sex. All of the women, with bare breasts typical of Minoan dress, were in various positions receiving oral from gods, satyrs, and of course, a Cretan white bull. Ever since Ward and I walked through an exhibit of ancient graffiti, he made sure to add some juicy comments and quips when it came to the sexually charged ones. Never failed to at least prompt a giggle, or at most, a hot make-out session in an isolated nook afterward.

Yes, the physical connection between us was undeniable, but that wasn't why I wanted him back in my life. Our attachment transcended physical intimacy. There was no one else in the world I could talk to and be listened to the way I could with him. He had the ability to understand the words that dared not escape my lips, and that silence was sacred and needn't be broken. I never had to explain how I was feeling—he understood. From my previous relationships, it exhausted me to no end to have to always advocate for my needs and my emotions.

Ward. I didn't show up after work. He'd be worried or, worse, thinking I'd stood him up on purpose—that I didn't want to see him again. I checked my pocket for my phone. The screen was black. Of course, nothing was working, yet my watch still was. The silence of this room amplified the ticking. The analog rose gold Seiko watch on my wrist had been a gift from my parents and was a good luck charm for my move to London. They chose the largest watch face available, which I preferred.

Tick. Tick. Tick.

I scanned the full shelves.

Might as well make myself useful.

I cataloged every item in the room and left the large rack of oversized items for last. The collection was nothing like what was being offered in the shop. These were genuine, priceless objects that would command a far higher selling point. The goods, while some could be rare, skewed toward the mundane— the personal jewelry, paintings, and pieces of furniture were for public consumption. Anything in this storage room was for wealthy billionaire private collectors, corporations, or national museums.

These spanned cultures from the Three Kingdoms period, to the Kush, to the Norte Chico. I could narrow down the time period and geographic region, but my knowledge was topical at best. In academic terms, I tended to be more of a generalist than to specialize in one civilization. More flexibility and career opportunities.

Behind me, the lock moved, clicking until the door swung open a few inches.

I checked my watch. Four hours and forty-four minutes.

I grabbed the door and readied the speech I wanted to give Mr. Samson—that I quit, effective immediately.

The front of the shop was deserted. No customers and, more importantly, no ghosts.

"Mr. Samson?" I called out in an even voice without a hint of animosity. "I need to talk to you."

Nothing.

He must be in his office with the door locked.

I unclenched my fists and returned to the counter to get my luggage and purse. Leaving was my only logical option. Extricating myself from untenable situations had become a specialty in my life. Self-preservation was a skill I learned at an early age—living as a brown, Asian American girl with immigrant parents.

The luggage wheels wobbled against the braided jute rug in front of the counter. Over my shoulder, the black candle's blue flame flickered, changing into a lavender color. It could change into a glittery rainbow for all I cared. I had no intention of waiting to find out.

I gripped the front door handles and yanked. They didn't even jiggle like they should have if they were locked. A dry laugh escaped my lips.

If Ward were in my position, he'd test everything—including throwing objects of increasing size to shatter the glass, or even climbing into the window display and stripping down to get the attention of passersby. After all that I'd witnessed today, resorting to anything logical or even extreme seemed futile.

Whatever force kept me in the storage room would be in play out here, trying to keep me in the shop. Something or someone wanted me here, whether I liked it or not.

I slapped my palm against the glass and then pulled it away.

No smear or even a trace of a fingerprint.

The morning sunbeams filtering through the clear surface didn't even provide a hint of warmth. My night shift had ended three minutes ago.

I gave the handle one more firm tug before slumping my shoulders.

Trapped.

I hated magic. Another hierarchical power structure where I was at the bottom, ready to be crushed at any minute. Learning the rules would be the only way to escape or survive.

"The least you can do is honor the terms you agreed to. I'm

supposed to have an apartment with regular grocery delivery."
I crossed my arms and stomped my feet, executing a perfect
imitation of my mother when she had to deal with difficult
people who never responded to reason. Emotion for emotion.
It was a language my parents used, but one I never called mine.

A new door swung open in the hallway at the back of the
shop.

A one-bedroom apartment was up a narrow stairway past
the door. A mural splashed across the exposed brick to reveal
a clockface with moving arms. The queen bed with a tufted,
modern dark leather headboard was tucked in an alcove with
fitted sheets. Beside the three-piece bathroom equipped with
a stacking washer and dryer was a small kitchenette with a
fridge, tiny gas stove, microwave, and an Italian single-cup coffee machine. The overall aesthetic married dark woods and
textiles with bright, lighter surfaces—maintaining the precarious balance of contemporary with traditional.

I opened the fridge door and found enough fresh food for a
day and night's worth of meals: stacked cuts of meat wrapped
in butcher paper, plump and leafy vegetables in the crisper,
fresh strawberries, table grapes, a pomegranate, and even yel-
low Philippine mangoes. There was also oat milk, pear juice, a
bottle of rosé, and Beaujolais. This was a better and more lux-
urious version of my fridge back home.

Did I still hate magic? Yes.

Perhaps a little less now, but not by much.

I was still a prisoner. Feeding and proper housing would be
the least they could do. This was still a glorified jail cell with
no windows, unlike downstairs. I sank into the leather love

seat with a dove-gray knitted throw and massaged my temples. I needed to eat and sleep. Tomorrow night's shift would come soon enough.

A GOOD NIGHT'S sleep or, in my case, a day, worked wonders for my frayed sanity. I ate a breakfast of Greek yogurt and strawberries and packed a sandwich and thermos, in case I didn't have access to the apartment during my meal break.

Somehow, I had to gain Mr. Samson's trust. He might not be an ally now, but he could be in the future. I had no one else. He could give me, at the least, information about this world and the mess I was in, and at most, what I needed to escape.

My supervisor was at the counter, examining the black candle whose flame now flickered a deep emerald green. He straightened his shoulders and bowed his head. "Ah, Ms. Buhay, I hope you are feeling better this morning."

"Much." I assumed a congenial expression—the kind I often used as a child to get permission for anything ranging from playing in the park to getting the extra slice of cheesy bibingka. "I apologize for my conduct yesterday. I assure you that it won't happen again."

He raised his snowy brows. "I honestly thought you'd be upset with me. I didn't want to do what I had to. I hope you understand. In any event, your resilience is quite admirable."

"Am I correct in assuming you're just as much bound to 'these rules' as I am?" I asked. His slight nod confirmed my suspicions. I had to ask the one question that I knew I shouldn't. "Are you trapped here too?"

He lowered his eyes. He placed his hands on the edge of the

counter and squeezed, turning his knuckles white while a long-drawn-out sigh escaped his lips. I doubted he could tell me because of these so-called rules. How long had he been stuck here?

"If you've been here longer than a year, tap your finger for me, please."

He rapped his index finger against the wood.

"Decades?"

He repeated the gesture. Mr. Samson then jumped from the counter, clutching his left finger as an invisible gale force dragged him from his spot, yanking him toward the hallway and to his office. The heavy door slammed.

Damn.

I put my boss in time-out.

If Mr. Samson had been here for decades, then it could be my fate too.

These rules were meant to be followed. There were still ones he had to adhere to which I didn't know about. Mr. Samson told me at the start that my primary task was acquisitions—which meant dealing with customers. I understood why I committed the infraction last night.

I pulled out my notebook and took copious records of all my observations, theories, and what happened today. Keeping a written journal always gave me a sense of control and certainty. My classmates often envied my thorough notes in college. I combined an eclectic mix of drawings with flowcharts, in addition to paragraphs—whatever it took to convey the idea best.

Ward once described them as something worthy of being hung in a gallery. We hadn't even started dating back then, so

I questioned his motives behind the outrageous compliment. It took me a bit to understand that he was genuine and spoke from his heart. I'd never known anyone who had that direct route from the heart to mouth without the brain being involved. It was refreshing.

I hoped that Ward was well and settling into normal London. Last night I envisioned him drowning his sorrows at the bar in the Shard. Nothing like getting over heartbreak in the tallest building in the city above the clouds. He would have assumed by now that I had ghosted him.

It wasn't the first time.

The bell above the front door tinkled.

A short, college-aged white guy walked in. His curly hair hid the tips of his large ears. The oversized neon orange hoodie wore him. The way he shuffled his feet and the crooked slope of his shoulders created an air of lazy ease. His hazel eyes studied me, lingering a little too long on the parts of me that I shared only with Ward.

I knew his type well.

"Can I help you?" I asked with a neutral expression.

He slid a folded piece of paper onto the counter. "Actually, I think I can help you."

6

Ward

. . . . .

DAY TWO

. . . . .

WARD DUNBAR HAD one of his basic necessities met. Quite interesting how the brain regained a little bit of function with a little bit of food. The riot led by his stomach had been sufficiently suppressed, and temporary order had been restored. However, the revolution was still scheduled if he didn't address the rest of his needs. Out of desperation, he asked Theo if he had a magical bed in his pockets.

The god didn't have one.

However, Theo did provide an alternative. Last night, Ward was handed a walnut and told to tap it on the floor three times. A colorful hammock sprang up, something plucked out of the beaches of Tulum right down to the halo of white sugar sand under it. Ward slept well despite his current situation.

He was sweeping the floor by the time Madam Selene walked out of her office the next morning.

"Mr. Dunbar, you must do something about your wardrobe situation and . . ." She wrinkled her nose and made a gesture toward his rumpled clothes, not even noticing the small pile of sand in the dustbin. "Hygiene."

A flush warmed his cheeks as he took a quick whiff of himself. Ward failed the sniff test and therefore kept his arms glued to his sides. "I'll try and get this addressed soon."

"Good. It's unprofessional." The bangles on her wrist jingled as she brushed an invisible particle off her black-and-white beaded caftan dress. "You have two appointments today."

"Two? Who are they?"

"Eryna and Mr. King, hopefully ready to make a purchase." Madam Selene made a sour face when she took a step toward him. "Don't move." She walked into her office and came back with a perfume spritzer. Before he could protest, he was bombed with a strong, heavy, feminine perfume with a prominent camellia note.

"Better." She sniffed the air and then leaned in. "A definite improvement."

That was subjective. He smelled like a seventy-year-old woman or a concentrated camellia bush. Take your pick.

Madam Selene rubbed the bridge of her nose. "We'll have to make do with the wardrobe situation. In addition to the rules in the ledger, you must remember that our clientele is quite exclusive and powerful."

Ward vaguely remembered the rules. It couldn't hurt to reread them before his first appointment. "Madam Selene, is there a place for me to sleep or bathe? Or is there any food that I could—"

"Mr. Dunbar, you never asked for any of these stipulations in your job contract."

"I didn't, but—"

"Your lack of planning doesn't constitute an emergency on my part. I need to get back to my work. Eryna will be arriving shortly. I suggest you review your notes and get moving. Try to make another restroom trip to make the best of your visual presentation." She waved her hand and retreated into her office.

His boss did nothing to help him, nor should she. Respect was earned, and all Ward had to show her was his inept, musty situation. It took a quick trip to the bathroom to make the most out of refreshing his appearance with the limited resources at hand. One point his boss made stuck in his mind like a tiny rock in his shoe.

Camille had always reminded him to engage in contract negotiations instead of accepting the initial terms. She advocated for knowing one's worth and being able to get it even if it were a titch more. Ward couldn't deal with the potential conflict. He'd rather accept the offered terms or decline and find something else that met his expectations.

The chime for the front doors rang.

Ward wiped the last rebellious strands of his hair down and headed back into the shop.

Eryna was a statuesque brunette with arresting emerald eyes and a low-cut, gauzy black dress that would normally draw every hot-blooded male gaze downward. Ward's blue eyes never wavered from her face. She moved with the grace of a python across marble—no friction from any direction other than from the ground itself.

"Ah, new blood," she purred. Her sparkling green eyes traveled up and down his body. Apparently, the courtesy he'd given her wasn't mutual. "Edward Auguste Dunbar. You look good enough to eat."

"Ward, please," he corrected her, before picking up the leather ledger and opening it to scan the rules. "Is there anything you wish to see today?"

"You smell like you've been sleeping with your boss. Tell me, do you like older women?" She reached out to stroke his cheek, but he moved away in time. She responded with a pout. "I'm sure that I can be a better fit. I can teach you things you can only dream about."

He cleared his throat and repeated his ask.

She huffed and crossed her arms. "Very well. I want to see three that you have on display: the pendant, the crown, and the ring."

The ledger was clear. Only one piece or collection could be shown at one appointment. Yesterday, he had shown Theo's girlfriend two. Whoopsy daisy. Granted, he hadn't known it was a violation at the time. Ignorance of the rules wasn't a viable defense in any court. He wasn't punished yet for his mistake, nor did he wish to further incur Madam Selene's wrath. As bad as his current situation was, it could be much worse. Ward was never the type to fuck around and find out.

"Only one piece at a time, I'm afraid." He snapped the leather portfolio shut. "Which one would you like to view?"

"Can't you make an exception for me?" She lowered her eyes and batted her thick lashes. "You can compromise, can't you?"

"I'm afraid I can't."

"Everyone has a price, Edward. You'll learn this in time, and when you do, I'll be here when you need me." She took a seat at the table. "So just one?"

"Yes, name it and I can get it out for you."

Like Theo, Eryna possessed a presence that came from power.

Ward still grappled with the recent awareness of the existence of gods and goddesses. His mortality placed him squarely at the bottom of the power pyramid, when, before any of this started, he assumed humans were the apex.

Immortals existed after the proverbial world was built. They had ample time to claim every single speck in the vicinity as theirs—the mountains, the air, the animals, and even the elements. It was total dominion because they arrived at the playground first.

Ward didn't recognize their names offhand, even after taking a few mythology courses in college. He assumed they must navigate this world with some sort of relative anonymity, at least toward mortals. In this case, his hypothesis was correct. These gods had their own rules to abide by; unfortunately for Ward, he'd never get access to them.

"But narrowing it down to one is so hard. Decisions are difficult, aren't they, Edward?" She twirled a dark strand around her fingers. "Out of everyone, I know you understand. Making the wrong one stings, especially once you can't take it back. No matter how much you want to. Imagine what it would have been like if you took the cushy position in LA the first time they offered. You would have avoided so much heartache, no?"

She plucked the information out as if she were browsing through his memories like pages in a book—highlighting all the juicy and damaging parts only to throw them back in his face. Ward's cheeks flushed despite not saying a word in response. He shrugged off the noise and regulated his breathing. Difficult clients, mortal or not, he could handle. Any tactic other than killing with kindness would only make this situation worse. Ward had murder on his mind.

"Eryna, what would you like to see?" he asked with genuine cordiality.

She pressed a matte-black painted fingernail against the corner of her pomegranate-red lips. "I suppose what I really want is in the vault. Could you go fetch it for me?"

He hadn't even known there was one in the shop. This was an upscale jewelry store, and of course it should have a vault. Before he could answer, his boss responded for him.

"Everything that is available for acquisition is on display. You know the rules of this shop." Madam Selene stood firm despite being at least three heads shorter than a now-standing Eryna. "You follow them as much as we do."

Eryna rubbed her palms together. Little sparks escaped from her fingertips as her hands glowed a deep blue. The lights in the shop flickered yet stayed on, changing to a more orange hue, flashing in long pulses.

Ward stood up and placed himself between the two women in case he had to protect or shield his boss, who he presumed was as human as he was.

Madam Selene placed a hand on Ward's arm before moving to stand beside him. "Consider yourself warned."

"I want whatever is in the vault." Eryna narrowed her eyes. "If you don't give it to me now, I intend to take it by force."

His boss remained unmoved by the threat. She raised her hand and made a slight gesture with her index finger. The front doors swung open and the hostile customer was sucked out into what appeared to be a galactic void of swirling stars and darkness. If it had been London as he last saw it, Ward would have been tempted to join her. The doors slammed shut, and the lights returned to their normal white glow.

"I doubt that will be the last we'll hear of her." Madam Selene pressed her fingers against her temples. "Don't worry, Mr. Dunbar. The shop itself is equipped to defend us and prevent any theft or robbery."

"Has anything like this ever happened on your watch?"

"My memory becomes cloudy with age. I couldn't remember the last time it happened. There are always those who want what they refuse to pay for. Our own world is very much similar to theirs."

"You mean immortals and gods."

Her genuine smile was a refreshing change from the usual sternness. "Ah. You're more observant than I give you credit for."

"Is she coming back, or is she banned permanently?"

"She can return once more. This place works with a two-strikes rule. She'll be behaving because it won't be easy for her to get out of the place she was sent to."

"They aren't all bad like her, are they?"

"They might as well be. I don't trust any of them, and you should take my advice and keep your distance. They lived far longer than you or I. This only breeds entitlement. They're all terrible, and if I wasn't . . ."

The rest of her words evaporated from her lips even though she continued talking. Her mouth vanished yet her cheeks and jaw kept moving. Ward recognized the phenomenon from films where parts of the body had been altered with digital visual effects, yet this was happening in real time. Something or someone in this world didn't want her to speak about this particular subject. Censorship was a concept across all dimensions, it seemed.

"Mr. King will be coming in soon. He has expressed his intentions of making a purchase. Be kind and courteous. I can't stress the importance of this sale enough." She walked toward the golden desk and ran her fingers along its smooth surface. "The scales will appear when you're ready to accept payment. If it doesn't balance, the sale can't be done."

The weariness on her face made her pale and aged her even more. Ward guessed her to be in her midseventies, but the way this world worked, she could be older. "How long have you been working here?"

She shook her head. "Far longer than you can imagine. I'm going back to my office. Please don't disappoint me, Mr. Dunbar."

There were so many questions he wanted to ask her. She certainly didn't lack strong opinions, and with her help, he might be able to get out of there. A prison breakout was more successful with cooperation and coordination between the inmates.

The chime signaled the entrance of Mr. King, the second appointment.

He was dressed again all in black, except for the vibrant lilac silk dress shirt under his suit jacket. A thick gold chain dangled from his neck with a dragon medallion. His powerful cologne was that of a clean bamboo forest—earthy, green, and refreshing.

Ward in his soiled state couldn't help but envy the god. He

needed a long shower, and if a car wash were nearby, he'd take the risk of chafing his bits for a chance at soap and water. If cleanliness was next to godliness, his mortality was the issue.

"You smell like the old lady that runs the place." Mr. King laughed, showcasing his perfect, white teeth. "It doesn't quite cover the offending odors though."

Ward bristled before donning his professionalism like a jacket. "Mr. King, it's so good to see you again. Madam Selene mentioned that you are looking to acquire today?"

"I am." Mr. King stretched out his arms and cracked his knuckles. "The jewelry set. It's time to put it back into circulation."

"Gifting it to a special lady then?" Ward strolled to the correct glass box display.

The god's grin was downright wolfish. "As a matter of fact, yes. One even a person with your discerning taste would appreciate."

"I'm sure she's as lovely as you are."

Mr. King guffawed at the veiled sarcasm in Ward's voice. "You and I have more in common than you realize."

"I doubt it."

"I didn't take you for a skeptic, Mr. Dunbar. You're a believer to the core. I mean, all this . . . wasn't it always within the realm of possibility for you? You still believe in Santa Claus."

The last comment wasn't meant as an insult despite the context and the messenger. The way the god said it almost conveyed a sense of wistfulness and loss. Belief in its core was a rare commodity for mortals and immortals alike. The prevailing sense of skepticism and ennui must infect gods because of their prolonged existence. As for humans, they lived with the constant threat that they would destroy one another. Nihilism bred disbelief, but not in him.

Ward did believe in Santa Claus. While he acknowledged that the jolly chimney interloper didn't physically exist, the idea of him was important, for Saint Nick was the embodiment of charity to children. Ward was always drawn to ideas and concepts, sometimes even more than the actual thing itself. Camille attributed it to his romantic nature.

"I *believe* you'll see her eventually. The gorgeous woman that's always in your waking thoughts."

"While I appreciate the sentiment . . ." Ward set down the black display boxes and stand on the desk. By now, he understood that thoughts were open season for his immortal overlords. "Deep diving into my brain without consent is considered rude in human terms."

Mr. King settled into the opposite seat at the desk. "Good thing I'm not human then."

Ward checked the drawers for the scale. The first one was empty, and the other two were as well. He scratched his head and checked underneath the desk, tapping for some sort of secret compartment. When that didn't work, he resorted to pulling out each individual drawer.

"Having problems, Mr. Dunbar?" Mr. King peered over the edge. "You seem to have more than your fair share of those lately."

"When it rains, it pours, it seems."

"What exactly are you looking for?"

"A scale. Possibly a weight scale. Though it could be a magical dragon scale for all I know." He returned to his seat and examined the top of the desk for any hidden buttons or an expanding leaf. "We need it to process your payment."

"Ahhh. You might want to steer clear of the table," Mr. King instructed. He leaned back in his chair. "I'm ready to make my purchase."

A golden balancing scale materialized from gold dust before them.

"First times are special, and it's fitting that I am yours."

Ward resisted the urge to groan at the terrible quip. "What's the next step?"

"Place the jewelry set on the left side. You'll be taking my payment and putting it on the right. The scale should balance."

"And if it doesn't, you do understand—"

"It'll *balance*."

Ward shrugged.

The shop itself would take any necessary measures to protect and defend, including vacuuming out gods into the cosmic dustbin. The overwhelming display of power wasn't a symptom of the shop's sentience, so much as it was a tool to be commanded—as demonstrated by Madam Selene, who wielded the hammer well.

While Ward removed the jade and gold jewelry pieces from their velvet perch, Mr. King was emptying out his pockets. An odd assortment of items littered the god's side of the table: a black-and-red matchbook with a twisting logo for the Diyu Casino, a pair of ancient bone dice, a monogrammed silk kerchief with the initial *T*, and a pair of literal brass balls.

"No, they're not mine, but they help me keep my dexterity." Mr. King took the two round objects into his left hand and twirled them with his fingers. They multiplied twice until he had six in his hand. The way the shiny orbs moved was hypnotic. He drew his hands together until twelve, rotating in a snakelike pattern, traveled back and forth. When he stopped, he tucked them back into his pant pocket. "They're impressive, aren't they?"

"They are, but apparently they don't measure up when it comes to the jewelry."

"See, you're learning. Given time, we could be friends."

Ward replied with a noncommittal shrug and returned to the business at hand. "What will you offer as payment?"

Mr. King plucked a toothpick from his suit's inner breast pocket. He placed it on the right plate.

Nothing in this world could be taken at face value. That sliver of wood could be anything, from a palace to a demon. The last thing it could be was an implement to dislodge an errant popcorn fragment from your teeth. If Ward ever gravely considered the amount of danger he was in, he'd be curled into a fetal position once again.

As the golden scale teetered toward its final outcome, Ward was certain the toothpick must be something else.

The two plates reached equilibrium. A series of musical chimes emanated from everywhere and nowhere. The song was in Ward's head, and yet his ears couldn't hear it. The toothpick in the right scale vanished into gold dust.

Mr. King leaned forward and grinned. "Pack it up, Mr. Dunbar. There's a very special woman waiting for that jewelry."

7

Camille

. . . . .

DAY TWO AND DAY THREE

. . . . .

THE FOLDED PIECE of lined paper might as well have
been a venomous snake in disguise. I didn't touch it.

"It's not a trap." The stranger's higher male voice had a bit
of a nervous hitch to it. "It's from Ward. You do *know* an Edward Dunbar. Tall, good-looking guy, easy to talk to, origin-
ally from the Chicago area, has two older sisters and one older
and younger brother, has a micro-scar above his left eyebrow
from when he was a kid and decided it was a great idea to para-
chute down the flight of stairs with a garbage bag—"

I had heard enough. "And you know Ward because . . . ?"

"He's stuck in the store too. Well, for him, it's a high-end
jewelry shop. All gold and light, not like this dark place. By the
way, I'm Theo. I promised him that I can deliver his message
to you." He approached the candle and ran his fingers through
the ever-changing flame. It flickered in varying shades of
blue—from the lightest wisp of clear sky to a deep cerulean.

Ward was as trapped in his job as I was.

How did this happen to us? It couldn't be a coincidence

that we had complementary day and night shifts. I had far too many questions, and I didn't trust this Theo enough to ask. I couldn't trust anyone, and even if it was Ward who sent me this note, the messenger could have read it and possibly tampered with it. None of this eased the knot between my shoulders.

"The paper won't bite." Theo rubbed the side of his neck. "And if you can, please write one back. He'd want to hear from you. He's worried about you, and I'm pretty sure he's still in love with you. He didn't want you thinking that he ditched you."

I reached for the note and unfolded it.

In Ward's very haphazard script, complete with oversized dots for the *i*'s, was a short and rushed note. "Camille, I'm stuck in the jewelry shop. I tried to get out and can't. Something's keeping me here. I hope you're safe and not in the same situation. Will write soon. PS Theo's a good guy. He's saved my ass here and I would be in worse shape if he hadn't come in. I know it's hard for you, but I think you can trust him."

I folded the paper into its original state. Theo offered me a crooked grin.

Ward might trust him, but I didn't. Trust was earned, and Theo had done nothing so far to earn it. I pulled out my planner and carefully tore a page from the back and wrote a short note.

"You should smile more. I bet you can sell this dusty junk faster that way."

The smile I gave him made him flinch. It was the one that never reached my eyes and implied that I was traveling spiritually outside my body to murder the other person it was directed at.

I folded the note into an origami heart before sliding it

across the counter to Theo. "I appreciate you delivering this to him. Thank you."

"You make the note sound like a root canal." He tucked the heart into his hoodie pocket. "I'll be back soon with another message."

The bell chimed at the door. A couple of new customers walked in, and these were definitely of the deceased type—ghosts. I swallowed and gripped the counter. I refused to repeat what happened yesterday.

"Yikes." Theo pulled up his hood. "Not sticking around for that. Good luck, Cam."

I ignored the unwanted nickname.

The translucent couple walked in holding each other's hands. They appeared to be South Asian. The wife wore a traditional sari whose once beautiful, vibrant colors were now muted in death. He wore a Western-style suit. The crispness of his shirtsleeves matched the faded line of his pressed pants. The couple must have been in their seventies.

She approached the counter and, with the help of her husband, unclasped her heavy golden necklace. She gathered the elaborate, multistrand piece of jewelry with both hands. The golden beads and tiny diamonds surrounded the centerpiece ruby pendant. She unhooked the matching earrings.

"Is this enough to secure our passage?" she asked in a British-accented voice.

"Passage to where?"

"The next place."

Heaven, purgatory, or hell. These were the choices that I was aware of as a lapsed Catholic. Future destinations that Lola and Inay were obsessed with reminding me were why prayer and religion were so important. My father imagined his version of the afterlife included a stocked fridge of imported San Miguel and being able to eat whatever he wanted regardless of cholesterol content. Ever the skeptic, I never thought about it. The instant consciousness left my mortal body, I'd cease to exist. Period.

I pulled the set of black scales from the shelves behind the counter.

"I would never part with this, but it's time. We're both ready." The elderly woman kissed her husband's cheek. "Dev and I have been together for many good years, and we've watched our grandchildren have children."

"We wanted to beat the rush." He glanced over his shoulder at the darkness of night through the windows. "I have a feeling it will be harder to make a bargain in the future."

She shushed him.

The black obsidian scales gleamed in the overhead lights. It appeared heavier than it was—at most, it felt like two pounds in my hands. The left scale had a painted, swirling golden symbol on the plate that I didn't recognize. Mr. Samson had mentioned the potential acquisition would be on the left, but I couldn't remember what I had to put on the right.

I placed the beautiful wedding jewelry on the painted scale and searched for something nearby for the counterbalancing weight. Everything within reach seemed too ordinary or unsuitable—a pocket watch, a ceramic dog, two dusty first editions of an obscure Victorian novel, and an antique telephone.

"Forgive me, I'd forgotten to give this to you." Mr. Samson appeared by my side, cradling a small wooden box in his hands. The pattern on the lid matched the one on the scale.

"May I?" I asked.

He nodded.

I opened the latched lid, and inside was a twitching, moving star. It reminded me of a sea urchin, but the tips were blunted. The spines moved up and down and left to right, creating an illusion that it was sentient. I touched one point to check and found it smoothed and rounded. The "weight" was almost buoyant in my hands. Tiny, moving lights of blues, purples, and pinks against the black crystal buzzed under the surface of its clustered center. I lifted the counterweight and held it toward the scale. It floated of its own accord to rest on the right plate.

We all watched as the scale moved, teetering from one side to the other until it balanced. The couple both exhaled with relief, held each other, and closed their eyes. Little by little they disintegrated into sparkling, flickering white motes. The peacefulness in their expressions made it seem painless, almost peaceful.

For someone who prided herself on being a skeptic, I was comforted by the fact that the transition into nonexistence could be beautiful. It was far better than what I'd imagined.

"You give them relief, these souls." Mr. Samson took the star and returned it to its wooden box. "They give us their memories so they can pass to the other side. Everything you see here is made of memories—theirs."

They were ghosts.

"How does this happen? How can a person's memories be turned into one of these?"

He scratched his temple. "As far as I know, I believe the dead are allowed to stay for a little while. Most eventually move on, but the artifacts in our shop are from those who tarried in this world a little too long to watch over their loved ones. Their memories coalesce and harden into objects that mean something to them. When they sell them to us, they forget about their past life before moving on."

"Then where exactly are we?" I asked.

I hoped my question wouldn't get him punished. He brushed a hand over his creased forehead. He seemed far more exhausted than when I first met him for the interview. The wrinkles around his eyes and near his jawline deepened—even his snowy hair seemed more white where there were stray streaks of silver. His shoulders stooped, compromising his height. Despite all this, his crystal blue eyes remained the same, with a telltale twinkle of mischief. I would have loved to meet this man in his youth. There were enough clues and whispers of a romantic charmer who probably swept women off their feet on a regular basis.

"We are *here*." His answer was a careful one.

I shoved away the list of unending questions and pivoted to something more personal. "Have you ever been married?"

The dry laugh that greeted me brought me joy. "I tried once. Perhaps I should clarify and say that I should have tried. She might have said yes."

"You definitely look like a man who had a sweetheart in the past." I returned the scales back to their place on the shelves. "I hope you didn't lose her when you got stuck here."

"It was long before that. Back when dinosaurs roamed the earth and that large comet seemed to be coming awfully close. And look at that, you made me remember that I did have a sense of humor at one point."

"It's not something you lose with age. Lolo Benjamin, my grandfather, pulled pranks on us even with his dying breath. He made sure that 'Hit the Road Jack' was played at his funeral. My grandmother always indulged him. They were complete opposites. She was serious and very religious."

"Being alike might bring more harmony, but opposites bring electricity, don't you agree?"

"I suppose."

"Ah, so there is someone in your life as well." He lowered his eyes. "I'm afraid you'll never see them again, Ms. Buhay. Such is the condition we find ourselves in. The sooner you acclimate, the better." His lids were beginning to droop while he stifled a yawn.

I asked, "Is there anything else that I should know before you return to your office?"

"Yes. If you find other guests here that aren't ghosts, you must treat them with respect. They will be looking to buy instead of sell." He waved, then shuffled off down the hall to retreat into his office.

What did "they" mean?

Eryna and Theo, earlier visitors and not ghosts, hadn't seemed to want to buy anything. While she was a threatening menace, he was more like a delivery service. Eryna wasn't human. Theo could be, but he reacted to the ghosts as if he'd known about their existence for as long as Mr. Samson.

Another visitor entered the shop. He was Asian, about a decade older than me, and dressed like he was one of my older cousins out to trap a rich cougar at the club. The matte-black suit and red silk shirt with exposed gold chains completed the look. The only thing missing was the gallons of Acqua di Gio.

He was handsome in a slick sort of way that made me uncomfortable.

"Can I help you?"

"I'm looking to buy something." He leaned against the counter, almost encroaching over the small gap between us. It wasn't an overpowering cologne; instead, it was the smell of clean air with an underlying, subtle hint of peaches. Odd combination and quite pleasant.

"We have antiques of all sorts. Can you specify what you're searching for?"

He drew closer to my face, and I retreated until my back touched the shelves. His intense study was unflinching, as if he were dissecting my mind. Golden flecks appeared in his dark brown pupils. They swirled into a hypnotizing pattern. Not human.

I cleared my throat.

"I'm not sure exactly what it is. I just know I need to buy it." He pulled back and held out his hand. "Mr. King."

I shook it. "Camille."

"Camille, I hope you can help me." He walked to a nearby table and picked up a bronze nude figurine. "It isn't this. It's something more complex."

"Are you looking for a particular memory then?"

He set down the figurine. "Clever girl. Yes, in fact, I am." He glanced around and rubbed his head, ruffling his short dark hair. "There are far too many minds in here. It's like wading into a river searching for one particular droplet. Where do we even begin?"

"Well, if you can narrow down whose memories you're

looking for, perhaps we can tighten the parameters." I lifted a glass perfume decanter from a nearby shelf. "Do you know whom you're looking for?"

"No. I'll know it when I see it." He rubbed his clean-shaven chin.

The glass was cool in my hand. Who could have sold this? When examining artifacts and antiques, provenance was important, and in this case, it meant everything. This bottle was an intimate part of someone who existed.

Mr. King joined my side. "You can't see them yet, but would you want to?"

"You mean the memories?"

"Sure. I can make it possible, that is, only if you want to."

I set down the perfume bottle. "I'm tempted, but not right now. I just became accustomed to the idea of ghosts. I need more time for my human sanity."

"Being mortal isn't a terrible thing." He fished a card from his inner pocket and handed it to me. In small printed, embossed red serif letters, it read: MR. KING. WEAPONS SPECIALIST. EASTERN FACTION. "If you change your mind, light this card with the candle's flame. I'll be here shortly."

"What are you?"

"Not human. If you aren't ready for memories, then you won't be ready for the true answer." He held a finger to his lips and winked. "Ah, and before I forget. This is for you. Consider it a gift and an incentive to help me find that thing I don't know. I'm asking for your help, Camille, and whether you help me or not, it's your choice. You get to keep the gift regardless."

He produced a large, flat, red velvet box from his front

pocket. Of course, it wasn't physically possible given the size. I chalked it up to a magician's illusion. "I suggest you open it as soon as your shift ends, and not a moment too late."

I accepted the present. It was lighter than it appeared—must be something magical like the star crystal. Every antique in this store felt solid, whole, and real, perhaps because they belonged to humans. I had more in common with the ghosts coming in than whatever Mr. King and his kind were.

I opened the box. The hinged lid pulled back, revealing a gilded headdress made of jade and gold. The cloud and rain motif implied sexuality and was completed by the soft budding peony clusters. It was crown shaped and meant to rest on the head like a tiara, with dozens of dangling golden droplets falling down like a curtain over the forehead and eyes. Ming, no, Tang dynasty. Priceless.

"If you're asking, it belonged to a court musician whose musical talents were equaled by her skill in bed and in political intrigue. I can tell you more the next time I see you."

"Are you sure you want to give this to me? It's far too precious for—"

Mr. King bowed his head. "She would have approved of you. Don't underestimate yourself, Camille. Only despair lies down that path."

He gave me a curt wave before exiting through the front doors. Sunlight streamed in the moment he stepped outside. My shift was done.

I put the headdress on.

I heard a voice that I never thought I'd hear again.

Ward.

8

Ward

DAY THREE

WARD WAS HAVING the best shower sex dream—vivid memories of their steamy morning ritual. He climaxed at the sound of her voice.

Her actual voice, and not from the depths of his explicit, pornographic imagination. "Camille?"

"Ward? Can you hear me?"

"Camille? Is that you?" He tried to get up quickly from the hammock, and it ended badly—he would have face-planted on the cold marble floor if not for his quick reflexes. "I'm here!"

"Are you running or something? You sound out of breath."

"Something like that. Never mind me. Are you all right?" He grimaced at the ruined state of his boxers and slacks.

"I suppose. No matter how you describe it, it's a prison. I got your note, by the way."

"Theo delivered it then. Excellent. You can trust him."

"We'll see." Hesitation coated her soft voice. Camille never did trust easily.

"Are you stuck with your boss? I think mine is human, which is comforting."

"I meet with ghosts. Yes, dead people. I'm helping them cross over by buying their memories. All of this is unreal." She paused and he could imagine her tapping her full lower lip in thought. "There has to be a reason why we're needed to perform some sort of job in this. What's yours?"

"Selling priceless artifacts and jewelry to the gods. Gods! Can you believe that they're real? We're talking about Zeus and company, though I haven't narrowed down who is who. Give me time and I can—"

"Ward, focus. I don't think it matters whom we're dealing with. It's more important to figure out the big picture. Why us? Are we stuck here until we behave or break the cycle somehow? There has to be . . ."

"Camille, I missed you and I wanted us to be together if we weren't stuck in this hellhole. I had plans to take you to the bar at the Shard. I've been thinking about how wrong it was to spend so many of those years apart. We lost so much time. I should have apologized or gotten my own head out of my ass. This is a really long and stupid way to say that I love you and I never stopped."

No response.

"Camille? Camille, are you still there?"

She was gone. Still, he was grateful for hearing her voice and connecting with her for a precious five minutes. It was the closest he'd come to being with her. The nocturnal emission was a technicality. Speaking of which . . .

Ward rubbed his eyes and groaned. After he cleaned up the sand, he scrubbed and hoped everything dried in time before

Madam Selene arrived. It would have been helpful to have one of those high-powered dryers in the restroom or access to laundry. This morning's mishap would only add to his already deteriorated hygiene situation. He had devolved into a smelly, damp dolt.

"IS THERE A plumbing issue in the restroom that I should be aware of?" Madam Selene scowled at his sorry state.

Ward Dunbar resembled a wet, contrite golden retriever who had frolicked in the rain for hours. "Sort of," he replied with a sheepish grin and shrug. "Unless you have a shower I could use or a change of clothes, I have to make do with what I've been given."

Before he could stop her, she whipped out her perfume bottle and spritzed him down. "We cannot offend our clients." She tsked. "One sale from Mr. King isn't good enough. We need to be able to move more inventory."

"How many have you sold on your own?" While wiping his watery eyes, he reached out to try to take the bottle.

She swatted his hand away. "None. That's why I hired you. I've never been good with people, Mr. Dunbar. I think you already picked up on this. My job is to make sure everything is managed and running. Dealing with clients is your primary duty.

"And speaking of which, it seems that you have a regular now. He'll be your only appointment for the day." Madam Selene tucked the perfume away before handing him the leather portfolio. "See if he can help your *dire* situation since he's been so generous to you in the past."

He winced at the sharpness of her tone. The woman could and would slice a person with a well-placed syllable. "Yes, ma'am."

"I pray that you will be more presentable tomorrow. I don't think fumigating the shop is an option for us. Very well, carry on." With that, she vanished into her office.

He opened the portfolio and saw Theo's name and sighed with relief.

The door chime echoed in the distance.

"Buddy, what did you do?" Theo walked in with a gray camo hoodie and loose cargo pants. "Did you try and take a bath in the sink?"

Din darted away and headed off to examine one of the displays on the wall.

"I . . . yeah. Something like that." Ward rubbed his greasy, wet hair.

Theo walked over to his side and placed his arm across Ward's shoulders. "I can sort of fix this, but it'll cost you."

Currency in this world wasn't reduced to paper bills, coins, plastic, or even fictional bits of data. Needless to say, nothing in Ward's wallet would suffice as payment. Gods had been known to demand anything from a firstborn child to eternal servitude. In his case, Ward was low on assets and unwilling to part with the measly lot he possessed.

"Dude, I don't want your liver or anything. I just want advice in the love department—you know, help with my girl. I saw yours the other day and she's hot. The best part, she still loves you. I need some of that with Din."

The god's ask was far more reasonable than Ward expected. He was relieved he didn't have to give up any of his organs or fulfill any of the other morbid scenarios he had cooked up. "Sure."

Theo withdrew a pack of mints from one of his many pant pockets. "It won't give you a fresh change of clothes, but it'll take care of everything else."

The small plastic case contained tiny white capsules. The label was again in Greek with a small golden lightning bolt as part of the logo. Ward popped the lid open with his fingernail and shook two into his opened mouth.

Down the gullet they went. The jolt that snaked through his limbs sent his heart rate skyrocketing. Everything was clean from head to toe, and his clothes looked as if they had been professionally laundered. It even revived his preferred cologne, which didn't contain any hint of camellia. Respectability was within his grasp once more—still well short of Maslow's hierarchy of needs, but he was still a prisoner after all.

"Thank you." Ward gave Theo a big hug. "I really appreciate this and everything else you've done for me."

The god shrugged and grinned. "What was I going to do? Let you continue to suffer? Mortals think gods are above it all. We do care, you know, but I'm not one of those types who claim that you're all my children. I'm not *that* kind of immortal. Nope. I just help on occasion or when the mood suits me."

Theo took a seat by the desk and kept his eyes on Din. She hovered by the glass case with the large blood ruby pendant. She wore a short, knitted striped dress over long suede boots. Her long auburn hair draped over her face, obscuring her perfect profile. The ambient light bouncing off the golden surfaces gave her an ethereal glow.

"So tell me all about your troubles, my friend." Ward settled into the chair across from him. "I'll do what I can to help."

Theo sighed. He stretched out his arms and threaded his fingers together. "Her mother doesn't approve of me. Okay, she hates me and always has. It's that whole 'I'm not good enough for her' thing. You look like the type that parents love. How did you do it with Camille's parents?"

It seemed like meeting the parents was a requisite ritual for mortals and immortals alike. The most accurate comparison in mortal history would be the Spanish Inquisition because of the sounds of internal and external torture being performed. In Ward's case, he was spared the figurative splint under his fingernails.

He met Nora and Jamie Buhay three months after his first date with Camille. She'd been worried at the time—not that they'd hate him on sight, but that they'd make uncharitable assumptions. They were far warmer than his own parents. Nora had fed him until he couldn't eat another bite. She showed him all of Camille's hula dancing recital pictures by the end of the visit. He and Jamie shared a beer on the porch for a bit. Camille's pensive nature came from him. Father and daughter both chose their words carefully and very well. For them, the silence wasn't accidental, it was intentional. Overall, the visit went as well as could be expected, which made it more of a shame when the relationship inevitably fell apart.

"Well, I had to prove to them that I wasn't just a rich white boy that was going to break their daughter's heart. It's about assuaging their fears about you. Nominally, they care about their daughter, and that's what it's all about. Start with a bit of empathy even though it might be hard."

Theo rested his chin on his hands as his thick brows knitted together. "And if it's not that at all? Her mother doesn't really . . . she's not the nurturing type and never has been. Din relied on her sisters the moment she popped into existence. And while her sisters are civil, they aren't exactly welcoming either."

"Is this a status thing then?" Ward asked.

"Of course." Theo rubbed his creased forehead. "I'm not the flashiest of gods nor blessed with good looks. Before you protest, I know what I am, and after thousands of years, I'm fine with it. I'm only impressive because you're not used to us. I'm a loser—"

Ward reached over and clasped the god's shoulder. "No, you're not. You've given me more kindness than anyone else. This is why Din is with you now. I bet she could have anyone she wanted and she chose you."

"You think so?"

Across the room, Din laughed to herself. Her laughter had a multi-tonal quality to it. Three voices ranging in octaves, almost singing in harmony. Even though it was yesterday, Ward barely remembered hearing her speak and couldn't confirm if her speaking voice was singular or plural. Anything was possible. Din was a goddess. If she wanted to speak in whale, she could.

"Yeah. She wouldn't be here with you otherwise."

Theo perked up a bit. The twinkle returned to his brown eyes. He glanced back at his girlfriend. "I want to impress her. Like a grand gesture. I don't have the capital to buy her something from here, at least, not yet. Got any ideas?"

"What does she like?"

"She's into some weird, spontaneous shit." He leaned back, tilting his chair on its back two legs. "Din likes flash mobs, unexpected fireworks, surprise parties. One time she couldn't stop laughing and smiling when I showed her how Americans treat Black Fridays. She wanted to be right in there with them, trying to fight for some useless flat-screen TV."

"Have you tried granting her wish? Personally, I wouldn't want to be trampled, but you gods are trample-proof, yes? Have that as a backup in the future. I'm sure there are other wacky phenomena around the globe that you can take her to in the meantime."

"I like the sound of this. I think she'll really like it. Thanks, man." Theo grinned. "I got an idea of where to take her to-night. She's going to—"

The alarm went off. The lights in the shop flared red as a high-pitched ringing assaulted Ward's ears. They both jumped to their feet. Din ran back to Theo, wild-eyed, clinging to him. She shivered and buried her face in his neck.

Nothing in the displays was amiss. The pendant Din had admired remained intact in its case.

"Shit. We better go." Theo fumbled in his pockets and re-trieved a paper heart. "Camille gave me this to pass on. We can't be caught here. Din's mom will kill us."

Ward accepted the note. "I'm sure it's just a mistake. Go. I'll deal with it."

"You sure?" He took a step toward the exit with Din. "Thanks. You saved my ass."

The couple hurried out before the doors locked. If some-thing were stolen, the doors wouldn't allow them to leave. The way the shop dealt with Eryna implied dire and immediate consequences. This was a triggered alarm like the one you'd see in a museum or art gallery where an unsuspecting person leaned in far too close or accidentally touched an artifact—most likely a clueless tourist or an uncontrollable child with grubby hands.

Madam Selene emerged from her office. The bangles on her wrist jangled with every furious step. "Mr. Dunbar, what is going on here?"

"It's a mistake. I claim responsibility." He raised his palms. "Nothing was taken."

"I see. You have violated one of the rules, Mr. Dunbar. You're to be detained until the appropriate time has passed." She snapped her fingers.

A whooshing, invisible force yanked him forward, down the hallway, into an open door that wasn't there before. The door slammed shut behind him and locked.

Ward Dunbar was officially in time-out.

Confinement in addition to incarceration seemed unnecessary. Actions had consequences, and though technically it had been Din who must have gotten too close to one of the displays, it was on his watch. He was relegated to the corner until the grown-ups had deemed the proper amount of time had elapsed.

His smaller jail cell appeared to be used for storage. The size was thrice that of the restroom. Various crates were stacked against the wall. Black velvet boxes in various sizes crowded the polished brass shelves. Three overhead lamps provided enough light to eliminate any dark corners. Of course, no windows and no vault.

The vault, if there was one, must be in Madam Selene's office.

Despite the punishment, Ward had no regrets about helping Theo. The god was the only one who had shown him any measure of kindness by bringing him news of Camille, and having spoken to her this morning, Ward was more determined to get the hell out of there. Theo gave him hope.

The paper heart was still in his pocket, along with the mints, chocolate bar, and walnut.

He pulled out the folded note and read it.

"Remember the heist-themed escape room we couldn't get out of? Think about the light puzzle box you were so consumed with—the one with the mirrors. We have to be aware of all the angles and which way to guide the light. We're the beams and everything else is smoke and mirrors. XO—Camille."

Before all this, being trapped in a confined space was not a joke. Somehow, humans made getting out of one a common, even enjoyable activity. Think of a magician's trick of bypassing a straitjacket but without the dislocated joints, attractive assistant, flapping doves, and rapt audience. Escape rooms were one of Ward and Camille's favorite date night pastimes. They loved the thrill of getting out and working with each other, though it was quite tense in spots. Her tendency to be quiet contrasted with his need to verbalize everything he was thinking. Despite the turmoil and conflict, they managed a high escape rate together.

Ward shook his head. The idea that they were pawns in some sort of game resonated with him. If he had any way of escaping, he'd need to think about strategy and communication, and figure out what the rules and who the players were—aside from himself, Camille, and their respective bosses.

Self-pity wouldn't help anyone out of any sticky situation.

A large, draped object caught his eye. The heavy black velvet cloth rustled under an invisible breeze. A low, distinct humming emanated from that side of the room—the kind that snaked under his skin, vibrating until all the fine hairs on his arms stood up. He ran his tongue along the edges of his teeth where the sound itched his gums.

Ward tucked Camille's note into his pocket and got up to investigate.

The heavy cloth was soft to the touch, with a slight bristly texture. He yanked it off to reveal an oval, gilded baroque mirror. The reflection was off but not distorted like one of those fun house mirrors at the county fair. The face staring back at him wasn't quite right.

He reached out to touch the surface, and his fingertips sank into it.

Two hands made of liquid silver reached out from the mirror, grabbing hold of his arms and pulling him in.

9

Camille

. . . . .

DAY THREE

. . . . .

"WARD?" I CALLED.

He cut out. There must be a time limit.

A sudden, ringing headache pierced both my temples. I took off the headdress and returned it to its velvet box. Magic. I had to accept it. Microchips and nanotechnology didn't explain anything in this world. I wished it did. It'd give me less of a headache.

I tucked the box under my arm and headed for my flat upstairs.

Hearing Ward's deep voice sent parts of my body aflame. The morning we last saw each other, he had his head buried between my thighs in the shower. His tongue carved out and thoroughly tasted every inch of me. God. He made me climax twice as I screamed out his name.

I squeezed my legs shut.

I hadn't been this horny since being in physical proximity to him. This was always his effect on me, and yes, it was very much mutual. I had better take a cold shower or I wouldn't be able to think straight for the rest of the day.

AFTER TAKING CARE of myself in the shower, I managed to collect my thoughts. The headache and the horniness onset weren't a coincidence, were they? The Tang dynasty jade headdress glittered from the overhead pot lights. When I set it up on display at a nearby side table, I almost missed the note included inside.

I lifted the cream-colored postcard with the same typeface and embossed quality as Mr. King's calling card. "Prolonged use will result in debilitating migraines and deterioration of physical health. The time limit is five minutes and for use only after the end of your shift. Use it well or not at all. Sincerely, Mr. King."

Ward had mentioned gods in our conversation. Mr. King, Theo, and Eryna fell into this category. Ghosts and gods. And where did Ward and I fit into this?

I sat by the kitchen table with my journal open. Every theory and scrap of information was laid out in sections. My habit of journaling provided me with control when my life wobbled and teetered on a precarious axis. I started it as a bullied teen when every emotion seemed to swallow me whole only to regurgitate me the next day. I outgrew my angles and awkwardness and lucked out in the looks department on the other side. Life got better, and I continued to journal. Ward had seen where I'd kept all of my old diaries, and he never asked for me to get rid of them—everyone else deemed them recyclable.

Some things were worth keeping.

Like Ward and me.

I clenched my left hand into a fist as I jotted down more notes.

When I lay down to sleep, my brain hurt from the information overload. I re-created a whiteboard covered with a tangled spiderweb of red string in my journal. Ward had more of a tendency to be a conspiracy theorist, but his belief in the goodness of people curbed his ability to visualize the worst-case scenarios. I had no such guardrails.

The only people I trusted were Ward and Mr. Samson.

Nobody else.

Everyone either conspired to keep us imprisoned or did nothing to help. Much like lying by omission, the crime of being a passive bystander fell on these ghosts and gods.

MR. SAMSON WAITED for me by the counter at the start of my shift. The windows outside showed a nighttime London—a world I was no longer a part of. I couldn't bring myself to stare out the windows of my cage.

"Can you believe that this store was empty when I came here?" He cradled a carriage clock in his hands. "This one was from a young thief from the Victorian era. He had quite a set of stories about the ladies of the age."

The antiques in this shop had been acquired in his lifetime. It made sense, since he seemed much better with people—or ghosts, in this case. I couldn't imagine how long it would take me to accomplish the same goal. He'd almost filled the shelves to the brink, yet he was still trapped.

I filed this information away before tucking my notebook behind the counter. "So that was stolen then?"

"It was a gift from a lonely baroness. Our thief's specialty was filching horses." Mr. Samson returned the clock to its spot on the back shelves. "There are times when they are reluctant to part with their memories but know that they need to."

The first woman appeared desperate to give me her locket, while the couple had offered their treasures without any trouble. Right now, I didn't want to have to persuade anyone. I hated client-facing positions. When the job was advertised to me, it mentioned involving minimal front-of-the-house work. If I'd known I had to talk to clients, I wouldn't have applied—though now knowing that this involved nonconsensual incarceration, I would have stayed on my side of the ocean.

"One other thing I forgot to mention. We have more visitors. They will try and buy something here, though they're mostly here to browse. I haven't had a sale when I was at the counter. They can be quite intimidating and difficult. Don't let them push you around."

"Of course they would be, they're gods."

My reply sent his snowy brows rising. "So that's what they are. I was trying to figure it out for decades. The woman and the man never aged. I never cared much for him, but she can be quite charming when she wants to be."

"You've been flirting with a goddess, Mr. Samson? How scandalous." I gasped for dramatic emphasis.

The poor man blushed and turned away to cough. In a wee voice, he conceded, "Perhaps a little. It's been so lonely being here by myself all these years."

"When did you last see her?"

"I can't recall. Perhaps a decade ago?" He rubbed his left temple. "My memories are quite fuzzy. It's probably why I was tasked to hire you, my eventual replacement. Has it been that long ago when I wandered in here searching for her?" The faraway look in his blue eyes accompanied the softness of his voice. "I can't even remember her face."

"The goddess?"

"No, the one before . . ." He covered his eyes and yawned. "I'm afraid I've reached my limits for today."

I placed a hand on his arm. "Go rest. I have everything handled out here."

He shuffled off down the hallway toward his office.

His memory and his energy levels were diminishing. Would Ward and I end up the same way? I realized that I didn't want to replace Mr. Samson. I'd take him with me when I got out. He shouldn't die here after giving so much of his life to this place. I refused to give more than I had to.

I'd been rearranging a stack of first edition novels when the bell tinkled.

Theo had returned, and this time, he had someone with him. She was tall, gorgeous, and way out of his league. She wore an oversized chestnut wool jacket paired with dark leggings and high leather boots. The pixie quality of her face made me wonder what kind of a goddess she was. Theo's usual hoodie and baggy pants ensemble did nothing to elevate my opinion of him.

It wasn't what he wore per se, it was how he *wore* it—with arrogance and a seething sense of entitlement.

The striking redhead wandered off down one of the aisles

while Theo made his way to the counter. His hands were shoved into his pockets, creating triangles below his hips.

"Ward says hi. No note today, though, because there was a mishap at the shop. Don't worry, our boy is all right."

Right. Ward trusted this fool. I should play along to cover my bases. "Thank you for passing my note." The smile I gave him was nothing like the resting bitch face I wore on the inside. "How is he?"

"Better. I helped him out with a few things. He's a really good guy. How did you two ever get together?" He leaned across the counter and glanced over his shoulder to check on his companion, who seemed enthralled with a plague mask at the moment.

"I'll tell you my story if you tell me yours."

"Deal." He clapped his hands. "Din and I go back to when this world had that brand-new smell. Had a crush on her since then, and last century, she finally remembered and noticed I existed. She's been with me since."

The truncated story reeked of plot holes. I decided to reciprocate. "Ward and I met in college. He was someone I didn't expect to fall for. Physical chemistry was definitely a factor."

"I mean, he is a good-looking bastard. Makes sense."

"Are you or Din seeking to buy something today?" I asked.

"She might. I don't really care for all these worthless tchotchkes."

I scrubbed the irritation from my voice. "Why do you think they're worthless?"

"Mortals have lived and died with such short lives. Most live unremarkable ones. It's nothing I haven't seen before.

Catch the fire of a star, sure. Humans are a speck in the grand scheme of things. No offense."

"Must be *really* awesome to be a god." Ward was the only one in the world who knew that the sweetness in my voice was a warning sign. "So much power."

"It is, actually. It has its perks . . . There was this one time . . ."

I nodded and inserted a syllable here and there while he rambled on. While he talked about himself, my attention wandered toward his girlfriend. Din had somehow donned the plague mask and was skulking around the store. Whatever dynamic held these two together, I had no clue. Theo proved himself to be a frat bro, long life and powers included.

"Ah, I hate to interrupt. Is she going to buy that?" I asked.

The mask was perched on her head with the pointed beak a foot up in the air. She admired her reflection in a nearby silver-framed mirror.

Theo whipped his head around and found his girlfriend. "Really, you want that, Din?"

She nodded, almost shaking the mask off her head.

"A girl wants what a girl wants." I turned to get the scales. Though Mr. Samson wasn't explicit in his instruction, every transaction in this place involved this magical point of sale. "I hope the price isn't too steep for you."

He winced and emptied his pockets, checking the items.

Din stood beside him. She bit her lower lip and clutched the mask to her chest.

Theo managed to scrounge up a few glass marbles. They rolled onto the counter and spun in place of their own volition. Nothing was ever what it seemed in this world. Though I wondered about their true nature, I dared not touch them.

"Please place your payment." I gestured to the left scale while I accepted the plague mask from Din.

The oversized item wouldn't possibly fit on the right scale, yet I'd seen stranger things happen here. I stuck the beak on the plate. The item shuddered, shrinking into the perfect size to fit on its pedestal. I stepped away to watch the scale teeter.

"Wait, I should add this." Theo tossed a piece of raw crystal onto the pile.

It was one of those that you see in geodes—uncut, with layers of rock clinging to the bottom. The cluster of crystals was violet, possibly amethysts, at least to the naked human eye.

The extra addition was enough to balance the scales.

The chunk of crystal along with the marbles vanished into disintegrating specks like the ghost couple.

Din clapped her hands and held them outstretched to receive her paid-for purchase.

I plucked the smaller version from the plate, and with a soft pop, it expanded to full size in my arms. I thrust it into her hands as if it were radioactive. She giggled and placed the mask over her face. Her striking blue eyes glowed from the darkness of the tinted glass goggles.

Of all the things in this shop, it was an interesting choice.

Theo turned to his girlfriend. "You love it?"

She nodded vigorously and giggled. The sound was a pure, hedonistic delight.

"I guess it's worth it then. Guess not all this stuff is junk." He turned to me. "Do you want me to pass anything back to Ward?"

"I'll wait until he says something back. Thank you for the offer."

"All right. Don't say I didn't ask." Theo took Din's hand in his. "Come on. Let's go show that thing off."

The couple walked toward the door. Din glanced over her shoulder at me. The blue spark of her eyes was still visible behind the opaque glass.

A three-voice chorus inside my head sang, "You both can't get out of here alive."

10

Ward

. . . . .

DAY THREE AND DAY FOUR

. . . . .

WARD PLANTED HIS feet and pulled himself away. Barely. He landed on his ass and safely away from the diabolical mirror. Once his heart stopped pounding like it wanted to fly out of his rib cage, he tossed the fabric over it and positioned himself at the opposite end of the room.

This was his first brush with despair in its concentrated form. The mirror invited those to fall into oblivion with its embrace. However, if there still remained a speck, a hint that hope still exists, then it would release its victim.

Though he was quite unaware of it, Ward's love for Camille saved him from this peril.

Love was often underestimated, derided, and reduced to a maudlin excuse for the simple and gullible. True love transformed even the most miserable creature. No one was impervious—no matter how adamant the denial.

Ward retreated to the farthest spot away from the dangerous object. After an hour, he took a bite of the chocolate, opened the walnut, and set up the hammock for the night. The mirror at the far end of the room continued to haunt him, and uneasiness crept into his sleep.

The door was unlocked when he awoke the next morning. Ward popped two mints and checked the clock on the wall. Thirty minutes before his shift. The punishment was grave for what he perceived as a minor offense.

"Ward? Are you there?"

It was Camille's voice again coming from everywhere at once. Hope rose in his throat that this might be a daily occurrence. "I'm here. I was in time-out."

She laughed. "I had that too. I freaked out on my first day when I saw the ghosts. What rule did you break?"

"The alarm tripped here. Nothing was stolen, but . . ."

"Did you cover for Theo? Ward, you can't trust these gods."

He frowned. "Who can we trust then? We're apart and there's no one to help us, and he's not as bad as you think. I'd be dead without him. It's impossible to get out of here without having help."

"Maybe. People always want something in return."

Camille wasn't wrong. Transactional relationships were common in nature. Remoras weren't evicted from swimming with sharks because they performed free grooming. In return, these tiny fish had the benefit of flashing the big predator as a friend at fun ocean parties.

"You did get help, didn't you? I mean, how else are we talking to each other right now?"

She snorted. "I guess. Tell me all the gods you've dealt with, other than Theo."

"Din, his girlfriend, Mr. King, and Eryna. No one else has visited the shop."

"I think Din is harmless. She's a bit odd though. Mr. King reminds me of my cousins, and as for Eryna—I don't like or trust her."

"Mr. King is an ass, but he isn't as terrible as Eryna. She threatened my boss, Madam Selene, and was kicked out. Apparently, she's allowed back in. They work on a two-strike rule at my shop."

"Eryna has an ability to control you. Be careful around her. Don't tell *anyone* we can communicate yet."

She meant Theo. "Will do."

"Before I go, Din said something to me—that we both can't get out of here alive. I'm not quite sure what this means—"

Her voice cut out. Their conversations had the lasting power of five minutes, as confirmed by his watching the clock. The white-faced analog timekeeper had two golden, ornate arms that moved with soft ticks.

Din's ominous warning rang inside Ward's head. He made a mental note to ask Theo about it the next time the god visited.

Madam Selene emerged from her office. She sniffed the air. "I appreciate the improvement, Mr. Dunbar. I'm sure you're as grateful as I am."

"Was my offense proportional to the punishment?"

She frowned. Her drawn-in brows threaded together. "I don't know how the punishments are meted out or the rationality behind them. In all my years here, I've followed every rule. Tell me what was in that room and what you were subjected to. You seem to be in one whole piece."

"Confinement on a smaller scale. I believe it's the shop's storage room. There were other boxes in there, and before you

ask, I never bothered to check. Oh, there was also a magic mirror that was determined to pull me in and kill me."

"Interesting, Mr. Dunbar. Have you noticed that the new
door remains? This place continues to be full of terrifying
wonders."

"Exactly how long have you been here?"

She narrowed her eyes and crossed her arms, bangles jingling.
"I can't comment. There are certain subjects that are taboo. I
have no intention of seeing the storage room anytime soon. Your
lackadaisical attitude toward your duties isn't mutual."

Ward continued to fish and see where it would take him.
"And your office, where exactly do you go? Is it another dimen-
sion where you have a grand mansion on a cliff and an infinity
pool?"

"You have such a vivid imagination. You might want to use
that to sell another piece to a client. I'm hoping that when all
these pieces are sold . . ."

"That we can get out?"

She gave him a slight nod. "It's what I believe. You've managed to sell one. There are five more items left. You give me
hope, Mr. Dunbar. I don't say that lightly." She pressed her
fingers against her temples. "You have only one appointment
today. I suggest you try and close the deal. And remember the
rules lest you get another date with that mirror you spoke of."

After she left, Ward reached for the leather portfolio and
found Theo's name. With his new sales goal in mind, he should
test out the theory and try to get his new immortal friend to
purchase something.

The hypothesis made sense. He was, after all, hired for
sales. He and Camille had a part to play in this grand game,

and it had to be within the realm of possibility that the key was the jobs they were hired for.

The front door opened. Theo wore a puffy bomber jacket with a loud tie-dye pattern in greens, oranges, and purples with canvas khakis. He came alone.

"Where's Din?" Ward asked.

"She's off, playing with a brand-new toy. I bought it for her at your girlfriend's shop. She'll miss me more when we're apart I think." He rotated the chair so that he straddled the seat. "Women are such complicated creatures. She's quite happy though. It's what you advised me to do. I was spontaneous and bought her a present. It cost me. Worth it though. She couldn't keep her hands and mouth off me last night."

"I'm happy for you." Ward walked toward the displays. "Anything you want to see today?"

"Sure. Bring me the jade necklace. I wouldn't mind seeing that up close."

Ward retrieved Theo's requested piece and brought the black velvet stand and necklace to the table before opening the portfolio and scanning the details. The jade beads of uneven size made up the strand. The ends joined in a brass hook clasp. The pendant was a Mayan carving of a head complete with a headdress, with angular lines and geometric features.

"This once belonged to Hunac Ceel," Ward read from the card. "A twelfth-century Mayan general."

Theo leaned forward and poked the pendant with his thumb. The audible zap singed the ends of his curly hair. He fell back and laughed. "Hoo boy! As potent as I thought."

This explained why Mr. King had been so careful not to touch the Tang dynasty jewelry.

Ward rubbed his gloved fingertips and was thankful for the added protection. "Are you all right?"

"I'm good. It's . . ." Theo lowered his voice to a harsh whisper. "You know what these are, right?"

"Relics and artifacts, mostly jewelry. Are you telling me it's something else?"

"When you mortals die, you give up— This won't work. I have to start from the beginning." He cupped one hand to the side of his mouth. "So, all the powerful figures in mortal history, they got there with a little bit of divine help. Most of them. It's rare for a mortal to rise above his brethren and live a remarkable life. How do they do this? They strike a bargain with one of us. So our boy Hunac did this to get some tail. Something about someone else's hot wife. At least that's what the zap tells me."

"You're saying that bargains between gods and mortals are common?"

"It depends on what you mortals want and how much of a price you're willing to pay for it. In *his* case, he gave up his own afterlife, and what you see here is his essence in a more elegant form." Theo patted down his hair. "We gods have a certain aesthetic standard to uphold apparently. Bargains are a big deal—not every god gives them out like candy. It costs us something too."

"What does it cost you?"

"We end up caring. When you exist for as long as we do, you stop giving a shit about the world, including mortals. We'd rather sharpen our grudges with each other and see who'll win."

"Like a war?"

"Yeah. We've been deadlocked since the Middle Ages."

"Do you mind if I write a note for Camille?" Ward asked.

"Sure." Theo reached into his pockets and pulled out a notebook and a pen. "I'll deliver it as soon as I can."

Ward jotted down all the information he had learned, tore out a page from the coils, and folded the paper four times. A small pinky-purple gumball wrapped in clear plastic popped out from the book. It glowed ombré and shimmered with an inner light. Ward picked it up and handed it to the god. "You dropped this."

"Oh, did I?" Theo wagged his eyebrows. "That, my friend, is another gift from yours truly."

"What does it do?"

"It's onetime only use. Trust me, you'll thank me forever for it. My aunt doles those out at her infamous parties. We know how to light it up in the West."

The bright gumball in Ward's hand pulsed with warmth. After having indulged in immortal sweets, he was intrigued by this one. Everything about the immortal world and its powers fulfilled his boundless imagination. He was the proverbial magpie, always distracted by the next big, shiny trinket.

"I'd wait until you're done with your shift and before Camille starts hers. This is a multiplayer co-op game." Theo rubbed his palms together. "Oh, you'll probably end up worshipping me after. Of all the presents I gave you, this is the best one."

11

Camille

. . . . .

DAY FOUR

. . . . .

AS WAS MY custom, I hopped into the shower right before my shift. The citrus-based shampoo helped me wake up from a bout of restless sleep. The pounding headache from the jade jewelry hadn't abated. The two ibuprofen I had taken might help get rid of it—then again, I wasn't dealing with an ordinary kind of headache.

I scrubbed my scalp harder, hoping the impulsive massage would bring me relief.

It didn't.

Through the fogged glass, a sparkly, somewhat translucent, spectral version of my ex-boyfriend appeared on the other side of the shower door. "Camille?"

"Ward, how . . . ?" I turned down the water and pulled the door open. "Oh."

Our time apart had almost made me forget how gorgeous he was. Slightly long wheat-blond hair that he often brushed away from his forehead. Beautiful sky-blue eyes, angular cheekbones, and full lips made for kissing and everything else. Hitting the gym in the mornings sculpted his arms, abs, ass, and legs. He was *here*. Naked and erect.

I stepped out of the shower.

"Theo. He gave me a little something that, uh . . . some kind of god candy? It has a bit of a side effect, as you can see." The pupils of his eyes darkened. "I'm not expecting anything from this. I just thought I could be with you in some way."

The way he looked at me was that of the famished and thirsty, and that was what I also saw reflected in his eyes. I reached out and grabbed *him*—expecting to feel nothingness, yet his perfect, thick cock was warm in my hands. This would be fun.

I pulled him toward me.

We both floated an inch or two above the floor. He captured my mouth with his, nipping my lower lip with his teeth. "God, you don't know how much I've dreamed and wanted this."

"The feeling is mutual." I ground my hips against him, rubbing myself along his length.

He reached behind me and cupped my ass, lifting me up so he bathed my breasts in hot kisses. Pleasure burst from inside me, clearing my lingering headache. He nipped an aching bud between his lips. I shuddered, crying out.

"And this, I want to taste all of you."

He hoisted me up onto his shoulders, balancing me as he buried his face between my legs. All of a sudden we were both weightless, floating in the air. His hands reached up to squeeze my breasts and tease my erect nipples. Ward's tongue traced every inch of me, licking, lashing, taunting my clit. I dug my hands in his golden hair and whimpered, tugging him on, until the stars burst behind my eyes. I came hard, screaming his name.

He lowered me into his arms. I reached out and guided his cock inside me. Wrapping my limp legs around his waist, I urged him on by rocking my hips. "Come inside me," I whispered, then added with a laugh, "I don't think we have to worry about birth control."

I was slick and ready for him. He groaned as he sank into me, thrusting, filling me up completely. His strokes were languid, angled to rub against my sensitive clit. "Harder. Don't wait," I moaned.

Ward kissed the side of my throat and growled. He thrust harder, grinding against me, filling me until we both climaxed and collapsed into each other.

"How is this possible?" I asked in a ragged whisper.

He brushed his fingertips along my cheek. "Gods and their magic. I don't know how long this will last, so I better say it now. I still love you and I've always loved you. No matter what happens to us, nothing will change this . . ."

Ward's words trailed off as he flickered in and out. His warmth was already leaving me. "I love you too," I said before he blipped out of view.

I hoped he heard me.

I DECIDED TO forgo the daily chat with Ward. We had already "spoken" this morning. Despite the fact the pesky headache returned, I didn't deny the bounce in my step when I started my shift at the antique shop. Sex with Ward had always been the easiest part of our relationship. When we spoke with body language and pleasure, there were no arguments. Conflict was always something simmering under the surface, and even now, I feared that something would puncture our somewhat idyllic state. We had bigger things to contend with and worry about than what had driven us apart years ago.

"Someone found a scrap of precious happiness this morning." Mr. Samson noted the silly grin on my face. "Could you spare a little for me?"

"I wish I could."

"Oh my." Mr. Samson withdrew a kerchief from his jacket pocket. He hurried toward me and dabbed my upper lip. He pulled the fabric away to show me the spot of scarlet marring it before he gave it back.

I held it against my nose. I hadn't had a nosebleed since sixth grade when I was hit in the face in a vicious game of dodgeball. The headache from behind my eyes flared with a vengeance. This was from the headdress only after two uses. The gods don't play. Still, it was worth it to be able to communicate with Ward without anyone listening. "It's nothing. Don't look too worried. I'll be all right."

"Pinch the bridge of your nose. Yes, that's it. It should stop soon."

I followed his instructions, and soon enough, the bleeding stopped. "I'm sorry about your kerchief. I can run a load of laundry and have it back to you tomorrow night."

"Ah, don't trouble yourself. It's yours to keep, Ms. Buhay."

He adjusted the shoulders of his dusty jacket. A few threads popped out of the seams. Things were beginning to unravel.

Something had been set into motion that day when Eryna came in and compelled me to light a candle. The changes I'd seen in Mr. Samson were far too coincidental. He'd been more tired, more aged, and more diminished. It was affecting him as much as Mr. King's gift had affected me.

Over his shoulder, the pink flame of the black candle danced before turning blue. The pillar of wax itself had a dripping skirt at the base. Despite the magic in this object, as evident in the strange flame colors, it was melting down. An invisible countdown was ticking. I suspected Ward and I needed to escape before the candle went out. It was already a quarter spent.

I pulled out my journal and jotted down this nugget of information.

"Congratulations on selling a piece in the shop!" Mr. Samson clapped. "I didn't think it was possible."

"It was an easier sell. A goddess took a liking to something in here, and her god-boyfriend was pressured to buy it for her. I'd never seen anyone so thrilled with a plague mask before."

"Ahh, that was what was sold. I vaguely recall acquiring it. It was from a plague doctor who was traumatized from the amount of death he experienced all around him. It was mayhem." He shook his head. "I'm fairly certain he was suffering from PTSD."

I picked up a painted wooden box of bone dice and shook it. "What's the story behind these?"

His blank stare worried me. I wasn't sure if he heard me or

if he was trying to remember. I waved my hand before his face. "Mr. Samson?"

He didn't answer. The faraway look in his eyes deepened. I touched his arm, squeezing with gentle pressure while watching to see any response. After thirty seconds, he blinked. The tension in my chest released, and I exhaled.

"Ah, Ms. Buhay, was I in the middle of talking about something? It's so easy now to forget. The train of thought is much harder to keep track of at my age." He noticed the box in my hand. "What do you have there? I don't think I've seen it before. Is it a new acquisition?"

I lied. "Yes. Yesterday, someone came in with them."

I didn't want to upset him or trigger another forgetting spell. This man was the only ally I had in this shop, and I didn't want to lose him. He'd been trapped here for too long. He shouldn't die here, and I had to save him and myself.

"If you're tired, you should go and rest. I'm starting to get accustomed to running everything in the shop because of your guidance." I mustered a cheery tone and threaded my arm through his. "Besides, semiretirement doesn't sound so bad, does it? You'll be here every morning to check on me."

"I suppose." He patted my hand on his arm as we strolled down the hall. "I have to tell you, I'm so glad that you're here. You've been a sheer joy to work with."

I walked him to his office. He opened the door and shuffled inside. Behind him were vague shadows and shapes, nothing I could make out. I hoped he had a flat of his own on the other side of the wall.

The bell jingled. I rushed back to the counter to see a surprise visitor.

A little Black girl, about the age of seven or eight, with round red glasses, box braids, and a school uniform, stood two feet in front of the counter. She held out a thick, dusty, well-loved volume of Carl Sagan's *Cosmos*. "Hi, is this where I can sell this?"

Her sweet voice had a slight Southern American accent.

"Yes, of course. May I?"

She pushed the book onto the counter.

She was so young and a ghost. Though I itched to know what had happened to her, I dared not ask. If I'd been in her place, I wouldn't want a stranger prying into how I died. It was my story to tell and not anyone else's.

"Can I take a look around before I sell it?" she asked.

"Go ahead."

I took the scales from the back counter and searched for the box with the star crystal.

She took about ten minutes—to discover and point out anything star related in the shop. She especially adored the gilded starburst mirror hanging on the gallery wall. Because of her intense interest, I waited until she returned to the counter before bringing out the wooden box containing the crystal counterweight.

"What's in there? The design is astrological." She peered at the box.

This was new to me. "Is it?"

"Yes. See this." She traced a symbol of two bent arches joined to each other. "That's Aries and my sign." The spot where her ghostly fingertips touched glowed, highlighting the fire sign. She then continued to point out the rest.

The carved box shone with shimmering symbols on every side.

"And this last one is Ophiuchus, the serpent bearer, and thirteenth sign." She trailed her index finger along a U-shaped sign with an undulating line across it. "Not many people believe in it, but hard-core astrologers do."

I didn't know about the thirteenth sign. I barely remembered my own. Astrology was something my mother believed in. Her superstitious nature encouraged her to make calls to psychics and get tarot readings—all of this while being a devout Catholic. She excused the blasphemous behavior by saying it was her hobby. Dad and I tolerated it as long as she didn't get too carried away.

"I thought astronomy and astrology are two opposing groups. One being science based and the other not."

"They are. Zodiac signs originated from constellations. I see it as two different photo filters over the same subject. Guess which one I prefer?" She let out an adorable giggle that broke up the overall seriousness in her expression.

"Well, the book says you're more of an astronomer."

She pushed her ghostly glasses up the bridge of her nose. "Correct."

I opened the box and showed her the star crystal. It pulsated with bright purple and pink lights under the dark surface. I would have offered to let her examine or even touch it, but I wasn't sure if it would harm her.

She cooed as I placed it on one side of the scale and the book on the other.

The scale balanced almost instantly.

The ghost girl grinned. "I guess this means goodbye. It's funny that we don't really spend a long time in this world. When I was close to dying, I felt it. Don't you feel it too?"

"What?"

"You should." She disintegrated into floating specks. "You're dying."

12

Ward

· · · · ·

DAY FIVE

· · · · ·

GIFTS CAME IN all sorts of shapes and sizes. The best ones were unique and often experience based. There's something more precious about enjoying the ephemeral. In Ward's case, he had been wooed with gifts from Theo, and the last one left quite an indelible memory.

Ward and Camille's relationship had always been physical, not only in the conjugal sense. Every time they were near each other, they connected through touch—whether it was sitting together in silence as they both read after work or holding hands when they navigated the stairs to hop on the L train.

The erotic gumball was definitely responsible for the insufferable shit-eating grin on his face when he showed up for work at the shop. Smugness dripped from every pore. He finally had his itch scratched—and not the one in the middle of his upper back where his arms couldn't reach. Any animal would reach the same level of contentment when its biological urges were met.

Madam Selene hovered over a display, wiping the glass

with a cloth. She paused her task and noted his blissful state of mind. "You look like the cat that ate a dozen canaries, Mr. Dunbar. I certainly am not responsible for *that*."

He chuckled. "Happiness isn't a limited commodity. You should indulge in it more often."

"Now you're implying that I'm a grump by nature."

"Not at all." He waved his hands. "I'm certain you are capable of being happy, giddy even."

She harrumphed and returned to cleaning. Her vigorous movements produced audible squeaks from the glass. "You have two appointments today."

Ward hoped one of them was Theo. He had to thank him for the wonderful gift.

"Not your best friend, unfortunately. It's Mr. King and Eryna. Yes, she's decided to return. I assure you that she will be on her best behavior. She knows the consequences if she's not." Madam Selene gave the glass one more harsh scrub before finishing.

"Can you tell me if there is a vault here?" he asked.

Any respectable establishment had a vault for the more valuable assets—far exceeding the array on display. Ward used his vast imagination to conjure up all sorts of hypothetical treasures that warranted protection. None of these flighty ideas made actual sense, but one couldn't fault him for trying. The concept of a priceless hoard being the epitome of mortal and immortal greed was understandable.

"There is. It has a mind of its own. I've only seen it appear once, a long time ago, and even then, I didn't have the combination or even an idea of how to open it. You'd better get it out of your mind, Mr. Dunbar. It'd be a foolish venture."

"Advice acknowledged."

She narrowed her eyes and snorted. "Why do I think this isn't the last I'll hear of this?"

Ward gave her a noncommittal shrug—one a child reserved for patronizing adults.

"Take care of your two clients and sell them something. Make sure you keep those appointments *separate*." She waved and headed back into her office.

Ward checked the portfolio to read Eryna's profile. "Western Faction. Lieutenant General. Handle with care and caution." These gods almost have ordinary titles. Mr. King was listed as a weapons specialist, and Theo's profile read: "Western Faction. Low-Level Freelancer."

He scratched his head.

Yes, these jobs sounded like those in the military, and this corroborated what Theo had said about war. Ward Dunbar still grappled with how this all fit together, and somehow he guessed that the vault was a crucial part of the puzzle.

He wasn't wrong. His goal was nebulous. He was trying to find a particular mountain but wasn't even certain he was on the right continent. All of this fumbling in the dark was frustrating at best and, at worst, agonizing. He never thought he had anything in common with laboratory rats, and now he could commiserate with them.

The front doors swung open. Mr. King walked in dressed in his customary black suit. This time, he wore a jaunty fedora. The metal plates on his wing tip shoes glinted from the lights. He carried a cane—one with a silver dragon head handle.

Ward greeted him with genuine courtesy. "Good morning, Mr. King. How may I be of service?"

"I don't know how to answer that question yet. Why don't we sit and have a chat first?" He pulled out the chair and took his place across from Ward's empty seat. Instead of leaning the cane against the table, he placed it on top. The dragon head had smoldering, fiery ruby eyes.

"Go ahead. You can take a closer look if you want." The god leaned back and clasped his hands behind his head, elbows out.

Ward lifted the cane up for inspection. It was far lighter than it should have been, which was typical of this world and this place where physics and science didn't apply. The shaft was made of Japanese cedar treated with shou sugi ban. The burning technique transformed the wood into a beautiful matte-black color. The intricately sculpted handle came to life when he touched the crown of the dragon's head. Its regal features shifted, blowing a puff of fire into the air. Incredible.

Ward returned the cane to its spot. "It's a weapon, isn't it?"

"Of course. You can't be a weapons specialist without a weapon or two." Mr. King studied his face as if he were trying to answer his own unspoken question. "You're handsome and quite vigorous. That's clear. There has to be something more that draws you to her. Camille. She's not one of those typical mortal girls that only care about—"

"Yeah, she's special."

"So physical appeal aside, what *does* she see in you?"

It was a question Ward had heard before. First from Camille's nosy cousin Racquel, who didn't have a clue about personal boundaries or a filter. If she had the option to whip out a ruler and measure him on the spot, she would. He often wondered what Camille saw in him. She could have any fellow she wanted. They often hung around her in swarms, but she was oblivious to all that.

"Not sure, honestly."

"She gets something out of the relationship. It's why she's in it. This isn't gleaned from millennia of enlightenment. Reciprocity. Mortals and gods are the same in this respect."

"Surely you have better things to do than talk about my love life. I hear there's a war going on."

Mr. King lifted his dark brows and laughed. "And you're smarter than you look."

"Who's winning?"

"No one. We're tied and have been since the bubonic plague. It's the worst form of tantric sex imaginable." The god picked up his cane and balanced it on the tip of his index finger. "The powers that be are more concerned about causing premature destruction of everything. Be prepared to take a side. You will be asked to. Remaining neutral isn't an option, Mr. Dunbar." The underlying threat in his voice shattered any semblance of nuance.

Ward countered, "How am I supposed to choose a side when I don't even know if anyone is on mine?"

"What if I make you an irresistible offer? Get me the thing I'm looking for, and I can help you and Camille leave this place." Mr. King tossed the cane in the air and caught it with a flourish. "I mean, you don't want to stay here forever. That's the alternative. It'd be a blessing if you died first . . ."

The door chime echoed, and Eryna strode in. She was dressed in a short, gauzy red dress and towering stilettos. Her long dark hair hung unbound past her lower back. Her green eyes blazed when she spotted Mr. King.

"What are you doing here?" She placed her hands on her hips. "I have a standing appointment."

Mr. King remained seated. He planted his feet and waved her off with his left hand while clutching the cane with his right. "This is still my time, Eryna. Be a good girl and wait your turn."

"Bullshit." She waved both arms and produced two wicked, curved swords out of thin air.

"Whoa, whoa, whoa." Ward held up his palms. "Weapons bad. Eryna, please put those away."

Mr. King stood and twirled the cane with his hands until it extended into a staff. The rush of breeze built into a gale-force wall of air toward her. She rushed forward, blades drawn, to clash her steel against his spinning staff. They moved in a blur and their movements reminded Ward of a zoetrope—a device where you spin the cylinders, and through the slits, the drawing of a horse in full gallop comes to life.

He stepped back and away to preserve his limbs. The magnetic force drawing them together sent electricity crackling in the air, zapping the ends of Ward's hair. This was far above his pay grade.

Madam Selene emerged from the hallway with her gray hair raised in a frizzy halo. "What in the world is going on, Mr. Dunbar?"

"That." Ward pointed to the dueling clients.

She cupped her hands over her nose and mouth. "I told you to keep them separate! Apparently, you can't even understand simple instructions."

Ward waved his arms in the air. "She came in early. I . . ."

Madam Selene hurried toward the wall near the desk. She

pressed her palms against it and whispered something inaudible. To anyone else, she appeared in prayer.

A low siren went off. Mr. King and Eryna froze in place. Madam Selene approached them with the expression and mannerisms of a stern schoolteacher. "This is not acceptable behavior from either of you. The shop has spoken. Consider yourselves warned."

They were both released.

Eryna brushed a stray strand of hair in her face. Her swords vanished as did Mr. King's weapon, which reverted to its original state as a walking cane. He straightened his jacket.

"Mr. King, you have ten minutes left in your appointment, then you must leave when Eryna has here," Madam Selene instructed the two. "In the future, if your visits are not the first one of the day, wait the allotted ten minutes before entering. I do apologize. Mr. Dunbar shouldn't have allowed this to happen. In all of my years . . ."

His boss had just thrown Ward under the proverbial bus. Ouch.

"No need. I'll leave now." Mr. King gave a jaunty wave.

Eryna stuck out her heel and made him stumble on the way out. She cackled to herself as she sashayed toward the desk.

"I trust that you'll not allow this to happen again," Madam Selene chided. She shook her head. "I can't spend all my time cleaning up your messes, Mr. Dunbar."

Before Ward could explain what happened, she was returning to her office, muttering to herself.

"Edward," Eryna called him over. "Come, amuse me."

He took a seat and watched her with caution.

"I don't bite. At least, unless you want me to." A surprising sweetness coated her voice. She dripped fructose with every syllable. "I can tell you something about your sweetheart. Would that ease your worries?"

He didn't respond.

The goddess said in a singsong voice, "I know you've been speaking to her in secret."

Again, he showed no reaction.

"A little bit every day. Did she ever tell you how this is possible? This little bit of magic?" She waved her manicured fingers in the air and produced a shower of sparks.

"No. I assumed she must have gotten a gift from a god somehow."

"And what a gift! You sold it recently."

The Tang dynasty jewelry set.

"Mr. King gave it to Camille. Such a generous boon." Eryna's green eyes twinkled as she cupped a hand to the side of her mouth and whispered, "It's poisoned. It's going to eventually kill her."

Ward tensed and clenched his jaw.

"See." Eryna reached out and touched his cheek. "I can be helpful. Now, what are you going to do to save your precious love from inevitable doom?"

13

Camille

. . . . .

DAY FIVE

. . . . .

AFTER THE GHOST girl departed, my nose bled again.

I used tissue paper and followed Mr. Samson's advice. Despite this, I intended to continue using the headdress. Getting rid of a private and important means of communication would be foolish at best. Working together without it was near impossible.

I threw the tissues in the garbage in time to see the odd couple returning. Theo and Din stood at the entrance. This time, Theo veered off into one of the aisles in search of something while Din approached me.

"You're looking pale." Her mouth didn't move. Her words echoed in my head in those three choral voices. "You must be sick."

"I'm fine. No need to worry," I replied aloud.

"But you're not. It's all because of a dangerous little trinket you've been playing with. I can take it off your hands if you like."

Her beautiful, flawless face broke into an unusual smile.

Her deep blue eyes glittered with mania, shining with glee. I'd seen these before. Every time my cousin was in a photo, she had the exact same face—eyes wide open past their natural range, with lips stretched, exposing gums and teeth.

"No, thank you. I'll be fine."

"You mortals are very, very fragile. Death becomes your companion the instant you are born. It's so hard to find meaning in your short little lives. Give me the trinket. I might even help prolong your existence for an additional two hundred years."

I declined again with even more politeness than she deserved.

Din shrugged. "It's your life. It's such a shame you're so easily parted with it. I thought you'd be one of those mortals who would fight harder for it."

I was. Holding on to that headdress and using it was one good way we mortals had the advantage in this game of the gods.

After not getting what she wanted, Din wandered off to browse.

Theo made his way to the counter. He dug into his pockets and produced two folded pieces of paper. "Mail delivery. He's written you more this time."

"Thank you." I tucked Ward's notes into my journal and started writing my response. "How is he doing?"

"As best as can be considering the circumstances." He tilted his head and narrowed his dark eyes. "On the other hand, you don't look too good."

"So I've been told."

"No, really. I wouldn't say you look like shit, because that would be rude, but you do look like shit. You look like you've been poisoned—not by mortal means. You've been naughty."

I glanced up from my writing to give him a patronizing smirk. "I'm fine."

He held his palms up. "Whoa. I'm just doing due diligence by making sure my guy's girl is doing all right."

"Duly noted."

Theo blew out his lips. "So . . . all this junk in here. How do you even begin to sort through it? I'm looking for something, and I can't find it."

"It'll help if you know what you're looking for. If it's specific, then I probably know where it is."

When I wasn't stationed at the counter, I spent the rest of my shift cataloging all the items in the antique shop. It helped me pass the time in between the sparse customers. The task itself was tedious and the best kind of meditative busywork I loved. Mr. Samson had acquired pieces from as early as the Dark Ages. In fact, one of my favorites was a medieval suit of armor with a prominent codpiece standing guard at one of the corners of the shop. I'd filled the leather-bound ledger Mr. Samson provided.

Theo raked his fingers through his curly hair. "Yeah, I don't even know where to start. It's not like it's obvious. *They'd* never make it too easy for anyone."

"They?"

"Oops." His cheeks flushed pink. He made a coughing noise and changed the subject. "Anyway, I guess I'm on a stupid treasure hunt."

Mr. King was on one too. He had mentioned almost the exact same phrasing.

"I hope you get a prize for winning this game."

"It'll be a game changer. If it isn't here, it's over there—where Ward's at. Those are the rules."

Their rules. These gods knew everything about the game, yet we mortals were left in the dark. I paused my note to Ward and scribbled the new information down in my journal.

"If you narrow down what you want in the future, then I can help you. In the meantime, as you said, there's too much 'junk' in here to conduct a proper search." I finished my note and folded it into a paper heart. "Please give that to Ward, and thank you."

Theo pocketed the note. He pursed his lips. "You sure you won't change your mind?"

"If it's about what we discussed earlier, I consider the matter closed."

"Ward's not going to be happy when he finds out about it. I can't keep this shit from him, you know this, right? Like I'm not going to lie—"

"I don't expect you to. Go ahead." My voice hardened. "This is between him and me, but it's ultimately my decision to make."

"And he is supposed to be okay with you trying to kill yourself? You can't make that kind of decision on your own. This affects him too. I hope you wrote this in your note, because lying to him would be worse. It's better if you tell him yourself. My boy's going to be furious and heartbroken."

Unsolicited advice from this frat boy god was the last thing I wanted. Ward wasn't his boy. They barely knew each other. Ward's uncanny ability to befriend strangers gave them ample permission to act as if they were on familiar terms. It was a habit I both admired and despised—admired that Ward allowed people in easily, much more than I ever would, and despised because of the liberties and entitlement near strangers took concerning my ex-boyfriend.

"Fine. I'm done. I said my piece." Theo shook his head and waved Din over. "If you don't want to repeat your breakup, you shouldn't be making the same mistakes over and over. I don't think either of you can survive the car crash of a relationship this time around."

Din sauntered over to Theo's side, and they walked out of the shop.

I closed my eyes and exhaled.

The last time Ward and I broke up, it nearly killed me. I buried myself in work in Manhattan—putting in sixteen-hour days, barely eating one proper meal a day, and limiting human interactions. Keeping busy numbed the pain every time. When my parents came for a visit, they refused to leave my apartment until I was taking better care of myself. It was the one thing I realized I took for granted with Ward. He had taken care of me when I'd forgotten how to.

We broke up because I didn't think he had the ability to change when I *needed* him to.

His fatal flaw had always been that he never questioned his privilege and how he drifted through his life with everything handed to him. I recognized this the moment we first met, yet I allowed myself to be swept away by our mutual physical attraction and his other wonderful qualities.

I couldn't be with a person who didn't fundamentally understand how hard I had to work to get to where I was. Every scrap of success I had to fight for, while his wealthy white family provided him with instant opportunities and a life devoid of hardship. I wanted him to strike out on his own and see if he was able to live and thrive outside of his family's influence.

Discomfort and change encouraged growth.

When he decided that his level of comfort was more important than mine, I left Chicago.

We never talked about it since meeting back up in London.

I never brought it up because I was afraid that doing so would wreck what we wanted to rebuild. Was it even possible to start over with a scorched and cracked foundation?

14

Ward

DAY SIX

· · · · ·

ANGER ELIMINATED RATIONALITY time and again. Emotions had a way of taking over and driving a person off a cliff. The volatility of this particular sentiment cracked continents and severed siblings. Ward Dunbar was throwing a justifiable tantrum.

His beloved had made a pact with the immortal equivalent of the devil. Of course, to clarify, Mr. King was a god of the Eastern Faction, and not Beelzebub, Lucifer, or the dark equivalent.

He paced back and forth in an attempt to keep his fury from boiling over. The source of his anger lay not with Camille's ability to make a decision for herself, but in his powerlessness to protect her from harm. Yes, Ward Dunbar was a feminist and not some controlling, lumbering Neanderthal. Otherwise, it didn't matter how pretty he was or how talented in bed, Camille would want nothing to do with him.

"Ward? Are you there?" Her voice rang inside his head. "We need to talk."

He took a deep breath and tried to calm himself down. "I'm here."

"So, I need to tell you how we're communicating now . . . like why it's possible. Mr. King gave me this Tang dynasty headdress. He warned me that it has bad side effects and that it's *my* choice to use it. It allows me to contact you for five minutes a day. I don't want to waste more of that precious time."

"And how is it affecting you?"

"Nosebleeds and headaches so far. It's nothing I can't handle."

"As far as I know, your degree wasn't in medicine. Who knows how it's fucking you up inside. Unless you have access to urgent care on your side, I don't see—"

"I knew you wouldn't understand. This is about being able to communicate privately. I got your note. Yes, there's a war between the gods and we're caught in the middle of this game. Theo is on one side and he's your messenger. He'll want you to take his side, and if we pick one, it'll pave the way for the other side to justify eliminating us. Being neutral is our best bet." Her voice cracked with frustration. "Both sides are looking for something. If we can get that, it'll be our key to getting out."

He gritted his teeth. "And if you die before then? Isn't the point that we both get out in one piece?"

"Tell me more about the vault. That should be your main task. I'm going to go through all the items in the shop and see if I can find them. So far, both sides don't even know what they're looking for. Once I get the parameters, I'll be able to figure out—"

"This isn't a group work call. We have to talk about you and that ornament. I don't think it's a good idea that you still keep using it. It's ridiculous, because we can pass notes to each other. It's not like we can't—"

"I don't trust *him*. He might be your bestie, but I don't feel the same. Having more lines of communication is better. For all you know, he's reading our notes back and forth, because I sure as hell would be."

"You're judging him too harshly. Theo helped me. It's because of him that I'm still alive. Not everyone is out to get you, Camille. It's not how the world works."

"Right, because everything is so damned easy in your world. Everyone is so happy to help and lend a hand. Must be nice to have been born with the silver spoon in your mouth and have everything fall in your lap without any kind of effort at all." Sharp resentment punctuated every word.

This was a classic lovers' quarrel. Ward had heard this all before. This sounded like the momentous one—the catastrophic argument that led to the big break. He could have stopped and capitulated, argued in a different way, but he didn't. He fell into the trap. Ward Dunbar hadn't reached enlightenment yet to escape the vicious cycle of reenacting the painful past.

"All I'm saying is that there are people who want to help. Jumping to the conclusion that no one is worthy of trust isn't productive. We can't get out of this without any assistance. I mean, you got help yourself even though it's laced with poison. At least acknowledge that." He paused to take a calming breath. "I'm not telling you to stop using the goddamned thing, because that's useless. I know you need to decide on your own. I respect your decision if you respect mine that I won't answer and continue enabling your destruction."

"You're being so difficult. All you're doing is wasting our time together. Damn it, Ward! This is the only way we can . . . I can't deal with you right now."

If there were a way to hang up angrily on a psychic phone call, Camille did just that.

He raked his fingers through his hair.

He'd fully intended to follow her to Manhattan and figure out what to do after they'd both settled into the city. She didn't want him to come with her. She was adamant he take the position in LA. "The long-distance relationship would be good for us," she had said. "It won't be forever, I promise."

His friends and family warned him that anything long distance was doomed to fail. He took it as her way of letting go of the relationship—living on opposite ends of the country would tank them. This was her way of saying goodbye without doing so. She asked him again to reconsider the LA job. He didn't. Instead, he begged her to let him come with her. She left Chicago the next morning.

Ward was adamant about not repeating his past mistake. He didn't want to lose Camille again.

All of this was moot. The future could only progress if they could escape the present.

MADAM SELENE WAS her uncharitable, grouchy self this morning. She wore disapproval as easily as the saffron shawl over her shoulders. She tapped the leather portfolio against the desk.

"I was hoping you would have another sale soon. It seems as if Mr. Theo is using appointments as social time. He has had ample time to browse what we have; surely he's interested in purchasing *something*." She thrust the book toward Ward.

He accepted it with a flourish. "He's trying to drum up funding. I imagine all of these pieces have quite the steep purchase price."

"These gods have all the wealth in the world. I don't buy that excuse. They're cheap, especially that friend of yours. Browsers can only be tolerated for so long. I'd suspect he was casing the shop, but I don't think he has the mental capacity to plan a heist."

Ward was again reminded to stay on the good side of her sharp tongue. "Yes, ma'am."

"Close the sale, Mr. Dunbar. It's in your best interest to do so."

"I'll work on it." He gave her a salute as she retreated back into her office.

Theo was the only visitor for the day. He and Din walked in ten minutes later. She headed to ogle and admire her favorite piece in the shop—the large ruby pendant. Theo rushed to his side and clapped him on the shoulder.

"I don't want to be the bearer of bad news. You're my boy, though, and I have to tell you that your girl wasn't doing too well the last time I saw her." He tapped his fingertips together. "I tried to talk her out of it. No go."

"I appreciate that. Thank you."

"You know I got you."

"Camille won't do anything anyone tells her to do. She needs to think it's her own idea. I just hope she doesn't die from this. I need to know what my options are. Do you think she will? Be honest with me."

Theo grimaced and shoved his hands in his pockets. "The way she looked, I don't know how much longer she has. The thing is, as a mortal, if you accept something from a god that has strings attached, those strings can choke the fuck out of you and kill you. She got herself into one of those shitty situations."

Ward balled his hands into fists. "It's her decision. I can't just override it."

"You keep telling me you love her and that she's the *one*. She's gonna die if you don't do something."

"I'm sure she'll be fine. She'll know when it's too much and stop." Ward acknowledged the last line was a lie the instant the words left his lips.

People often lie to reassure themselves. The action was equivalent to an ostrich burying its head in a hole in the ground. The mental exercise did nothing to eradicate the current problem at hand. Denial was a heady drug.

"She's not fine. This whole stoic thing she's putting on is for your benefit." Theo fished out a glossy black compact from his pocket. "Before you ask, it's Din's. She told me to hold on to it, and I think she even forgot I still had it. Anyway, watch this."

The god opened it and whispered something in an ancient language, causing both mirrors to fog up. He cleaned it with his sleeve to reveal Camille in both reflections. The top showed her in her current state. Her brown eyes strained at the corners with dark circles. She brought her fingertips to her temples to massage them. Her furrowed brow creased in pain.

The bottom showed her internally, almost like an MRI or CAT scan. This one focused on Camille's brain and its dark areas. Her brain was bleeding out.

"Is the bottom showing what's happening now, or what will happen?" Ward asked with palpable panic in his voice.

"It's what's going on now. She's not gonna make it if she uses that thing one more time. Listen, I'm not telling you what to do, but if this was Din, I wouldn't hesitate to do something."

"What can I do? I'm stuck here. She wouldn't listen to me even if I told her I know she is dying." Ward pressed his fists against his temples. "This would be different if I was physically with her. I'd get rid of the damned thing. Yeah, she'd be mad at me and it'd be worth it. I'd be saving her life."

"Attaboy. That's the spirit." Theo patted him on the back. "Then why don't you do it? Why don't we go and save your girl?"

"You'll help me? You've already done enough . . . I can't ask you to."

"Yeah, so that. It can't technically be a freebie. I'm going to interfere with another god's business. It's going to be painful and risky on my end. There are consequences. I'd do it in a heartbeat otherwise."

Din made a little wiggly gesture over the necklace display with her hands. She giggled to herself and cooed over the glass box.

"You want the necklace in exchange, I take it?" Ward asked.

"Not asking you to steal it. I'm only asking for a discount. A small one that gets me over the edge so I can finally get her what she's been begging for?" Theo lowered his head and shrugged. "I would never ask you to steal for me. You know that."

"And you would . . ."

"I'll figure out a way to get the poisoned gift from your girl and save her for you."

The difference in crime was minor. A transgression was still a transgression despite the rationality or intentions behind it. Ward was agreeing to commit a felony in order to save his beloved. Hypocritical at best, dangerous at worst.

"What do you need to do to get that—whatever it is—from Camille?"

"Did she say what it was? That's a start."

"Tang dynasty headdress. You've seen it here. Mr. King purchased it and apparently gave it to her."

The piece was stunning, with its floating embellishments that cascaded down to form a makeshift veil over the forehead and eyes.

"The Eastern Faction is responsible for your girl's situation then. Wouldn't put it past them. They'll do anything to win this war. Dirty, cheating gods." Theo punched his open palm. "They think they're richer than us. We'll show them."

"Are there only two sides to this? The East and West?"

"Yeah. It used to be so many different groups. It's gotten simpler over time. The easiest way to explain it is to break it down by geographical regions. Asian, Pasifika, and African gods are the Eastern Faction. European and American gods form the West. It's been this way for the last three millennia."

Ward wrote the information down in the planner he had bought for Camille.

"Oh right, all this almost made me forget the mail delivery." Theo tossed a paper heart on the desk. "You're going to send something back to her, too, right?"

"Yeah." Ward scribbled the letter to Camille on an empty page in the back of the planner.

Theo tore out a page from his notebook. "You sure you don't want the usual paper? The girly stationery might confuse her."

The planner Ward had picked out for her was quite feminine with its pastels and subtle gold accents. The pages followed a soft lavender-teal ombré color scheme.

"No thanks, I'm going with this. I'm hoping it'll surprise her."

"Make sure you tell her to bring the hair scrunchie thing to work with her. I wouldn't be able to get to it otherwise. I need to be in physical proximity. Not sure if I can do it without seeing it. Dealing with another god's magic is very dangerous and tricky. I promise I won't take it until you give me the go-ahead. I need time to figure out how to pull this off anyway."

"Sounds good. It'll give me time to figure out on my end if I decide to go through with it."

"Cool, cool. I'll leave you to your love letter writing." He headed off to join Din. He whispered something in her ear, and she responded by throwing her arms around his neck and leaning down to kiss him.

The god must have disclosed their potential deal.

Ward wrote an apology, because those were the best to lead off with. It was far easier to ask for forgiveness for a future sin. The mental gymnastics he needed to go through to justify his foolish action were impressive.

Oftentimes, nothing but trouble awaited those with the best intentions.

15

Camille

. . . . .

DAY SIX

. . . . .

I POPPED TWO more ibuprofen for the headache, knowing full well they probably wouldn't help. The intensity was increasing—almost enough to interfere with my getting a good night's sleep and put a cramp on my quality of life. My field of vision was also compromised. It blurred along the edges, making everything look like a watercolor painting left out in the rain.

I had no one to blame but myself.

It didn't matter. The sooner I solved my end of the puzzle in the shop, the sooner we'd get out. All of us.

Mr. Samson waited by the counter when I came downstairs. He was studying the catalog I'd been working on. He pored over each page, all the while scratching his head. "You've done so much work, Ms. Buhay. I realize that I can't remember most of the items in here."

"I'm not done yet. There's still a small section left to go through. I'm hoping the list would give us a good idea of everything in here. Gods have been coming in asking for certain items, and I'd like to be able to help them buy whatever it is they need."

"Ah, right. Wait, did someone come to purchase something? I don't think that's ever been done before." The alarm in his voice was palpable as he almost dropped the ledger. "What do we do? I'm not sure—"

I placed my hand on his arm to calm him. "It's okay. We'll be okay if that happens. Don't worry. I'm here to help you now."

"Right, right. I'm not alone anymore." His hand shook as he placed it over mine. "Not anymore."

"Why don't you go rest? I'll keep an eye on things around here."

"I do feel tired." His voice took on a distant quality.

I hid my worry when I walked him back to his office. His mental and physical decline was happening faster now. The day when he wouldn't make it out of his office would come sooner than I wanted or was prepared for.

After Mr. Samson was deposited in his room, I went to work finishing up the last section of the store. The catalog spanned fifty pages to list the two thousand seven hundred and thirty-one items in stock. The way I set it up made it easy to narrow down each item's location quickly. This was what I needed to do before I had my chat with Mr. King.

I took out the business card he provided and lit the tip with the black candle. The flame changed to a deep, impenetrable black. The entire card was devoured by the void. I barely got my fingers out of the way.

Mr. King appeared at the doorway with a surprised grin on his face. "Ah, just the mortal I wanted to see. Is it too soon to ask if you're willing to help me?"

"Yes, it's still too soon. I have questions I need answered first."

"Mortals are ever the source of unending questions. I'll try my best and answer what I can." He approached the counter and stopped a few feet away. I was certain the added space was for my benefit.

"First, what is this candle?"

Mr. King lifted a brow and approached the color-changing flame. He slipped his fingers through the lavender fire and wiggled them around. "This marks time. I'm certain you already know or suspect this. When the wick was lit, it signaled the beginning of this whole thing."

He confirmed my hypothesis. I'd had to start with an easier question before I proceeded with my probe. "Will finding this item you're searching for turn the tide for the Eastern Faction in the war?"

His dark brow arched. "Ah, you are ever so surprising, Ms. Buhay. I do wonder what else you have deduced in your short time here at the shop. To answer your question, yes. While it won't ensure ultimate victory, it will pave the way for that scenario."

I didn't care much about the power struggle between these gods because they might be the ones responsible for all four of us being trapped here. Once we left, they would continue bickering as they had since the beginning of the world.

"Do you believe that if Ward and I find it, then all of us mortals can be free from here?"

"Yes. It's why you are here. I believe you two are the key. Though I still haven't figured out how one place plays into the other." He wandered over to a nearby shelf and picked up a lacquered chinoiserie trinket box. "You have your part to play and so does he. You can call it destiny or purpose—whichever you feel comfortable believing."

I jotted down some notes, filling out some makeshift charts in my planner. "Then I am supposed to find this one thing in the shop and give it either to you or to someone in the Western Faction?"

"Correct." He tossed the box in the air and twirled it on his fingertip.

"Why aren't you asking me to give it to you and take a side?"

The tiny container spun even faster, blurring the bright colors into a smudged rainbow. "You do as you please. You will be asked to choose, but not by me."

"Playing hard to get? Not a tactic I picture you using." I leaned against the counter and watched the unnatural display.

"While it isn't my greatest virtue, I can be patient when needed." He waved his other hand over the box, freezing it in midspin. Mr. King flicked his index finger. The trinket box flew through the air to land in the same spot he had plucked it from.

"You have no idea what you're looking for? Another god came in here, who I'm guessing is from the opposing team, asking for the same thing. This scavenger hunt is futile if neither of you has any concrete clues. Otherwise, what's the point of all this?"

Every game had parameters. I had figured out that Ward and I both needed to solve a puzzle that was confined to our location. While I had to find a relic in here, Ward's task was sketchier. He believed he had to find the vault. Anything else beyond that he hadn't solved yet. His last note contained far more information than I expected. He filled in the gaps in my knowledge.

Mr. King searched through his coat pockets, patting them. "There might be something. Our illuminating conversation has given me a brilliant idea."

He fished out a wriggling translucent thread from his pocket about eighteen inches in length, with the width of the chunky yarn Lola Nene loved to use for her knitting. The way it moved wasn't the smooth undulations of a snake—instead, it wriggled like a fresh dew worm on a hook.

"Is that alive?" I asked, taking a step back when he placed it on the counter.

He poked it with his finger and it recoiled. "Does it matter?"

"Is this your clue?"

"It might be. Try touching it."

I made a face. It wasn't that it appeared slimy or un-attractive; my concern was disturbing something sentient. This fiber-optic creature was eerie in the way it squirmed. Its aversion to Mr. King caused it to travel to my side of the counter.

I inhaled. I already used a magical headdress that gave me wicked migraines. Why was I drawing the line at touching some magical larva? With one eye closed, I stuck out my index finger. The worm reacted, gravitating toward me. It was cold, yet warm at the same time. It wrapped around my finger and then exploded into mercurial droplets. The pools of liquid shifted, forming letters.

Mr. King hovered over the message. "Interesting. I can't read it. This must be for your mortal eyes only."

I didn't read it aloud; instead, I committed it to memory. "You must seek the one with six heads but no face, and twenty-one eyes that cannot see."

The message vanished shortly afterward.

"I hope you paid attention." He leveled his gaze at my face. "You'll know what to do next."

I had to figure out who in the Western Faction had the other clue. Theo, Din, or Eryna.

Mr. King tilted his head and narrowed his eyes. "Before I leave, I highly suggest that you limit using the gift I gave you. You might have one or two uses left before it kills you. Be careful." He placed another card on the counter. "Don't hesitate to contact me again. It has been a pleasure, Ms. Buhay."

The moment he left, I jotted down the clue in my planner.

I had no idea what the riddle meant. Ward had always been better with them than I was. The next time we talked, we would figure it out together. I refused to allow such an important piece of information to be written down and passed through Theo.

Speak of the devil, Ward's messenger boy had arrived without his girlfriend.

"You've got mail." He placed a folded piece of stationery on the counter. "It's from him. He's using some sort of girly notebook."

"Thank you." I tucked the pastel ombré paper into my journal.

Theo tapped his lips. "He also told me to relay a verbal message: '*Stick to passing notes.*'"

I expected that after our last argument. Ward wouldn't go as far as to tell me what to do. He'd do everything else in his power though. He might even not answer the next time we talked.

"Got it."

Theo swiveled his head to take in the shop. "So much junk in here. Just when I think there isn't that much, there's even more shit that I didn't notice the first time."

"I'm feeling generous today." I leaned over the counter. "I think I can help you with your problem. First, tell me, do you have a magical worm in your pocket?"

16

Ward

DAY EIGHT

TRYING TO CONVINCE any sentient being to do anything that was against their mindset was nearly impossible. For Ward, it was his ex-girlfriend, and that came with its own set of dangerous land mines. He was royally fucked.

"Ward, I had a breakthrough yesterday!" Camille's voice was downright giddy. The good mood was a great sign that maybe reasoning with her, later on, was possible.

He matched her enthusiasm. "Awesome! What did you find?"

She told him about the two clues in the form of riddles, and how each faction had one that only they could decipher. Her task was to find these two objects. And his . . .

"Your job is the vault. I have no idea what else, but that's what you need to focus on. Theo and Mr. King had my clues. I would suspect Mr. King will have another for you in the future since he's the only one in the Eastern Faction. You'll have to figure out who holds the other in the West."

"And this is how we get out?"

"It has to be. Keep the clues to yourself and we'll be set. Speaking of which, do you have any idea how to solve them?"

"Can you repeat it again?"

"The first one: 'You must seek the one with six heads but no face, and twenty-one eyes that cannot see.' The second is: 'Find the thirteen hearts with no organs.' I was thinking something like a pineapple with a hundred eyes. Or potatoes. I couldn't find any carvings of them in the shop."

Riddles were Ward's specialty. His inquisitive mind was tailored to solving them. This skill had no real-world value, but here, he might redeem himself. "No clue for the second riddle. Maybe it's something like an anatomical model? The first though, twenty-one and six. Six and twenty-one." He thought aloud. "One's a prime number. The other is not. Six heads."

"I can try looking for hearts around here. I think there's at least one in the catalog." The sound of paper flipping must be Camille going through her ledger.

"Six sides? What has six sides? A hexagon, but that doesn't explain the number twenty-one or the eyes. Eyes can be dots and not literal eyes . . . dots, dots, dots. DIE!" Ward clapped his hands together. "It has to be a die! As in dice! It has six sides, and if you add up all the numbers on the sides from one to six, it totals twenty-one."

"You're so damned hot right now. I'd totally give you a kiss if I was there. That makes so much sense! You've solved it. I'll see if I can figure out the second one on my own. Have you tried asking your boss about the vault?"

"She's not exactly, uh . . ."

"Charm her. There's never anyone you couldn't befriend.

People love you. Play to your strengths. It's probably the fastest way to get the clues out of the gods too." The compliment was genuine. Camille might be stingy with them, but when she did give them out, it came from her heart. "Once you get those and know what you need to do, we can all get out."

He exhaled and decided it was time to do the unpleasant task he was dreading. "So, can we talk?"

"About?"

"How are you feeling? Are the headaches getting worse?"

"They're the same. Look, I don't want to waste any more time on this. I can only use this thing for at most one or two more times before it kills me."

"Camille, you say that so casually. You can't minimize—"

"I'm good with this. If it wasn't for our private line, I wouldn't know that I have to go find dice now."

"There's always the notes. The notes don't at least freaking induce a fucking brain hemorrhage." The bite in the last sentence was a product of his rising frustration. "I'm not going to do this again. You said so yourself, you're going to die if you keep using it."

"I don't trust Theo!"

"You can't keep living your life thinking everyone is out to get you. I trust him. Shouldn't that count? I mean, you still do trust me, don't you?"

"Of course I trust you. I *love* you." She let out an exasperated sound. "You do know that all these favors Theo is doing for you aren't all an act of altruism. He'll want some payback, and he'll be collecting. You can't keep accepting gifts without thinking there are strings attached. He's with a faction and will be asking you to pick sides. *His.*"

"And what if I choose *his* side? What's wrong with that? He's been nothing but kind to me. Repaying kindness isn't a crime. How much kindness have you gotten?" He paused. "Right, you got *poisoned*."

"I chose this. It's all about taking the harder road to get to where we need to go. I do what needs to be done, and yes, it involves work."

"Working hard won't make people love you or respect you more. Camille, you don't need—"

"Fuck you, Ward." She ended the conversation with a ragged sob.

That had gone smashingly well.

They should be married in a week and trot off into the sunset to have those 1.93 children.

Ward covered his face with his hands.

To be clear, he was quite aware of how much of a shitshow this was.

His affluent upbringing had always been a pain point for Camille. She resented his family's generational wealth—the country club memberships, charity galas, and the easy connections to powerful people. His father's ancestors had oil and gas money, and his mother and her family owned one of the larger regional banks in the Midwest. They advocated going to the right schools, getting good grades, and being a productive member of society. They were all about taking advantage of every single experience their privilege afforded. His first job out of college was a position at a gallery owned by one of his father's friends. Ward worked his way up and managed to reach director in a few years. He maximized the advantage he was given.

His parents and siblings loved Camille, yet she was adamant that they as a couple wouldn't work. He offered a solution—to move to downtown Chicago, enough miles away from their families, and start over in a new place and city.

It had worked until he got the job offer in LA and turned it down.

He couldn't understand her discomfort or think that she could even be uncomfortable. After all, he was an attractive, wealthy male and an overall kind person. It wasn't that Ward dismissed Camille's concerns as mere drama. He just couldn't wrap his thick head around the fact that she had to maneuver across racial and class lines—and the implications of that for herself and her family. By extension, because he never had to truly work hard a day in his life as she had, she was concerned about whether he'd put in the effort in their relationship.

The lovers picked at the same scab to reveal a deep, infected wound that they hoped had magically healed. It was still there festering, and no repeated declarations of love fixed it. They relived their past with every argument and thus dwindled the chances of any viable future happening. Giving power to the past only led to regression and stagnation.

"YOU HAVE ONLY one appointment today, and it isn't your regular cheap friend." Madam Selene snapped the portfolio closed. "I'm hoping you have encouraged Mr. Theo to come up with the funds for a purchase."

"Who is the client for today?"

"Eryna. If you can convince her to buy something, that

would be good for us. Our pool of clients is small. Mr. King and Eryna should be your focus. Their pockets are deep."

"And if they buy everything here, what then?"

"This all ends. That is my hope."

"You must miss the outside world." Ward tipped his head toward the windows, where London moved in the daylight. "You must have seen it change in all the time you were trapped here."

"I don't even remember my life before this place. Don't waste time contemplating on what you can't change." She crossed her arms and glared. "No one cared that I was here all these years. Why should I care about them?"

"Surely you must have family or people waiting for you out there. A sweetheart maybe?"

She snorted. "If there was, they'd have moved on. I know I would if I was in their place. You can't live with regrets, Mr. Dunbar. They'll eat you up eventually."

His boss reminded him of a snappy crocodile—all teeth and hard ridges. If there had been any softness in her, there was no trace of it left. Ward surmised that her prickly nature might be why she had survived in here for so long by herself. If it worked for porcupines as armor, Madam Selene wore it well.

"When we get out, what would be the first thing you'd do?"

She rubbed the bridge of her nose. The bangles on her wrists jostled from the gesture. "Leave London behind and die with dignity somewhere far from here."

"That's grim. I know I'd take my girlfriend out for a drink and we'd likely go on a very long vacation together after this."

"I doubt your girlfriend will still be around, Mr. Dunbar.

She won't understand any of this or why you've disappeared. No one will miss you, and when or *if* we leave, you will find yourself out of time and out of place."

"Oh, do cheer up, Madam Selene. It's not as bleak as you think. *When* we get out, I'll take you on a date at the Shard, where I can get you a proper drink or two."

"Focus on the task at hand, Mr. Dunbar. Eryna will take some convincing to get her interested in any of these pieces." She handed him the appointment book.

"And what if she brings up the vault again? What should I tell her?"

"Tell her that you don't know where it is, and even if you did, you don't have the combination or key. It's the truth. As I stated before, I only saw it once and I never opened it." She shook her head. "I must get back to my office. Do your best and try to sell something to your client today."

ERYNA DECIDED ON an interesting, demure librarian look for her visit. Her long dark hair was in a high chignon. Her choice of a high-necked lacy cream blouse was complemented by a hip-hugging mint-green pencil skirt. Camille had a similar work outfit in her closet. In fact, Ward remembered ripping the buttons of the blouse open one night when they both had too much Beaujolais.

He placed the leather portfolio strategically over his groin.

"Aah, Edward." She licked her lips and sauntered over to him. She touched his arm. "Aren't we frisky today?"

Ward blushed and cleared his throat.

"I chose this outfit for you. I'm glad you appreciate it." She twirled and winked. "Perhaps it will help you see me in a different light."

"Shall we sit and then you can tell me what piece you'd like to see in greater detail?"

"Oh, fine." She waved her hand. "Bring me Amanishakheto's crown."

He retrieved the requested item, all the while thinking of differential calculus to try to get his erection to subside. The crown was an impeccable piece of jewelry. It was a thick gold band adorned with female figures with malachite wings. The owner was the warrior queen of Nubia.

"She destroyed Roman armies." Eryna leaned in close to examine the crown on its black velvet cushion. "I would have loved to ride with her in battle. Nothing matches the feeling of a massive stallion between your legs and a sharp sword in each hand."

"Are you on the winning side in the war of the gods?"

"Yes." The hiss of the *s* was punctuated by a flash of perfect teeth. "Edward, you should join us. The Western Faction has much to offer a pretty mortal like you."

"I'm not interested in taking a side right now." He extricated her hand from his arm with firm gentleness. "Why don't we talk about something you mentioned before—the vault."

She licked her glossy red lips. "Have you found it? Have you seen what's inside?"

"No and no." He leaned forward and whispered, "However, I can confirm that it exists. The problem is that I don't know how to find it."

The spark in her emerald eyes ignited. "I see."

"Purchasing the crown might help."

"And this will make you happy?"

"It will make my boss happy. You did say that Queen Amanishakheto was a formidable force. Wouldn't you want to experience her memories when you wear it? All of these priceless relics are more than mere mementos of the dead, am I right?"

She threw back her head and laughed. "Clever boy. Fine, I'll buy it."

Four more items left to sell, and if what Madam Selene believed was true, they'd be set free.

17

Camille

. . . . .

DAY EIGHT

. . . . .

"WARD?" I CALLED out. "I know you can hear me."

Nothing. Two precious minutes had already passed. The pounding headache behind my eyes had made it impossible for me to see anything as clearly as I had before.

"Ward, answer me, damn it. Don't waste this time. I just want to hear your voice again, please. We need to work with each other to figure things out. Do you remember the time we didn't escape?"

We had booked a room with an airport baggage theme. We were sorting through the luggage, trying to find out the right combination to open the door to make our flight. I'd been hung up on decoding a series of geographical coordinates while he was staring at a crew manifest. We didn't get out because we didn't work the puzzles out together—we didn't realize that the two were linked.

"Everything here is connected. Whatever I solve will be bound to you somehow. I feel this. We have one last time we can talk, and I hope that you'll talk to me then."

I did my best to understand and respect his position of silent protest.

We were still recovering from our knockout fight, punching in the same places that we knew would hurt the most.

Being called frigid or cold was a badge of honor I wore from childhood. I'd been bullied for being brown and too smart, and for my humble upbringing. My father worked as a bellhop at two hotels, while my mother was a seamstress. I didn't go to sleepovers or many birthday parties. I didn't need friends when I had more cousins than I knew what to do with. I didn't trust anyone that wasn't family. As for boys, I didn't trust them either. Puberty was kind to me, and their newfound interest was discomforting. Since I wasn't able to guess their ulterior motives, I defaulted to assuming the worst or ignoring them altogether.

Ward was different. We met in an anthropology class. He kept recruiting me into group work in class, urging others to listen to my ideas, and his general sweetness allowed him to slip through my defenses—that and the constant bribe of thoughtful snacks he always seemed to have on hand. At first, we talked, and talked, and talked some more until I trusted myself not to lose my wits if he kissed me.

Seeing him in London rekindled the dream that we could be together. This was as far away as I imagined him to be. It was why I kissed him then, without hesitation, knowing that he and I might make it work here.

I missed him and craved running my hands through his hair and over every inch of his skin. Our addiction was mutual. No one else satisfied every part of me.

The moisture on my upper lip signaled another nosebleed.

While pinching the bridge of my nose, I reached for the box of tissues I carried down from my flat upstairs. At the rate I was going, I'd collapse after using the headdress one more time. Mr. King had warned me of the dire consequences.

I was willing to risk it once again if it meant Ward and I made progress with our escape plan.

THE NEXT EVENING, Mr. Samson wasn't at the counter. I walked to his office door and rapped my knuckles against the wood. No answer. He might've been feeling too ill or exhausted to make it out tonight.

In the little time we had spent together, I found myself growing attached. It surprised me that I even anticipated our short chats. Our age difference didn't inspire some sort of grandfatherly relationship or anything in that vein. It wasn't weirdly romantic either. If anything, it was a comfortable familiarity I somehow found in him—a complete stranger whom I barely knew. It was a strong gut feeling, one I rarely got, but when I did, I'd never been steered wrong.

I trusted him and cared about him. It was the opposite situation with Ward and his boss. From his notes, he had, at best, grudging respect for the woman, and, at worst, he maintained civility while trying to follow her exacting standards. Despite their less-than-ideal relationship, he was still determined to save her. I expected nothing less from him.

I waited for a response at Mr. Samson's office door for three minutes before I returned to the shop counter.

It took me a moment to remember what I was looking for past the throbbing pain in my head. Dice.

There was a painted box of ancient dice I picked up yes-terday, or was it the day before? I couldn't recall. The concept of time slipped through my fingers, but I still had a firm grasp of every item and its location in this shop.

I picked up the box and examined the geometric pattern painted on each side. A set of three red and black lines criss-crossed along the border, interchanging when they connected. I flipped it open and examined the weathered dice inside. Each die's "eyes" were made of two concentric circles with a dot at the center.

Age and use had shaved and chipped the edges of most of them save for one. I held the lone die with decent edges in my palm. This must be it. What was Theo's riddle again? Thirteen hearts and no organs. There were two anatomical hearts in the shop, and they weren't the answer. It must be like the die. Fig-urative hearts, instead of literal.

A middle-aged ghost shuffled through the door. He wore a lime-green velour leisure suit reminiscent of the eighties, with a gold chain against the bare V of skin exposed by the unbut-toned floral-printed shirt. He swung his hips to an inaudible beat accompanied by fingertips snapping.

"Oh, hello, sexy lady. I'm here for a trade."

I shot him a trademark glare I often used on overreach-ing men.

He held up his palms and straightened his spine. "Sorry, it was a compliment. I swear."

"I take it you want a ticket to the afterlife."

"Yes, ma'am." He took off his gold wire-framed aviator sunglasses and perched them atop his gelled, thinning dark hair. "I'm tired of hanging around here. Seen everything there is to see. Time to move on."

I asked, "What are you offering?"

He shrugged. "I'm not sure. Could you help me?"

"I suppose I can try."

This was a first. All the other ghosts that had visited the shop already had something specific in mind. With the amount of inventory in the shop, it wouldn't surprise me if this was something Mr. Samson had done for others in the past.

He emptied his pockets on the counter: a wrinkled pack of Virginia Slims, a dented can of Altoids, a souvenir pack of cards from the Tropicana, and a worn, wooden rosary with a few of the beads missing.

The choice was obvious. "The rosary is your lucky charm, I take it?"

"Yeah. My mama carried it around when she left Warsaw for San Diego. Gave it to me before she died. Thing is, she knows I don't pray. She said it'll mean she's still praying for me long after she's gone. It's not that she thought my soul was in need of saving. This was her way of saying that she'd be with me always. She was the best of mothers. Best."

"Did the charm work when you gambled?"

"Every time. So much that I kept to the East Coast casinos after wearing out my welcome in Vegas. My mama would kill me if she ever caught me telling the tables that the Virgin Mary was my queen of hearts."

Hearts. Thirteen. His set of cards.

There were no other playing decks in the entire shop. This had to be it. I wasn't going to let him leave without separating him from that deck first. Asking him for it, however nicely, might not equate to him acquiescing though. If he left without giving it to me, it would vanish.

Think, think, think.

"Maybe I should pick this?" He lifted the rosary and wrapped it around his semitranslucent fingers.

"Yes. Before you do, I have a proposition for you. Why don't we play a game?"

He perked up and set down the beads. "What kind?"

I withdrew the box of dice from behind the counter. While going through statistics and probability in my head, I picked out four dice. "Roll it all at once or one at a time. Closest to twenty-one without going over wins."

"What's the prize?" The ghost rubbed his palms together. "I didn't think I'd get in one last bit of fun."

"Your pack of cards. I get bored in here, and having a few games of solitaire would liven up my evenings. Since you can't take your possessions with you anyway, I'm basically providing you with entertainment. Might be fun for you. Does this work?"

The gleam in his eyes matched the twitch in his fingers. "Deal me in."

I grabbed the four dice and rolled them all on the counter. The rattling sound echoed against the polished wood. The odds of rolling over twenty-one were low at best. Six, five, four, and four. Nineteen. Pretty good.

"Not bad, not bad." He collected the dice in his hands. "Not going to try your method. I'm opting for one at a time."

He transferred three dice to his left hand while he shook the fourth in his right. He threw down the die and it landed on six. "Good first number." He threw down the second and it came up again with a six.

Twelve with two more to go.

He kissed his fist with the third die before casting it. Another six.

Eighteen.

"And now it gets interesting." The ghost winked at me. "I have a fifty-fifty chance of winning and losing. If I roll anything from one to three, I'd be able to tie or beat you. Anything more and I'll bust."

I kept my expression calm. In the best-case scenario, I'd get the cards. Worst case, I'd have to beg some god to get me another deck and probably lose my soul in the process. At least I knew what the answer to Theo's riddle was now.

He shook the last die for what seemed like forever—holding it above his head, dancing with it, all the while humming "Groove Is in the Heart." If it hadn't been for the stakes, I'd have laughed over the absurdity of the moment and song choice.

"And. Here. We. Go." He released his grip, and the die tumbled from his hand.

We both watched it dance. It teetered on its rounded edges. This was one of the well-worn ones damaged with age. This could go either way. I didn't know ghosts perspired, but this one did. Dots of moisture covered his forehead. The die alternated between three and six. Salvation and ruination.

Six.

I blew out my lips and sent out a silent hallelujah.

He clutched his belly and roared with laughter. "What are the odds? Rolling all sixes. I should have been at the craps table more instead of blackjack." He pushed the cards across the counter toward me. "There you go, pretty lady. You earned it."

"Thanks." I rubbed my hands together and laughed. "That was fun."

Fun because I got the right outcome.

I tucked the deck behind the counter by my planner before retrieving the scales.

"Sometimes you have to gamble to live a little, you know? It makes me feel alive. It doesn't matter if I lose in the end as long as I get that high. Don't worry, I never gambled more than I could afford to lose. Going to riverboats on weekends made the days running a forklift at Home Depot less painful."

I accepted the rosary, placed it on the left scale, then put the star crystal on the right. It achieved balance almost immediately.

The ghost closed his eyes and lowered his shoulders. "Name's Benny by the way."

"Camille. It's been a pleasure, Benny."

"Likewise." He gave me a salute before he disintegrated into evaporating flecks.

Decent guy and someone I never would have talked to otherwise. Ward would have liked Benny. My ex always had a way of bringing out the best in people, because he saw it in them in the first place. I asked him once what he saw in me. His answer was "Someone who is capable of so much love, far more than even what you imagine. You are one of the most affectionate and loving people I know."

Because previous ex-boyfriends had always told me otherwise, Ward's comment was a revelation—to be seen in a way I wanted to be.

I winced when a sharp wave of pain throbbed from behind my eyes.

The Tropicana deck of cards was ordinary by any means. Blue background with white diamonds in a hypnotic pattern with two white rectangles showcasing the green casino's logo and the website with the phone number for reservations. While I debated between taking out only the heart cards and keeping the deck intact, the wording of the riddle implied it stayed whole.

"Thirteen hearts and no organs," I repeated to myself.

I placed the die at the head of the boxed deck. Before I changed my mind, the two items fused together, sparkling in a brilliant light. I shielded my eyes, and when I opened them, I was staring at a black obsidian key.

It followed the Victorian skeleton model. The ornate filigree making up the bow tapered into a long, skinny stem leading to four different pins with varying wards. A very unusual key for a lock that didn't match anything in this shop.

Every locked item either included a key or wouldn't take this particular one. However, nothing in here was ever as it seemed.

I walked down one of the aisles and pulled out a burgundy, faux-alligator train case from the sixties. The brass opening was tiny compared with the magical key. I pressed the oversized key against the lock. The luggage popped open to reveal a dusty and tattered interior.

Huh.

I snapped the train case closed and rushed back to my catalog on the counter. There were hundreds of items ready to be opened—ranging from lockets, pieces of luggage, jewelry boxes, drawers, cabinets, padlocks, two diaries, and even three safes.

Providing no other ghosts walked in, I had my work cut out for me for the next few days.

This key was the next step in getting out.

"Ms. Buhay," Mr. Samson called out from the hallway. "I'm so sorry I'm late. I overslept and lost track of time."

I scrambled to my feet at the sound of his voice. "Stay there. I'm coming."

He gripped the walls for support as he emerged from the doorway. His steps were shaky. I ran to his side and wrapped my arm around his waist to help steady him.

He was slightly out of breath. "Have there been more customers? I do miss talking to them."

"You don't need to concern yourself with that right now. I'd rather you rest." I guided him to the counter, where he braced himself with his hands for support.

I pulled out the skeleton key and placed it before him.

"What is that?"

"It's a way for us to get out. I'm sure of it." I told him everything—of the clues, the gods, Ward and his boss, and the other shop. To his credit, he listened and didn't question my sanity.

He asked the question with tears in his blue eyes. "You truly think we can get out of this place?"

"Yes. You'll be out and about in London again, wooing all the beautiful ladies." I covered his hands with mine. "We will see the sun soon."

18

Ward

. . . . .

DAY EIGHT AND DAY NINE

. . . . .

WARD DECIDED NOT to answer the psychic telephone call from Camille this morning. His silent protest was driven by his decision to now accept Theo's offer. Thievery would have dire consequences in any situation, but especially this one. He was ready to accept any punishment for his crime if it meant saving his beloved's life.

"I see that you've sold the crown to Eryna." Madam Selene's tiny smirk transformed the harsh features of her face. He had almost thought her incapable of such an emotion. "Now sell the rest."

"Do you know what the gods do with these pieces when they leave the store?" Ward asked. "I doubt that they prance around naked wearing these things."

"These precious items are a drug to them. No, no, not in the way you think. They don't use it the way humans do. They get intoxicated and high off the essence of the mortal who owned that piece. When you're immortal, some emotions are harder to feel than others. What better way to remember the whole range?"

Theo reacted potently when he touched the Mayan jade necklace. It explained the effect they had. Godly emotional cocaine. It was logical that immortals would evolve their methods to alleviate boredom. Nothing was more fatal than enduring a timeless existence in perpetual ennui.

"So you're saying they're basically immortal robots with no feelings?"

"Not robots, but sociopaths. Manipulative by nature and incapable of having empathy, let alone remorse."

"Surely not all of them."

"Yes, *all* of them. They're also stingy. Why do you think it took this long to sell anything in this shop? But you, Mr. Dunbar, you've proven that it's possible to get them to buy." She patted his arm. "I've never been able to convince them, yet you have leverage."

"Leverage?"

"Yes, you use everything you have and weaponize it. The sooner this shop is empty of its wares, the sooner I'll stop nagging. Anything that loses its purpose loses its worth." She handed him the leather book. "Your friend will be dropping by today, and Mr. King. Do I need to remind you that you should keep the appointments separate?"

"I remember." Ward tapped his head. "Oh, I do have one question."

"Make it quick, Mr. Dunbar."

"What happens if the payment is short? Or if it is too much? It isn't like the price and currency are listed and we have a firm guideline."

She rubbed her fingertips together and made a tsking sound. "Interesting and relevant questions. I don't have the answers right now, but I will hopefully by tomorrow morning. My understanding is that these transactions are our responsibility the way retail businesses in our world are on the hook for counterfeit currency. If any transaction fails or is deemed suspicious, you'd be the one accountable."

"What is the harshest punishment, theoretically?"

"Damned if I know, Mr. Dunbar. I don't break the rules, nor do I want to in the future. Don't get any ridiculous ideas now. If you're done with the inquiries, I'll be off to research." She retreated to her office in a huff, ending the conversation.

Ward scanned the appointment list. Theo was due in the morning and Mr. King in the afternoon. There should be plenty of time to hash out his deal before the next client.

BY THE TIME Theo walked in, Ward had already finished writing a long apology to Camille for what he had put into motion. It wasn't a plea for forgiveness, but one asking for understanding. He feared that this would damage their relationship beyond repair. Ward's concern was warranted. To say that Camille wouldn't be happy would be an understatement. Chickens would be more pleased knowing a fox had moved into the coop—and that they could be murdered at any moment.

Theo wore a navy Manchester City cap and a matching navy hoodie. "So, have you made up your mind about our group project?"

Din's vintage black leather jacket matched her thigh-high boots and plaid skirt. Her long hair was bound in a herringbone braid that swung like a pendulum as she rushed to the ruby pendant display.

"Yeah, I'm in. There's a complication though. I'm still figuring out how to hold up my end of the deal."

"I know you're good for it." The god clapped Ward on the shoulder. "I did a little thinking, and I might be able to steal your girl's poison pill without it being in physical proximity. It's going to test my godly hacking skills to pull it off."

"Hacking?"

"I'd be messing with another god's magic. It's not considered ethical by immortal laws. Frowned upon, more like it. Don't worry, it's not going to send me to Tartarus for an eternity of torture or anything like that."

"And you're okay with going ahead first? I really hate that I can't get you what you want sooner. Camille's life is in danger. If she uses that thing again—"

The thought of Camille's death caused Ward's voice to crack.

"Dude, I know. She's your girl, you love her, and you don't want her to die." He tipped his head toward Din. "You'd do anything for her. I get it. That's why I want to help you. It'll help seal the deal between us. For me, it'll be a win for the Western Faction, and my girl will be over the moon for it. And maybe her mom might start getting used to the idea that Din and I are together for the long haul and not because 'Din is slumming it and is going through a rebellious phase.'"

"Ouch. It's funny that she thinks you're still teenagers. Aren't you older than dinosaurs?"

"The biggest pain in the ass you can ever imagine. Nothing I can do about the future monster-in-law." Theo rubbed his palms together. "However, I can save your girl. So the heist is on then? Not going to change your mind?"

"I'm not. Camille's my highest priority."

"All right. We need to make it official." The god held out his hand. "This is a bargain—I will steal and destroy the headdress, and in exchange, you will sell the ruby pendant at a discount."

Ward reached out to clasp the offered hand. "I agree to the bargain."

The jolt of energy snaked through Ward as soon as they made contact. It traveled through his body from his toes to the tips of his hair. "And what are the penalties for reneging on the deal?"

Theo scrunched his nose. "Death and your chance at the afterlife. Shit, I should have cleared that with you before I offered. My bad."

"No, no. It's fine. I'd have agreed to it regardless. So, how are we going to do this?"

"I'll visit Camille tomorrow and accomplish my end. You said she doesn't have much time left. Last I saw her, she looked pretty far gone. I'm sure that once I remove the poison, she can start recovering. That's usually the case with these things."

"I need her alive and well when we leave."

"She's working on that. She helped me realize that I was carrying a clue all this time. Not sure how she'll solve it. I have a hunch that y'all will get out once our side wins."

"The Western Faction."

"Yeah. This war has been going on for far too long. I'm tired of it. No one wants to move on until we have a clear decision though. Can't settle for a tie." Theo snapped his fingers and conjured a tally with two columns. The total was even on both sides. "We've been doing this shitty square dance for centuries. Something has to give."

"All the while, we humans don't even know this is going on."

"The brilliant part is that you kinda do. The bubonic plague was our doing. It was an accident, really, when someone in the Norse Guild let loose their pet project. Whenever you see something that catastrophic and can be explained by science, that's us." He tapped his chest.

"So all the world wars . . ."

"Not us. That's your mess. We sit and watch, and place our bets."

"You take credit for the natural disasters then?"

"Sure. Most of them. Intense hand-to-hand battles."

"And plagues and diseases then."

"Yeah, personally, you don't want to know how that happens." Theo eyed the bubble cameras around the shop. "The store's setup is pretty foolproof. I feel like I got the easier end of the deal. All this . . ." He made a twirling gesture with his index finger. "Is all beyond us."

There was a higher power above the gods. Anything was possible. An ant could think that nothing was bigger than an elephant, but it hadn't yet seen a blue whale. To be clear, Ward Dunbar was well aware that he was the puny ant in this scenario.

"Can you say whom you're referring to?"

Theo shook his head.

Answers were difficult to get in this world. Madam Selene was unable to entertain some of his questions, but when the topic strayed to the taboo, she was muzzled. The trick was making the right query.

"What are your plans when you and your girl get out of here?" Theo asked.

"Not sure. We'll need time alone together to figure out how to go forward."

"You think she won't forgive you for this?"

Camille wouldn't. Ward was caught in a lose-lose situation of his own making.

19

Camille

DAY NINE

I WAS ALMOST done unlocking everything in the shop, and yet I found nothing of substance. I even tried the key out on the most obvious choice—the front door—and it didn't unlock. Any buoyancy I had from yesterday's revelation was almost gone.

The obsidian skeleton key in my hand was destined for a lock I hadn't found yet.

What if the lock wasn't here, but where Ward was?

Was it possible to get it to him?

I wouldn't trust any of these gods with the key.

Theo came in through the front door. He wore a black beanie, an oversized puffy jacket, and ripped baggy jeans. He reminded me of a kid who constantly borrowed his bigger brother's clothes. Din was nowhere in sight.

I tucked the key into my pocket. "No girlfriend this time?"

"She'll drop by in a bit. She has something she has to take care of before she comes in. Why, do you miss her? I mean, we're open to having you join us if that's your thing." He wagged his brows.

Even if he was joking, it was inappropriate as hell.

"I'm kidding." He laughed and waved his hands. "If you do change your mind, though, it's an open invitation."

I had no idea what Ward saw in this horny fool. "Anything I can help you with today?" I switched to a formal tone.

"Yeah, kind of. So the clue I gave you yesterday, did you ever figure it out?" He brushed his fingers through his curly hair. The twitch in his hand betrayed his anxiety.

"Not yet."

"Oh, that sucks. Let me know when you do. It's probably something cool or important. Ward will want to know about it. He's trying his best to get you both out."

"I'm sure he is."

"He's busting ass, my guy. Always hustling. Was he like this out there? Gotta be. You know, I have a few people in my circle who're just as motivated. I bet . . ."

I busied myself by rearranging the apothecary bottles on the shelf behind the counter. Whether he was unable to read the room or he didn't care, Theo seemed to be the type who either liked to hear himself talk or needed to make as much noise as possible to cover up the lack of brain activity.

He checked over his shoulder. "So where are all the ghosts? Slow day?"

"I don't control who comes in. Since I've been here, the most I've ever gotten were two visitors at a time."

"This place isn't exactly a club." He laughed at his own joke.

I cracked a painful half smile.

"Seriously though. Maybe if you cleared some of this junk out, you could do something decent with the space. It's so damned depressing in here."

If I had the option to usher him out, I would. Mr. Samson never gave any guidance. As far as I knew, my duties involved catering to every customer—no matter how annoying or inconveniencing they might be.

"Do you have a note for me?" I asked.

"I do, but I can't give it to you until later."

"I see." I pulled out the note I'd already written and folded it into a heart. "I have this for him. Can you please deliver it?"

He plucked the note from my fingertips. "Will do."

Din sauntered in. She wore the plague mask pointing up on her head and had to duck to clear the front doors. Her singsong choral voice echoed in my head. "I brought them."

"Brought who?"

Theo snapped his fingers. The Tang dynasty headdress that Mr. King gave me materialized in his other hand. The glint of gold and jade sparkled in the light. The droplet veil tinkled as he tightened his grip.

"Wait, that's mine!" I called out, rushing from behind the counter. "What are you doing?"

Din put the beaked mask on her face and raised her arms. A circle of ghosts rose from the floor. These were nothing like the ones I'd dealt with—these were specters, no human faces or features, amorphous shadows with grasping claws.

I wanted nothing more than to run forward and take back what was mine, but the cluster of spirits gave me pause. I remembered the terror of encountering my first ghost, and this was far more sinister.

Even Theo took a step back from the crowd of phantasms.

"Give it back, please," I pleaded from the counter, reaching out my hand toward him. "I need that—"

"I made a bargain." He tossed the headdress to the ghosts. "*Factum est.*"

The piece of jewelry was devoured, ripped into a hundred pieces by the specter mob.

"No!" I sobbed.

My sole means of private communication with Ward was gone. I didn't even have a choice in the matter. The throbbing migraine in my head dissipated, yet I was too distraught to even care. I sank into a helpless heap in front of the counter.

Theo tossed a folded note at my feet. "Ward sends his regards."

When Din and Theo left, the unwanted ghosts did as well. I cared about none of this.

I curled my hands into fists and pounded the cold marble floor. Damn it. I dashed the hot tears away from my cheeks. *Ward, you just screwed us both with your ridiculous sense of chivalry.*

"You asshole!" I screamed, hoping he heard me.

He had good intentions, but it was my choice to make. He had robbed me. I *knew* the risks, and I was fine with the consequences. Now I didn't even know whether I was able to forgive him or if my relationship with him was salvageable.

Was there even a "we" to save?

Anger flared inside me along with the worst sense of impotence. That was the source of the tears, and I hated it. I sobbed into my knees. Hiccups vibrated through my chest, causing me to gasp for breath.

I was alone.

Ward wasn't on my side.

No one was.

The folded sheets of paper lay by my feet. I didn't need to read them to know they were a written apology. Nothing Ward wrote down had the ability to coax forgiveness from my lips. I pulled the papers toward me and unfolded them. The infuriating bastard. They were written on the teal ombré paper, from a planner he had purchased for me from a little stationery shop on Carnaby Street. The note read:

Camille,

I know you're pissed. I'm sorry, I had no choice. I had to do it. Nothing was worth the price of your life.

This isn't about sacrifice or martyrdom. You have to be alive when we leave, and I know we'll still be able to get out of this place. Whether you still want to be with me, I don't know. I'd rather you be alive and screaming at me than the alternative.

I know I'm selfish because a life without you isn't one worth living.

I've already lived that.

It took me living six months in Chicago in our apartment before I realized you weren't coming back. I didn't go to LA because I wanted to. I went because it was easier than to be reminded of where you used to be, in all the places where you should be.

I still wonder why you left—how much of it was because I couldn't do what was hard.

*Deciding to take the headdress away from you was
far more difficult than you can imagine. I didn't want to
be the unwanted, savior knight. You're more than
capable of saving yourself.*

*I did this despite knowing how it would make you
feel. Be angry. Hate me.*

I'm grateful that you're still alive.

*Even though your feelings have changed, know that
I'll always love you.*

Always.

Yours,
Ward

Taking care of me in his own way to the very end, knowing
I'd hate him for it.

I leaned back and covered my eyes.

Rage might burn bright and hot, but sustaining it consumed far too much energy. I used to be able to. I lost the
stamina after I left for Manhattan. Living in the city alone
taught me that having anger as a constant companion wasn't
ideal—it was exhausting. Pettiness didn't fuel my existence,
unlike some that I knew.

The version of me he remembered wasn't who I was anymore.

I gathered myself and got to my feet. Any form of communication with Ward going forward would be compromised. I
sure as hell knew that Theo would be reading each note if he
hadn't already done so. He and Ward had made some sort of
bargain.

What the hell did Ward offer in exchange?

It would bite him in the ass. Dealing with gods with an already screwed-up power dynamic was dicey at best. I prayed he hadn't sacrificed something as ridiculous as his own life. He better not have traded his own for mine.

"Breathe," I muttered to myself.

Worrying about him overrode any lingering resentment on my part. Theo wasn't the type to give freebies without collecting on a massive favor in the end.

My bargaining with a god would lead to more trouble. The headdress was a mitigated risk and classified as a gift. I wouldn't have negotiated for it—I refused to be bought.

My ex was likely in some deep shit he didn't even know he was in. He trusted Theo with everything, and this misplaced loyalty would inevitably lead to betrayal. Ward would argue with me about my inability to trust people until he was blue in the face, but my gut instinct told me I was right. Theo was trouble.

In order to get out of here, I had figured out the puzzles on my end. Everything left was up to Ward. He had to fish out two riddles from both factions and solve the mystery of the vault. I didn't see a path forward with collaboration.

How was it possible to work out anything in the future if we had to deal with not only a time delay but also surveilled correspondence with the potential of sabotage? Any kind of planned action would be impossible to pull off.

Any leverage I had was gone.

Wait.

No, it wasn't.

The skeleton key was still in my pocket. I fished out Mr.

King's card and burned it by the green flame of the black candle. He appeared moments later, dressed in black and wielding a shiny silver cane.

Mr. King stepped forward. "Ah, Ms. Buhay. What's on your mind?"

"What if I've found the thing you've been looking for in here?"

"I'm listening." He narrowed his eyes and leaned on his cane. "Hypothetically speaking, you'll need to decide whom you want to entrust that item to. Both factions would be eager to get their hands on it."

"When I hand it over, does this mean the experiment is done here? Is my part done? Will I and Mr. Samson be set free?" The questions tumbled from my lips without pause.

Mr. King held up a finger. "First, we need to clarify what you think this game is. How did you come to the conclusion that it is one?"

"The riddles. The fact Mr. Samson has been here for decades. If this was a glorified prison, there wouldn't be an endgame—we'd be trapped, and that's it. Why have riddles? Why have mortals like me here?" I stretched out my arms. "All of this has a purpose. It's too well designed not to have one. This is an escape room."

He laughed. "Ah yes. I know what you're referring to. This is a way to settle the war of the gods. A nonviolent, nondestructive method meant to keep both sides from pulverizing each other and everything else in the process. A civilized chess match."

"And the answer to the rest of my questions?"

"I don't know if you'll be set free or if your work is done. I do have the feeling of déjà vu—that I've gotten to this part before." He winced and tapped his temple. "Memories are tricky and easily manipulated here. Gods aren't immune."

This might explain what was happening to Mr. Samson.

"Eventually, you and Mr. Dunbar must choose a side, and it has to be the same side. We can't end in another impasse." The dragon head of his cane breathed fire.

"Then I must choose."

I didn't even know which side was which. These were sides of a war I didn't even care about and that I doubted cared about me or my kind. Ward and I were caught in an untenable position. I didn't want to burden myself with all of the implications of making this decision. Ward probably would. He'd wrestle with the agony of his indecision till kingdom come.

"How much will my choice matter?" I asked.

"To us, it means everything." He twirled the cane with his left hand until it spun into a whirring circle. "The gods can't interfere with bribery. It's not allowed. There are severe penalties for both parties involved."

"So many rules."

"Yes. It keeps things civilized and fair, mostly."

"I don't even know half of them. All I was told was to sell and acquire in this shop. How is it fair that I don't know the full situation I'm in?"

"That might be for your protection or to keep everything unbiased. While it certainly helps, knowledge isn't always the solution to every problem. I doubt you'd believe me though."

All my life, I relied on gaining knowledge to get ahead. I had to know all the options and outcomes. Yes, it stemmed from the need to control and diminish my anxiety. It didn't matter that what I unearthed was more destructive than beneficial. More knowledge meant I made the best decision possible.

None of this applied here. Mr. Samson wasn't allowed to tell me everything even if he wanted to. I didn't trust anything these gods said. As for Ward, anything coming from him going forward was suspect.

The black candle beside me flickered red. It was past halfway melted.

I trusted myself.

"I've chosen a side." I held out my hand to Mr. King with the skeleton key. "Take it."

20

Ward

DAY TEN

WARD CARRIED THE heavy weight of Camille's anger on his shoulders. Nothing kept one on their toes better than knowing that someone they cared about was mad at them—such was the power of said emotion. A veritable sword of Damocles over his head, and he accepted it like a martyr. After all, he was trying to save her life.

"Mr. Dunbar, you have a very busy day today." Madam Selene emerged from her office. A few stray strands escaped her tight bun. "And I've also concluded my research. There is no such thing as counterfeit in immortal terms. Yes, they have the capacity to fool mortals and their own brethren, but not this shop. Therefore, there is no corresponding punishment."

"And about illegal transactions?"

"I don't appreciate your line of questioning, Mr. Dunbar. They either have enough for payment or they don't. There isn't a middle ground. You wouldn't be allowed to finish the transaction otherwise."

"Ah, but what about—"

She shot him a quelling glare. "You have three clients to see today. I suggest you focus. There are still four items for sale. I fail to understand why the prospect of freedom isn't enough of a motivation for you."

Every morning, it seemed like someone had spit in her breakfast or that she had fallen asleep and woken up with a crease between her brows. To be fair, there was no such thing as a cheerful prisoner.

"It is. I'm confident we can get out. Oh, I happened to come across an interesting bit of information. Somewhere in this shop might be riddles. Maybe if we—"

"If that's what you want to think, then use these fanciful riddles as a selling point to your clients. Riddles are for children and adults with too much time on their hands. How ridiculous, even for your active imagination. There's a time and place . . ."

During the impromptu lecture that he never asked for, Ward's spirit and mind left his body to focus on the clues. Madam Selene did mention that she had never made any sales in her tenure. He introduced change, and it had to be for the better. Maintaining the status quo wouldn't help matters. The sooner he could escape this level of hell, the faster he could patch up his relationship with Camille. Provided she had forgiven him or was able to in the future. In the arena of love, nothing was ever guaranteed and only a fool would bet on certainties.

Madam Selene snapped her fingers. "Are you paying attention, Mr. Dunbar?"

"Yes, ma'am. Sell, sell, sell!" Ward flashed her a motivating grin.

She covered her eyes and shook her head. "There better be at least one fewer item on display when I see you tomorrow morning."

Ward rubbed his palms together. If there was anything he did well, it was selling. It was never about the money; the thrill was in getting someone excited about something. This comported with his idealism and romantic nature. The actual exchange of goods was a forgone conclusion.

He picked up the ledger Madam Selene left on the desk. Eryna, Mr. King, then Theo. The appointments were spaced out enough to avoid any conflicts. Ward needed to make at least two sales today to test the riddle theory and to decipher how to apply the discount. The first two were his marks.

Eryna walked in thirty minutes later. She wore a dress made of smoke. Literal gray wisps both covered and uncovered all the important parts. Again, he kept his eyes focused on her flawless face because Ward was a gentleman.

"You should see how a group of soldiers react when I appear like this in the middle of battle." She dragged a finger across her collarbone. The smoke vanished, leaving her naked. "Or like this."

He didn't dare look. "My supervisor believes in a formal, strict dress code. I hope you can comply."

"Oh, Edward, you're such a prude." She made a vague gesture with her wrist, and the smoke returned. "If I were your lovely Camille, you wouldn't be so uptight about nudity."

Ward cleared his throat and pulled out the chair for her. She took a seat and wriggled into place by the desk.

"The crown that you purchased, did it have any unusual properties?" he asked.

"Nothing out of the ordinary. Why?"

"That's a shame then. I was hoping it would be . . ."

She nibbled on the tip of her index finger. "What are you suggesting?"

"That it would contain a riddle. Camille has found two at the antique shop. I think she's close or has already found the item you are looking for there." Her emerald eyes flared with fire. He continued laying the bait. "Isn't that why you keep coming in here? You and Mr. King. You're searching for something similar. Perhaps these riddles would lead to that vault you've mentioned."

"I didn't realize there was a devious mind behind that pretty face and delectable body. You've been very busy, I see." She craned her neck to stare down the glass gallery. "And one of these will contain something valuable?"

"Two. Four items left and two riddles. The odds are in your favor."

"I can only afford to buy one for today."

"Think of what it would mean for the Western Faction to secure an advantage. I bet the war has gone on for long enough on both sides. I can only imagine what it'd be like for the general who eventually wins it for the faction."

"You're trying to seduce me, Edward."

He was. Getting anyone to buy anything could be construed as an enticement to open one's wallet. "Not seduce, but get the game moving so I can escape."

She reached out and caressed his chin. "Are you that eager to leave this place?"

He said yes without hesitation.

"But this is the only place where gods and mortals can

interact on a regular basis. In ancient times, it took special circumstances for us to appear to humans, and a purpose—we had to make bargains. Here, you can revel in the presence of magic. Why choose an ordinary life?"

If he weren't in love with Camille, he might have chosen this life. The glamour, magic, power, and possibilities of this world intrigued him. Ward wanted to meet each god and guess their identity. He wished to walk through Olympus and Valhalla, if they even existed. The wonder of this world wasn't lost on him, yet none of it mattered without Camille. She made every day he spent with her magical.

At this point, if she didn't forgive him, he would wither away as a lonely hermit bachelor with a volleyball for a friend on some deserted island populated by stray cats.

"Because it's what I'm used to. We mortals like our comfortable bubbles. Anything too much would test our sanity. It might be why we can only take gods in limited doses. Even in recorded history and myths, there are instances where divine contact resulted in insanity."

"Yes, I have seen this for myself." Her laugh was a high-throated giggle. "You mortals are very fragile."

He turned his attention to the display cases. "Which one are you interested in?"

"I'm torn between the pendant and the earrings."

Ward's bargain with Theo would be jeopardized if Eryna chose the pendant. "Might I suggest the earrings? The ruby pendant was inspected before by a client. It didn't yield anything unusual."

"Fine. I'll listen to your suggestion, Edward. I do pray for your sake that this proves your theory instead of invalidating it."

He walked to the display that held Electra's golden earrings. The glittering pair was sculpted with impeccable detail. The top was the torso of a muscled figure who he assumed was her father, Agamemnon. The figure tapered off, transforming into a thick, curling serpent with an open mouth at the end.

Ward brought the velvet stand to the desk. The goddess moved forward for a closer inspection of the earrings. She closed her eyes and took a deep breath. "I can still smell the blood. Yes, this is the right bauble for me."

"Shall we proceed to payment?" he asked.

She uttered the key phrase, held up her right hand, and rotated her wrist. Gemstones and three daggers materialized on the tabletop. He touched the golden scales before putting on the pair of gloves in the drawer.

This was the perfect time to test the system. In order to fulfill his bargain with Theo, he needed to learn more about the transaction system. Economics and mathematics weren't his strong suit, and even if they had been, he wouldn't understand how immortal currency worked. These gods and goddesses had an almost infinite amount of time to dispute the value of any given object. Yes, one would assume there'd be a standard by now, but never underestimate the potency of pettiness marinated and brewed over countless millennia.

Ward placed the earrings on the left plate and then piled the assorted glittering gems onto the right. Between the stones and the dagger, the choice of which to leave out was easy. He deliberately pushed out a small emerald that "fell" underneath the scale while arranging the three daggers on the plate.

The scale teetered and came close yet didn't balance. He

reached out and tried to remove the earrings from the plate. They didn't budge. No removal was possible midtransaction.

"Oh, Edward, you missed that. Silly boy." She pointed to the gem. "It should balance now."

He corrected his "mistake." "I apologize, Lady Eryna."

The scales balanced with the added weight. The precious stones and weapons on the right scale vanished in a sweep of gold dust. He reached for the earrings, and they came off the plate without resistance.

"Let me have them." She held out her open palm. "One at a time. The effect is always so potent at initial contact."

She licked her lips as he handed her the first one. The corresponding effect was frissons of energy. Eryna threw back her head and moaned, crying out in ecstasy. Orgasms. She arched her back and bucked in her chair. Her smoke dress vanished from the vigorous movement. "Now the other one."

With his eyes closed, Ward gave her the matching earring. He covered his ears with his hands and waited until the X-rated show passed. This hadn't happened with the other sales. Mr. King reacted with nostalgia to the Tang dynasty ornament. Theo was zapped with what he described as lust by the jade pendant.

Each piece drew out the strongest emotion from the mortal who owned it. Theo mentioned Hunac Ceel's lust and it matched his life story. Electra's tragedy centered on revenge and matricide. Wrath. Eryna was titillated by bloodlust and rage. Ward hypothesized that the remaining pieces in this shop must embody the rest of the deadly sins.

By the time he finished guessing which sin belonged to

which piece, the goddess regained her composure and returned to the approved dress code.

"Oh, that was delightful. So delightful." She was still out of breath. Eryna fluttered her fingers over her hair to restore it to its normal, unfrazzled state. "I almost forgot about the riddle part."

Camille mentioned that her riddles came in the form of glowing worms that reacted to her touch. The earrings on the desk retained their original shape. No worms so far. Ward pulled off the gloves and touched one with the tip of his left pinkie— it was the finger he was most willing to sacrifice in case it was incinerated.

The gold earring wobbled and had no zap. His digits were left intact.

"Edward, what are you . . ."

A strange, glowing worm with moving lights under its skin snaked out. Eryna reached out to touch it and it recoiled, moving toward him. He followed Camille's instructions, and his touch disintegrated the creature, and its essence formed letters on the smooth surface of the desk.

"What does it say? What does this mean?"

Thermopylae and the Water Margin.

Ward committed the words to memory per Camille's warning.

"It's not a riddle. I don't even know what to think. At least not yet."

"You'll decipher its meaning soon. I can feel the climax to this war is nigh. Know that the Western Faction has brought you this gift." She snatched the earrings from the table and put them on. "You will choose the right side when the time comes, won't you, Edward?"

She departed shortly after.

He'd better clean her chair before Mr. King's appointment. Extra bleach, hand sanitizer, or whatever he could scrounge up in the restroom cabinet.

21

Camille

· · · · ·

DAY NINE AND DAY TEN

· · · · ·

MR. KING EXAMINED the key in my hand without touching it. "You're certain you want to entrust this to me, Ms. Buhay?"

"Aren't you supposed to be happy? Thrilled even. I chose *your* side."

"I am. Forgive me, I'm trying to understand the future implications. It would make Mr. Dunbar's choice much more difficult." He plucked the key from my hand and rushed to deposit it into his inner jacket pocket. "Remember what I said about both sides? That if he chooses a different side than yours, we would all lose."

"Oh. You didn't mention that part."

"Anything but a decisive victory for one side is not good for either immortals or mortals. This war has gone on for far too long. I'll take the key back to my faction and we'll figure out what to do with it . . ."

"I think you're supposed to give it to Ward."

He winced and smacked his forehead. "Your boyfriend hates me. I can't give it to him. Any gift given by a god to a mortal should be accepted willingly. You were receptive to the headdress, therefore the transfer worked."

Mr. King was right. Ward's disdain for him bled through our letters. I had never pinpointed why. Ward liked Theo for the same unexplainable reason. It wasn't that I trusted Mr. King—I picked the lesser evil. I didn't forget that this god had supplied me with the means to kill myself if I wasn't careful.

"Speaking of which, you shouldn't be using the gift I gave you anymore. Another use and it will be fatal."

"That won't be a problem. It's gone and eaten by spirits. Ward struck a bargain with Theo."

"Shit and even more shit." He groaned and covered his face with his hands. His cane remained standing on its own. The dragon's head spit fire.

His response confirmed my worst fears. "What do you think Ward promised him in return?"

"Something bad. It's never anything minor. It could be anything from his soul to his firstborn son. Bargains are inviolable. No god or mortal can interfere, and they must be fulfilled. Ward is compelled and must complete his end. Reneging isn't an option. The punishment is worse than death."

"What's worse than death?"

"Eternal torture. Death is something you'd be wishing and praying for."

Fuck. Of all the times when I gloated over being right, this wasn't one of them. Theo had taken full advantage of him. I had to find out what Ward was sacrificing to keep up his end of the deal. The only way to do this was to get on better terms with Theo. I'd rather get an unanesthetized five-hour root canal.

"Any words of advice on how to handle your ex?"

"Ward already doesn't like you. I suggest you try not to piss him off. Also, he won't take to you buttering him up all of a sudden. Personality changes will only make him more suspicious of you."

"You two make an odd pair. On the surface, you both are very beautiful mortals. I understand the physical attraction. Everything else is a mystery."

It was a common question many had asked. Ward and I were opposites. He was laid-back while I was considered type A. I made sure we arrived at social functions on time while he wrote the thank-you cards and followed up after the event. The ways we complemented each other often became the cause for conflict. Ward wasn't my better half—he filled in the missing parts of me.

"When you get to know him, you'll understand. Don't let the pretty boy looks fool you."

Ward was often underestimated not only because of his appearance but also because of his kindness. Some equated both traits with stupidity. His intelligence was one of the many reasons why I loved him. Still loved him despite what Theo had done.

I BEGAN MY next shift trying to relax my resting bitch face when all I remembered was Theo's horrible invitation to a ménage à trois. Theo had never seen me with any other expression, and for good reason. He would be visiting soon, and I had a note ready. Nothing I'd written would be intelligible to anyone other than Ward.

Mr. Samson hadn't made an appearance. I knocked on his

door a few times and talked as if he heard me. I worried about him and his declining health and memory. My fondness for him surprised me after my turbulent first day. He'd been sweet and supportive—the sole source of comfort in this hellish nightmare. The fact that he'd survived for decades under these conditions made me even more determined to see him freed.

I brushed my worries aside when Theo walked in with a sheepish expression on his face. Din wasn't with him. It didn't matter if she was. Something about her terrified me, and I didn't understand the root of my fear. It went beyond the disconcerting sensation I had in her presence.

He fidgeted with the zipper of his hoodie. "Are you still mad?"

Lying and saying everything was fine between us wasn't an option. He wouldn't buy it. "Yeah."

"My boy had the best intentions. He wanted to save you at all costs. I don't think he'd last a minute here if you were gone. He feels terrible about it. Knew you'd be pissed, but he had to do it." Theo spread his hands. "He was stuck between a hard and an even harder place."

"Doesn't change the fact he did something that I never asked for."

"His heart was in the right place though? Doesn't he get points for that?"

Theo was campaigning hard for Ward. I still didn't buy the motivation behind it. "I guess. What if Din were to do something to you that you never asked for?"

"Depends on what it is." He licked his lips and wagged his brows. "I'm open to anything she wants to do to me."

Pervert. He probably didn't show this side to Ward often. These gods had an even greater capacity for deceit, as if they

were a more concentrated form of human emotion. Every god
I met exceeded the parameters of mortal conventions—even
the subdued, philosophical version of Mr. King. The side he
had chosen to show me likely didn't match what Ward saw,
and the same case applied to Theo.

A person's true face was their worst side.

For the longest time, I waited to see what Ward's anger
would do. I wanted to see if he would be cold, petulant, or
even violent. After the terrible experience with my first relationship in my teens, I was ready to leave at any hint of trouble.
Ward handled his anger the way he approached every emotion—
better than I ever would. He processed them at an appropriate
and healthy rate. My tendency was to burn everything down
and cut out people in my life.

"You'll forgive him eventually though? Don't tell me you're
one of those chicks that will treat him like scorched earth. Disposable. You women love to weaponize your rage to get us to
beg, contort, and submit. Manipulative as fuck. Don't be *that*,
Camille."

The edge in his voice didn't surprise me. I'd been waiting
for it to surface all this time because, to me, this had always
been there. This justified every single one of my suspicions. If
Ward ever caught a hint of this, he'd disengage and distance.
But Theo wouldn't make the mistake of letting his mask slip.
He was using Ward with this bargain and would continue to
do so until he got what he wanted.

"I won't allow my anger to change what I have to do. People
argue all the time. Ward and I will sort this out on our own."
I pulled out the folded heart from my pocket and placed it on
the counter. "See. No burned bridges."

He scooped it up and slapped down a note from Ward. "He found a clue. The brilliant guy worked out that the pieces being sold at the jewelry shop contained the clues. He needs your help with it."

"Ah, thank you." I tucked the note into my journal without reading it.

"Western Faction's got the first. There's still one more left to find there. If we get it, it's going to be a decisive victory. Say, have you found anything here yet? With those two riddles we got you?" His brown eyes drifted again to my breasts. "It should lead to something really interesting."

I turned my back to him to avoid the ogling. "Not yet. Still working on it. Did Ward say anything else?"

"Yeah, he thinks the Western Faction is the way to go. That's the side he's leaning toward. He knows he has to pick a side. It'd help if you two are on the same page."

Lie. Ward would never make such a rash decision about this and this early. He'd want more information. Mr. King's warning echoed in my mind. "I guess I'll have to sort it all out once I get those riddles solved."

"We'd treat you well. I know someone who can make it possible for you and Ward to be together forever—like eternal youth and immortality. Sounds good, right? It's technically not a bribe if I frame it as a reward."

His hot breath was suddenly on my shoulder. I wanted nothing more than to scream, which wasn't an option right now. "So where is Din?" I turned to slide past him out from behind the counter. "She must be missing your enchanting company."

"She's busy. You know, off with her girlfriends doing who knows what."

He followed me as I busied myself by heading to the far end of the shop and rearranging a set of teacups and saucers at a nearby side table. His proximity was unwanted, and I couldn't even tell him to get lost. At least not yet.

"Ms. Buhay, might I speak with you in private for a minute?" Mr. Samson was standing in the back of the shop by the counter. He stood ramrod straight, as he had during my job interview.

Theo backed off and waved as he slipped out the front doors.

I clapped my hands. "Oh, Mr. Samson, that was brilliant."

My boss swayed and then slumped against the side of the counter. I rushed to his side to check on him. "Are you all right? I know you've been tired. Though I appreciated the help, please don't overexert yourself."

"Can't help myself." His words came in gasps. "Seeing a damsel in distress is a weakness."

I steered him toward a high-backed chair with ornate, filigree-carved arms. We stayed there in silence until he was able to catch his breath. If we hadn't been trapped here, I'd be wheeling him to the nearest hospital. His decline grew worse each day.

"You have an unwelcome immortal admirer." He patted my hand. "The shop will not allow us to expel these kinds of . . ."

"Jerks. I thought as much. The worst part is that this pervert already has a girlfriend."

"Then perhaps telling her about his abysmal behavior might get him to behave?"

It was what I was planning to do. Din would certainly have thoughts about how her boyfriend was acting. I didn't care whether this would break them up. Anything to dissuade Theo from his mission to get into my pants.

"It's on my to-do list." I squeezed his warm hand. "And how are you feeling?"

"I can't say I haven't had better days. Sometimes I feel like I can't tell where I am or who I am. Yet somehow, when I see your face, I remember."

"I'm doing what I can to fix our situation. I've heard from Ward. He has found a clue. I haven't looked into it yet. Would you like to help me with it?"

Mr. Samson nodded.

I fetched the note and did a quick scan. Ward didn't write much about anything other than relaying information. Given what had happened between us, he must have assumed that I'd still be furious with him.

"Thermopylae and the Water Margin. What does this mean?"

Mr. Samson rubbed his chin. "The first is an ancient place in Greece where a famous battle took place. I don't remember any more details. My memory isn't what it used to be."

I tapped the paper against the floor. "If I had access to my phone or even the internet, this would be so easy to look up. Nothing I have that uses information technology works. All the times I took for granted that I was able to search for something as mundane as the weather. I should have been more explicit about what I wanted when you asked about any requirements I needed to accept the job."

"You might not have the internet, but wasn't there the workspace request when you asked for a fully furnished flat?

I'm surprised there isn't already a bookcase with specific books related to antiques and antiquity in place. One of your duties was to deal with acquisitions."

Which meant dealing with cataloging and research. There was a small desk area upstairs with a drawer full of stationery and writing implements. I hadn't needed the books until now because I hadn't finished completing the catalog until recently.

"Does this mean I'll have access to a library soon?" I asked.

"I don't see why not. You were very clear and shrewd about your requirements. This type of thoughtfulness and preparation is why I hired you in the first place. Your other wonderful qualities are why I look forward to seeing you every morning."

I blushed. This man had gotten under my skin.

"You can check and see after your shift. I know accepting all of this magic is hard for you to digest. The most pragmatic and grounded would find it hard. Lucky for me, I'm comfortable with the idea of faeries, gods, and the like. Spirit me away on a flying hippo and I'd be fine with it." He paused to let out a dry chuckle. "If you don't mind, can you escort me back to my office?"

"Of course."

After I dropped him off, I headed up to my apartment. Sure enough, there was a bookcase waiting for me right beside the tiny desk, which had expanded in size. I was more comfortable thinking that contractors let themselves in and made the adjustments or that the grocery delivery service restocked my fridge when I was at work. Rationalizing all these minor miracles helped me maintain my sanity.

I repeated the clue to myself as I pored over the books in my new bookcase. The shelves had the standard furniture and antiquities manuals sprinkled with the occasional art text-book. There weren't any history books on the shelves—especially ancient Greek ones at first glance.

"Oh." I spotted a thick tome on the desk and picked it up. "Ancient Greek history, huh? Very convenient. Now flip to the right page I need, just like Google."

The book did as I commanded, opening in my hands to the right section of the momentous battle. Now wasn't the time to figure out *how* this was happening. Of course it was magic. I took down general notes on the event where a small force of Spartans held off the massive Persian army.

The information meant nothing until I put it into the con-text of the clue. The Water Margin might refer to the Aegean, geography, or something wholly different. I spoke aloud as if I were using a typical virtual assistant AI device. "What is 'the Water Margin'?"

A geography book and a novel appeared on the desk. The larger, thicker volume opened to a section on bodies of water. I picked up the less obvious choice. The cover was in Chinese with an English translation. "*The Water Margin: Outlaws of the Marsh*," I read to myself. The novel had to be the right answer.

The clue contained both a Western and an Eastern ref-erence.

How did a military battle relate to this novel? What was the connection? The nature of the riddles of the antique shop was far more straightforward. It led to finding an actual object. This set of clues didn't give me the impression it was another scavenger hunt.

It had to lead to the mysterious vault in Ward's shop or be related to it somehow.

I took out Ward's letter and read it again. Key lines stood out—all centered on my perceived anger. He was certain I'd already cut him off from my life and was proceeding with a no-nonsense approach to collaboration. This was so far from the truth.

Yes, I was upset with what he'd done, but I was still in love with him.

I wanted to walk away from here and see what the future held for us together.

We handled disputes well when we were together. We talked and made sure we didn't sleep or make love that night with it still looming over us. None of these options were available to us now. So much nuance was lost in translation through these pages.

I wrote my letter addressing this. He needed to know that I still believed in *us* before I even began to tell him about my theories. There wasn't a point in getting out unless we went together, hand in hand. All of us.

22

Ward

. . . . .

DAY TEN

. . . . .

MR. KING WALKED in thirty minutes after Eryna left.

Ward had everything tidied and ready for the visit—though it was highly improbable the chair would pass a black light test. He had proven that the cleaning supplies in the bathroom were quite inadequate.

The god appeared more at ease today than he had been. Granted, the last time Ward saw him, he was engaged in hand-to-hand combat with Eryna. Mr. King pulled out the chair and sat down. "While I appreciate your efforts, Mr. Dunbar, I am aware of what happened here. It's one of those things that gods *know*."

Despite Ward's valiant efforts, nothing would wipe away any glowing immortal residue. He should feel no shame, but he did. Guilt worked in mysterious ways.

He cleared his throat and drew Mr. King's attention to the other end of the shop. "As you can also see, there are only three items left for sale."

"Ah, she also bought something. I mean, it's the least she

could do after making a mess." The god brushed his hands together in a wiping motion. "What prompted the spending spree? That's what I want to know."

"I may have the answer to that. Do you remember when Camille found a riddle in one of your possessions? She believes that there is something here for me to discover, and I've proven her theory. Eryna's purchase yielded a clue. One of the remaining items has the other. There should be two, the same number as there was in the antique shop."

Mr. King gripped the edge of the table. "So she's ahead. This isn't good for the Eastern Faction."

"Which piece would you be interested in today?"

"Humor me and choose, Mr. Dunbar. I want to see what you think is suitable."

Of the remaining pieces, Ward had to reserve the ruby pendant, and if he wanted the Western Faction to keep their advantage, Hunac Ceel's jade necklace was the right decision. He retrieved the jade necklace and placed it on the desk before Mr. King.

"Interesting choice. Tell me your reasoning."

The smooth, polished green stones shone under the shop's lights. "I think you'll enjoy the emotion behind the artifact. It will jive with what you're into." Ward recalled the god waxing nostalgic about some fling he had with a courtier in their first meeting. The lust side effect should be a welcomed outcome.

The possibility that Ward might have to do another cleanup after this was very likely. Janitorial services weren't a requirement stated in the job description when he signed up. Then again, he never bargained for being imprisoned either. He was in the running for the unfortunate circumstances award.

"Jade is a good stone. I'd wear this." Mr. King took a closer peek at the carved pendant without touching it. "You think that a clue might be in here?"

"It could be. There are two other choices left if you buy this one and eliminate it from the field. Your chances are as good as any. The sooner the clue is found, the faster we can settle whatever this is. I think it's only then that your war will be decided and Camille and I will be set free."

"And what do you expect to do afterward with your new-found freedom?"

"Take Camille out for a drink at the Shard, then figure out if we want to stay in London."

Ward still wanted to be with her but wasn't certain that his feelings were reciprocated. Ultimately, if her happiness meant being away from him, so be it. Most believed in the adage that if true love was meant to be, you set it free. In reality, the expectation was that it would return like a boomerang. It was far nobler to declare the former aloud and not the latter.

"You're very confident about this 'we,' Mr. Dunbar. I heard that you are responsible for destroying the gift I'd given to Ms. Buhay."

"That could have killed her. Did you at least warn her about it?"

"I had. She decided to use it in spite of the consequences. You can't tell me that you didn't appreciate hearing her voice again after all of this time spent apart?"

Ward did, but the cost was far too high to pay. "I can't deny that. But there had to be another way."

"You're trapped in here. The choices left to you are very

limited. Some things that come your way have a price. Nothing is ever free, especially when dealing with gods."

"Kindness, Mr. King. Not everything has to be quid pro quo."

The god narrowed his eyes and gave him a once-over. "Tell me. How many things in your life were given to you or handed to you? Was the motive behind them all 'kindness'? How much of it was because you happen to be a good-looking bastard? Or because you come from a wealthy family? Or because they needed a favor in the future?"

"Obviously, I can't assume the motive behind everything. However, I do approach it from a charitable place. I don't find any advantage in living my life as if it's purely transactional." Ward uttered the last sentence with a bit more edge than he had intended.

"You don't like me at all, do you, Mr. Dunbar?"

Ward put on a pair of gloves to handle the necklace. "How I feel doesn't affect how I do my job."

"But it does." Mr. King leaned back on his chair, tipping it on its back legs. "It's important when you choose a side. You must pick a side that is the same as Ms. Buhay's. Any other choice is meaningless."

"Right. For this war of yours. I don't even know what side stands for the interests of mortals. I doubt your two factions would hold a town hall where I can ask as many questions as I want. I doubt Camille would make such a rash choice."

"If she had, you wouldn't know what she decided. Collusion is against the rules, though collaboration to solve any riddles or clues is allowed. How else can you untangle whatever it is that will lead you to choose a side?" The god paused to take in Ward's surprised reaction. "Yes, Mr. Dunbar. It all leads to you and her reaching the same conclusion. All these games are designed to settle the war."

"Games that imprison me and three other mortals. We're forced to play without our consent."

"You must do what you can with the cards you were dealt. So do we."

"Do you have the payment ready?"

Mr. King uttered the phrase, and the scales reappeared. He opened his jacket and fished out a few items from his inner pockets. The god produced a bundle of incense sticks, a gold chain necklace, and a jar of preserved peaches.

"What happens if you don't have enough and you try to take the item anyway?" Ward kept his tone casual. "Would the alarms go off and we'd go into lockdown?"

"If this is your roundabout way of accusing me of future theft, it won't work. You might want to ask your friends in the Western Faction. They're more known for that kind of shit."

"I doubt that your side is full of law-abiding angels. I'm sure both have their own list of dirty deeds."

"No one's hands are clean in a war that is this long and bloody."

"Can you humor me? I want to know what happens if you pay too much." Ward placed the incense, jar, and necklace onto the right plate. "It's fascinating to see how immortal currency works."

Mr. King tossed a silver coin with a square hole in the center of the desk. "If it will make you happy, why not?"

Ward piled the coin with the others and studied the scale as it moved to balance. The right side tipped downward.

"It has a way of correcting itself. Nothing is as cut-and-dried as your mortal means of money." The god played with a set of brass balls between his fingers. It was a familiar toy Ward had seen him fiddle with before. Mr. King scrunched his face in a look of concentration as he lined all six of them up in the air in a vertical line.

While he was distracted, Ward tugged the gold chain off with a quick sleight of hand. The chain slid down, hidden, to land on his lap. He pushed aside the burning tinge of guilt and shame for the theft. This was what he needed to uphold Theo's "discount."

Any crime could be justified with mental gymnastics. Ward was limber as any in this respect. He was still committing a felony, and no amount of justification would change this. An entire Broadway musical was built around a man who stole bread and how his entire life went into the toilet. It was highly doubtful that such a production would be made for Ward and his choices.

The scale balanced without the missing item.

"Ah, perhaps I'd been mistaken then." The god snapped his fingers and the spinning balls vanished. "Payment is always about estimation—it was never an exact science."

All the items on the right scale vanished.

Ward handed him the jade necklace. "Looks like. Shall we see if this yields a clue?"

"I doubt it. I can smell Theo from it. If anything were to happen, it would have then. I know where your loyalties lie. I'll be back to claim one of the remaining pieces. Don't forget, Mr. Dunbar. *I let you have this one.*" The god deposited the jade necklace into his jacket pocket.

Whether the god meant that Ward had taken away his chance or that he knew about the stolen necklace, Ward wasn't sure. Uneasiness settled on his shoulders and remained long after Mr. King's departure.

WARD TUCKED THE filched necklace into one of the shallow drawers.

Gods were far more complicated than he had ever realized. Mr. King's unpredictability threw Ward for a loop and increased his mounting mistrust.

"Bro, you doing all right?" Theo tapped Ward's arm.

Across the room, Din already hovered over her favorite glass case.

"Yeah. Just thinking stuff over. Trying to figure out how to fulfill my end of the deal."

Theo turned the chair over to straddle it. "Have you made progress with that?"

"Sort of." Ward traced the drawer front that held the gold chain necklace. "Give me a day or so to work out the last of the details."

"Awesome! Din's psyched. I even told her mom."

"And?"

Theo threw his hands up in the air. "The bitch is satisfied! Can you believe it? It's like for the first time, she didn't look at me like I was a fuckup."

Ward laughed.

"Normally I wouldn't care what the old witch thinks. Din cares, so yeah, I have to." The god's gaze wandered to the object of his affection. "She's the best thing that's ever happened to me. Like when she's happy, everything doesn't suck as much."

"Camille's the same way."

"Is she though?" Theo turned his attention back to Ward. "She's still pissed. Like 'I don't know if she'll ever talk to you again' pissed. I'm not sure you can fix this long distance. I mean, maybe if you were together in person, it'd be easier to patch up."

Ward slumped in his seat and covered his eyes. "That bad?"

"Yeah. It sucks. It's the kind of mad that you can't fix easily. Normally, I'd say let her cool off and eventually she'll get over it. Not sure about this though. She said something like she remembers exactly *why* you two broke up in the first place."

The god continued to state his case. "I'm guessing she's been this mad before? If it were any angry goddess, you'd offer a sacrifice and it'd be done. Somehow, I don't think she operates like that. Sorry, guy, it's one of the downsides of dating a superhot chick. At least she didn't say outright she hated you. Is she one of those types that do like revenge hookups? If so, I'd be umm . . ."

"What are you saying?"

"Well, you and she are physically separated. Now, I'd never go out and even take a two-second look at your girl. I'm not sure about *him* though. You know who I'm talking about."

Mr. King. A good-looking bastard of a god that Camille didn't hate on sight. "She wouldn't do that. She's not like that."

"She might not be, but he is. I can see him going after your girl. He's a sneaky asshole. Those Eastern Faction gods are manipulative as fuck. I'm saying this from a friend's perspective.

I gotta watch out for your best interests. Speaking of which, you'd better keep your note as profesh as possible. Don't want to make her even madder."

Writing another heartfelt apology would do no good. The damage had been done—no use in performing CPR on a corpse. The sole viable option was for Ward to disclose what he had discovered and not make everything worse.

23

Camille

. . . . .

DAY ELEVEN

. . . . .

AFTER I NARROWED down that "Thermopylae" referred to the battle—which occurred in 480 BC—I skimmed the novel. Its author and the date it was written were disputed, but I doubted that was what I needed. The correct guess would be AD 1120, when the story was set.

The instant library was far more helpful than I had imagined. Though the internet was faster, this was a decent alternative. Ward would have been delighted at such a marvel. He had a better appreciation for all these incredible miracles facilitated by magic.

I wanted nothing more than to see him again—in the flesh and not by some fanciful glittery means, as fantastic as it was. I wanted normal, like taking a walk on the South Bank and watching the sunlight on the river, or eating a bag of mini cinnamon doughnuts from the food truck that reminded me of home, then sitting for a fancy high tea at Harrods, or seeing the wonder on his face when we ducked inside Shakespeare's Globe to see *A Midsummer Night's Dream*.

We had none of these things.

We were in separate cells in the same dungeon. Like prisoners, all we had were our memories and the luxury of ruminating over what we might have done differently.

I rubbed my forehead to shake away the mild headache. After Theo destroyed the headdress, the pain had dulled yet never went away. The nosebleeds had stopped, thankfully.

The note I had written Ward was more emotional than anything I'd written before. There were no metaphors or secret coded language. I rationalized it as the toll of being alone. Lonely by choice was different from enforced separation. I *missed* him and had forgiven what he'd done.

No point in holding on to grudges that added to my misery.

When this was all over, there should be a California king–size bed we'd make a nest in for at least a week at some hotel in the city. We would order in and spend most of our time naked in each other's arms. Together. We'd figure out what we wanted to do afterward because there would be time.

I folded the note into a heart and tucked it into my planner.

The black candle on the counter continued to burn down. When its flame was snuffed out, it'd be the end of this experiment or game, whatever it was. Ward needed to find that vault and what was inside. The numbers I had might be the combination he needed to open it.

By then we'd be free.

THE SHOP WAS deserted when I arrived downstairs for my next shift. Mr. Samson was nowhere to be found. I didn't give up hope that he might make an appearance later.

I examined the black candle and checked how much it had burned since yesterday. The violet flame danced in a steady flicker. Ward and I didn't have much time left to unravel all of this. Most of the heavy lifting was in his hands.

Theo walked through the front doors alone. "Just checking, you still mad?"

"No. I'm over it." I dangled the folded heart in front of him. "I have something for him. I figured out his clue. Please and thank you."

"At least you're still doing the group work. I was concerned that you'd rage quit." He stuffed the note into his pocket.

His thin veneer of pleasantry had worn away. I wasn't surprised. What I didn't understand was why. Why try to pretend to be nice in the beginning only to drop the act at this point? Then again, he might have given up all pretenses because I wouldn't give him what he wanted.

"I still want to get out of here. That hasn't changed."

Theo rubbed his chin. "Yeah, but not with him? You're gonna fly solo after this, right? Leave my boy behind and just move the fuck on. Maybe try and find another city ten thousand miles away from him and the wreckage you left behind."

"Is there a point to this? None of it is your business. I doubt Ward wants you discussing this with me."

"I'm doing it for him. Even if he was here, he's too fucking scared to talk to you about it. Scared you'll pull a déjà vu— leave him when shit doesn't go your way. You can't do your usual power move because you're already apart. For somebody who prides themselves on busting ass and working so hard, you don't put in the effort when it comes to relationships, especially with Ward. So much easier to light everything on fire and walk the fuck away, isn't it?"

That slid under my skin. I didn't go to Manhattan because I wanted to get away from him. The job in New York had a better promotional track and would help me heal my own wounds. The painless option was to stay in Chicago, marry him, live the life of luxury, and smile and watch as Ward inherited his parents' vision of his future. I'd lose the man I loved as he acquiesced to a life he never wanted.

"What happened with Ward is between me and him. He doesn't need you to—"

Theo made a circular motion with his hands. A scratchy vision of Ward appeared between his fingertips. The quality reminded me of grainy closed-circuit television. In it, my ex was talking to Theo. His words were muffled at first, then became clearer with each passing second.

". . . she wants what she wants, and if I didn't go with it, I'd be the bad guy. Camille has such high, impossible standards." Ward's handsome face contorted with pain. "I've never been able to live up to them. Nothing I do is ever good enough. Even when I try to save her, I end up fucking it up."

Theo clapped his hands, and the vision of Ward vanished. "Are you sure you're even good together? Do you even listen to what he wants, or is that not as important as what you want?"

I raised a hand and pressed it against my chest.

This wasn't a lie. I'd seen this version of him haunting my dreams in Manhattan.

I hurt him, and I didn't know if I was able to fix it or *us*.

Would Ward even want me to?

We hadn't talked about the past, thinking it wouldn't matter, or that it wasn't as important as our decision to be with each other in the future. We treated it as if speaking about it or addressing it would break the spell of our future.

Unspoken led to broken.

I had believed that starting over would mean we didn't have to reexamine the wreckage. I chose to smear mud across my own rearview mirror as I drove toward another try with Ward. The good would always outweigh the bad. Love healed and fixed everything. Given time, we'd have that talk we said we would, and everything would be sorted out without reopening old wounds.

"I'm still passing on your notes. The least I can do is help him get out so he can find someone better for him out there. Someone who won't make him feel like a fuckup all the time." Theo shook his head and left the shop.

I never wanted Ward to feel like a failure. I did everything to encourage and motivate him to want more and be more— with the caveat that it was what he wanted, what he was passionate about. Did I push him too much and out of this idea of a future together?

I stewed in mental self-flagellation for hours until the door to Mr. Samson's office opened. I dashed away my tears before running to the hallway to help escort him out.

"Ms. Buhay, are you all right?" He reached out to touch my tearstained cheek. "I hope you didn't have a terrible run-in with that lecherous god."

I shook my head. "It's not that. It's something else. I screwed up, and I don't know if I can fix it or if it's fixable."

I maneuvered him into the ornate chair he'd sat in the last time. The deepening wrinkles around his blue eyes accentuated the darker shadows underneath them. His once pristine suit jacket was tattered at the hem and cuffs. He had diminished far more than I wanted to acknowledge.

"Everything is fixable to a certain extent. What can I do to help?" He leaned back against the chair. "It can't be all that bad. Start from the beginning and humor this old man."

I told him everything. I treated it like he was my priest at a Catholic confessional. It was my form of exorcism to see if it was possible to absolve myself of my failings. I was truthful almost to the point of pain, and unflinching about how much I had failed Ward and our relationship—how I wanted more from him and how this had destroyed him in the end. Blaming Ward for everything was the coward's way. I bore the responsibility for shattering *us*.

"You do realize that there are two people in this relationship. You can't be selfish and own all of the shortcomings." The distant gaze in his eyes held such affection. "I loved someone once before all of this madness. For the life of me, I can't even remember her name or her face. Every time I try, it's like squeezing water in my hands. All I have left is my love for her. It drove me to keep going and living even during times when I couldn't."

"Don't tell me you tried to—"

"Yes, multiple times. This place won't let you. Death will only be granted on their terms. Whoever is running this place. I feel as if I'm being kept around because I haven't finished or fulfilled my purpose yet. You don't know what it's like to be trapped here for decades. You lose your memories and sanity the longer you stay." He blinked and then gave his head a quick shake. "Ah, but you were talking about something else. What was it?"

"Love problems with my ex-boyfriend."

He smacked his fist onto his open palm. "He's the fool. He's wrong on all counts. Yes, I picked a side and it's yours."

I laughed at the absurdity of his statement.

The twinkle in his eyes made me grin even more.

"If I were still a young man and you were mine, I know I wouldn't let you go. I'd tear down the walls of this place to get to you."

He truly was the sweetest old man. I patted his arm. "I appreciate you being my knight in shining armor."

"You deserve everything, Ms. Buhay." He covered my hand with his. "I will do everything in my power to make sure you leave here."

24

Ward

TODAY WAS THE day.

Ward planned to pull off the grand larceny this afternoon. If he didn't, he'd be in for immortal retribution for reneging on a bargain. He'd prefer whatever punishment Madam Selene or whoever was in charge of the shop had in store.

Basically, Ward might have signed himself up for death and dismemberment in his white knight quest to save his lady love. He never asked for a complete rundown of the terms. Most bullheaded knights don't when they go charging at the angry dragon. They don't stop to ask about insurance, write wills for any of their families, or set up bereavement funds for their widows. It was all about the spectacular act of courage—didn't matter what the consequences were because they might not live long enough to suffer them. Pity.

Madam Selene tapped the leather portfolio against her palm as she walked out of the hallway. The smile on her face was new. It didn't quite reach her eyes, and it showed a bit too much gums and teeth. She must not be used to emotion. "Only two more! You need to sell two more, and then we'll get released. This is why I chose you for this shop, Mr. Dunbar."

He returned her smile. "You're in a good mood."

For now.

She spread out her arms and flapped them. "This is monumental. We are this much closer to freedom."

"Are you sure this is the way out?"

"Of course it is. It has to be. Things are happening now that didn't in my tenure. Don't lose momentum. You have to close the deal with Theo today. He's your only appointment." She handed him the book. "At this rate, we might be out tomorrow."

"Hopefully."

"Sell, sell, sell!" She waved her wrist, jingling her bracelets. "Get your vagabond friend to buy something! That cheapskate has been visiting for years and browsing with empty pockets. Surely he must have saved up enough by now."

His boss wandered off to her office, muttering some choice words about the god Ward called friend. The battle-ax had no tolerance for thrifty gods, and Theo was the worst offender in her eyes. According to her, nothing was worse than being immortal and broke—this meant one spent far too much time being lazy and foolish. Admirable logic for a mortal.

When Theo and Din walked in, she didn't run to hover over the ruby pendant, because Ward already had it on display at the desk. "Today is the day."

Din clapped her hands and squealed. She took a seat, vibrating with childlike glee. Theo stood behind her. He reached out and handed Ward a paper heart. "Sorry, bud. She's still ridic pissed. At least she's committed to group work. She mentioned that she wants out of this place and not with you."

Ward tucked the note into his pocket.

He didn't blame her. Camille had every right to walk away. The least he could do was make sure that she was able to get out of this place. It was the living without her part that had crushed him before and would again.

To him, the time apart was a blur—the kind one felt when spinning so fast in a teacup ride when the colors swirled together and one lost all sense of time and, inevitably, their lunch. He went to parties, met new people, and did well at his job to get promoted. All the while, he showed that the idea of thriving was a facade when inside was a prevailing numbness.

The first time he felt alive again was when he saw her at the bookstore.

He didn't know if he would survive this time.

"Bro, there are so many other hot chicks out there. There's plenty to be had once you get out. You'll be able to find someone hotter and better—an upgrade. I know you loved her. You've been there and done that already though. Some things you can't fix, no matter how many times you try over and over again." Theo cupped Din's shoulders. "No shame in knowing when to quit."

"Yeah." Ward turned his attention to the ruby pendant necklace. "Din, do you want to try it on first?"

She shook her head.

"She's waiting to try it on in private. She promised me some fun times when we get home." Theo rubbed his palms together, wagged his thick brows, and then uttered the key phrase.

The scales materialized, and Ward placed the necklace on the left. While the god sorted through his pockets for the payment, Ward pried open the shallow drawer and hid the necklace on his lap.

"Okay, so this should cover most of it." Theo pushed five black pearls across the table along with a fancy silver fork. He crossed his fingers and closed his eyes.

Ward transferred the items to the scale. As expected, it didn't balance. The gap was noticeable, and he wasn't certain the necklace bridged it.

The god stared down the uneven scales. "Whatever magic you have up your sleeve, you better work it now."

Ward added the gold necklace to the right plate, and its effect was immediate—achieving balance. Once the payment was taken, he packed the ruby pendant necklace into a velvet box and handed it to Din.

"Oh, man, you really pulled through." Theo clapped him on the shoulder. "Thanks, buddy."

Din held the black box against her chest and giggled. She grabbed Theo's hand and yanked him toward the exit. Theo laughed and waved with his tongue hanging out like a beagle on a summer car ride with the window down.

It was done.

Ward's chest deflated as his heart hammered in his chest. He rubbed his sweaty palms against his pants while he waited for the other shoe to drop.

"Mr. Dunbar." Madam Selene emerged from the hallway. "What did you do?"

The invisible force that had swept him up before did so now, and he was thrown into the storage room. Two seconds later, Madam Selene was tossed in right beside him. She rubbed her hip as she tried to get to her feet.

"I'm sorry." He helped her up. "I didn't mean for you to be in here with me."

She crossed her arms. "Whatever you've done, it's clearly frowned-upon conduct. You haven't done something so egregious that the penalty is severe. What happened?"

Ward confessed to everything—the bargain and his motive, how he got the necklace and his adding it to ensure the transaction went through. She listened and said nothing, her lips clamped into a thin, unforgiving line.

"I love her and I can't let her die. Anyway, she hates me now, but we're all still trying to get out."

"Camille is right to be upset. I'd throttle you myself if you made such an important decision for me. You don't know what's best for her. You acted on what's best for *you*." She pointed a finger at his chest. "You treat her and your job here with such carelessness. Have you always had this sense of entitlement?"

He took a step back. The other person who had called him out this way was Camille. It was very early in their relationship. She freaked when she found out about his family. She wanted out, but he convinced her otherwise. Something Camille said back then always haunted him. "You live in this glorious bubble where everything is easier for you. You don't see it because how can you? You don't know what it's like to live without it."

His boss clucked her tongue. "This shouldn't be the first time you've heard this. If it is, there is no hope for you."

Madam Selene had a fantastic bullshit detector, and it was

a pillar of her no-nonsense personality. Ward wasn't spared, and he should be grateful for the refreshing dose of honesty he was force-fed during this crisis.

"How long do you think we'll be in the penalty box?" he asked. "The last time, I can't remember how long it was."

"It doesn't matter. You sit here until the time of punishment has elapsed. You can't change everything despite your desire to. Did you think I wanted to be stuck here for decades?" She leaned against a nearby rack full of velvet boxes. "If I could find a way out of here, I would have by now. Nothing in my research has ever led anywhere."

"Then you do know about the gods, their war, and how we fit into all this?" He glanced at the draped mirror across the room and kept an eye on it.

Madam Selene wrapped her arms around herself. "They don't care about us. We are put here to perform a task. Until we do, they will not let us go. Your girlfriend, Camille, is working with you now though. More minds, better chances."

He remembered Camille's note in his pocket and read the letter. She gave him two numbers—480 and 1120. In between the information and her theories were sprinkles of anger woven in. Little jabs, pricks, phrases like "disappointment, failure, laziness." She had never been this vicious to him, yet he'd seen her wear her rage, and this fit. Of all the emotions, rage and love burned brightest with her.

Ward slipped the note into his pant pocket. His wounds could wait.

"Did she give you any important information? No offense to your abilities, but I believe she has a higher processing speed when it comes to these things."

He winced. "She gave me two numbers. She believes that they could be part of the combination to open the vault."

"I only saw that vault once, and even now, I'm questioning my memory." Madam Selene pressed her fingers to her temples. "I think I saw it in the store decades ago. It wasn't in the hallway like the doors that would pop up. Oh, and it had a wheel. I didn't even think it was meant to be opened, because it disappeared the next day."

"You don't know what caused it to appear?"

"No. How could I?" She leaned to the side to try to see around him. "Ah."

He didn't realize he'd been standing in front of the mirror. Madam Selene skirted around him and walked toward it. She reached down and flung the heavy velvet away. She stood before the black mirror and assessed her reflection.

"Don't get too close . . . it—"

She held up her palm. "Do you know you get pulled into the other side? If you let yourself, you can slip in, but you need to be committed. I wasn't at the time, so it released me."

She had lied about breaking rules and misled him.

"I'm dying, Mr. Dunbar," she declared. "If you can't sell the last item in time, I won't be able to see the outside world again."

25

Camille

. . . . .

DAY TWELVE

. . . . .

THE LAST TIME I checked, it wasn't Black Friday.

The number of ghosts in the shop tonight was close to capacity. They huddled together in masses, streaming through the front doors as if they were late for some important event. The transparent bodies overlapped wherever there was space. There must have been close to at least one hundred and fifty ghosts.

The sound of the desperate crowd flooded my ears. They cried out in many languages I didn't recognize. The scale on the counter had been in constant use. I'd started stacking the acquired items on the floor when I filled up the available shelf space.

I stood behind the counter and tried to talk to the nearest spirit. "I can help the next in line."

The ghost was an elderly woman who thrust a small greenware vase into my hands. "Please. I need to move on now. Help me."

I placed the vase on the scale, and it didn't balance. "I'm sorry, I can't—"

"No, you have to take it. I need to get out of here." She shoved the vase back into my hands as I tried to return it. "Make it work, I have to move on. You don't understand. Existence as we know it is ending."

"She's right," the male ghost beside her chimed in. "It's my turn. Here, take this!" He threw a Frisbee at my head.

I ducked in time to avoid it. Before I had the chance to chastise the wayward ghost, five more took his place begging, pleading in desperation. They reached out to grab me by the arms. They tugged on my sleeves and almost pulled me across the counter, dislodging a few of the objects already there.

"Stop!" I tried to smack away their hands but met a rush of cold air when trying to make contact. "Please, let go. I can't help you this way."

They dragged me down to the floor. My body shivered, shaking me down to the bone. With every ghost's touch on my skin, the coldness seeped in and lowered my internal temperature. This was an inescapable, nightmarish mosh pit. So many ghosts were crowding me that I'd lost count. My teeth chattered, clicking together until I closed my eyes and hugged my knees, sobbing as I did on the first day.

Too many voices. So cold. Unable to move, think, or scream.

I didn't know how long I lay there on the floor.

Heat. Someone picked me up from the floor. Yelling. Mr. King. He deposited me into the chair that Mr. Samson often used, before driving away the ghosts. Once the spirits left, the shop's temperature climbed up to its normal level, yet I was still shivering.

"Here." Mr. King whipped out a red silk kerchief from his pocket, and it transformed into a thick blanket. He draped it

over me, anchoring it between my shoulders and the back of
the chair. "The shop should have a capacity limit. There were
far too many in here. Where is your boss?"

My words were punctuated by lingering teeth chatter.
"He's not doing too well. I don't think he would have been able
to handle crowd control."

The blanket was warm and far cozier than I expected. The
scent of crushed pink peppercorns and peonies rose from the
embroidered silk. I settled into its embrace and held the edges
tight. "Thank you for the rescue."

"I'm not about to let you turn into an icicle. I confess that I
still need your help." He squatted down into a sitting position,
resting on his heels. He took out the skeleton key from his inner jacket pocket. "So this is happening."

The obsidian key was starting to evaporate into thin air.
Tiny, dark particles rose off the small key on his open palm.

"I don't understand. Why is it disappearing?"

"Because I'm supposed to give it to your boyfriend, and
he's not ready to accept it yet. Gifts from gods always need to
be accepted willingly, remember? Otherwise, it doesn't work."
He tossed the key into the air and then caught it on his fingertip.

"And if you can't give it to him in time?"

Mr. King sprang up to his feet. "Then it's game over. We
haven't gotten this close before."

"I don't understand."

"Why do you think you were hired and brought in?" He
paced before me in a tight line. "The ghosts are right. This 'experiment' is millennia in the making. You happen to be a participant in the last declared iteration."

I hated all of it. Ward and I never wanted this—we never would have signed the consent slip if we had known. My idea that this was some sort of escape room or game was right.

Being stuck here halted both of our lives and those of Ward's boss and Mr. Samson. Otherwise, I'd be living out there rebuilding my relationship with Ward in this fantastic city. I still wanted to go on train trips into the rest of Europe and weekend getaways to Paris with him. We would sort out our differences and find a way forward, even better than what we were before. If there was an upside to any of this, it was that I was more determined than ever to make it work with Ward.

He was my one.

"Have you tried talking to Ward?" I asked. "Something more in-depth. He's very philosophical. You should show him that side of you."

"I opted to do something else instead." He then proceeded to tell me about the gift he'd given to Ward. "I helped him with his bargain with Theo. He'd be screwed otherwise. Reneging on one never works out well for a mortal."

"Thank you." I blew out my cheeks. One fewer worry in my head about Ward being decapitated or worse. "As much as I appreciate what you've done, I'm not sure if that's the way to get him to trust you."

"It's not about trust. You don't trust me, Ms. Buhay. Oh, don't look surprised. I know. You don't need it to accept a gift. The condition is that you must be able to handle the responsibility and all the ramifications that come with it." He paused and scratched his head. "I'm honestly lost on how to get this key to him."

"Could you say it came from me?"

He shook his head.

Of course not, because that would be too damned easy.

Ward would see this as some sort of surprise cobra in a box, given their past interactions. Writing it down in a note wasn't an option when Theo could read it. The thought of coaching Mr. King like Cyrano de Bergerac might be the solution.

"What if I told you what to say?" I folded the blanket down to my lap. "If I were to train you in gaining his trust. I'm as invested in this as you are. You'll win your war, and the mortals jailed in this place will be free."

He narrowed his eyes. "You're offering to teach me how to woo your ex-boyfriend?"

The comical expression on his handsome face made me laugh. He appeared to be around the same age as my oldest cousin and displayed the same kind of irreverent approach to the world. If Ward saw this side, he'd warm up to him. The problem was Theo and whatever lies he might be feeding him.

"Theo already went the bro route. I'm saying you have to break them up."

"This isn't a romantic comedy. It's too much work. I can't woo the man and break up his bromance at the same time." The voice Mr. King used was literally that of a Valley girl. I giggled at the ridiculousness of it all.

The humor shocked me far more than the magic. My expectations of the gods matched my experience so far except for this. I anticipated the pain, the struggle, the superiority complex, and the violence, but not this. Having grown up with Catholicism, I believed in a different god—one that was benevolent and selfless and that transcended all of humanity's foibles. Nothing resembling the supposed immortals I'd encountered so far.

I sobered. "Ward trusts Theo. Don't say anything that will contradict what Theo would say. Open trash talk won't work. It's about planting doubt without outright challenging him."

"You're saying break them up first, then the wooing comes afterward."

"Yes."

Mr. King's gift might have bought Ward some goodwill, but even then, Ward wouldn't be able to deal with any kind of ass-kissing at this point. Right now, my ex was probably trying to decode what Mr. King's gesture meant. I doubted he did the same for Theo's generosity.

"Mr. Dunbar's friendship with that god is problematic, to put it mildly. How deep does this go?"

I told him about the letters and the gifts.

"With the completed bargain on top of this, it's almost like a marriage. It'd be difficult for him to break free of Theo's influence. Every gift comes with a caveat. I'd been explicit about mine and you accepted the terms. For Mr. Dunbar, I doubted he even would have contemplated that there would be strings attached if he wasn't told beforehand what the terms were. Disclosure is up to the god."

"Then Theo didn't tell him for a reason."

Mr. King shrugged. "It would be anything from a small- to medium-sized consequence. Judging by what you've told me, it's in that range."

"I wish I could write him all this. We exchange notes and Theo delivers them. I'm pretty sure the messenger reads everything, and I wouldn't be surprised if he edits the content as well."

"Well, shit." Mr. King covered his eyes. "You didn't tell me this earlier."

"What?"

"Your boyfriend's definitely more fucked than I realized."

My chest tightened. "Tell me."

"All of these favors that Theo has given to him accumulate like a tab. Think of it as a hotel room charge. When he comes to collect, it would be almost impossible for Mr. Dunbar to resist it. Everything that this implies means that the chances of him choosing the same side as you are . . ."

"Wait, if this means that the game ends in a tie, you said that it would—"

He stroked the back of his neck. "End of existence. The ghosts aren't wrong. They're panicked for a reason. If I were you, I'd talk to your boss and see what kind of crowd-control measures, if any, he can enact. This will only get worse. I doubt we have much time left before everything ends badly."

26

$$\sim \!\!\! \sim \!\!\! \infty \!\!\! \sim \!\!\! \sim$$

Ward

. . . . .

DAY THIRTEEN

. . . .

"DON'T FORGET WHAT we discussed yesterday," Madam Selene told him at the start of his next shift. "We have little time left."

One last item left to sell. This game was progressing. Finding the vault and opening it would be the end. It had to be—at least for the weary mortals suffering in imprisonment. With all of the hidden parameters and unspoken rules, they were making some sort of progress.

She handed Ward the book. "Mr. King and Theo today. Be the closer I hired you to be."

"Wait, before you leave, I want to know what you think. Why were you left alone for years on end, then all of a sudden given the opportunity to hire someone else? It's a drastic change."

"I don't think I was alone. My memory is telling me I was, while my heart and gut tell me that I wasn't. It makes no sense, Mr. Dunbar." She winced and pressed her palms against the sides of her head. "I don't like how this makes me feel. I think I'm going to be ill."

Before he could offer to help, she hurried to her office and slammed the door.

Not alone. Insanity would be the result of years of isolation, and Madam Selene still maintained her clarity and mental faculties. Ward jotted down his thoughts and theories in Camille's planner. He'd been so consumed with making sure that everything was coherent that he jumped at the sound of Mr. King's polite greeting.

"Good morning, Mr. Dunbar."

Ward finished the sentence and then tucked the pen and planner away in a drawer.

"Letter writing is an ancient art form. Glad it hasn't lost its relevance in this modern age." The god took a seat and folded his hands on his lap. "I'm here to purchase the last piece on display."

Ward nodded and headed off to bring him the gold ring. As he passed by each vacant case, he remembered when they were all full and how the jewelry shop appeared when he first arrived. Somehow, the emptiness of the store was unsettling— the way that any space that lost its purpose was diminished.

The gold ring had a carved face on either side. He read the short description aloud. "Once the property of Erysichthon of Thessaly."

"Do you know about him? If so, enlighten me."

Ward scoured his memory, recalling the classics and mythology courses in college. "He was a king who chopped down Demeter's trees for a banquet. He was cursed with infinite hunger for his misdeed. Definitely a cautionary tale or allegory of some sort."

Mr. King tipped his head. "And this will yield our last clue then?"

It must. Everything in the store was gone.

"It was a rhetorical question, Mr. Dunbar. Don't worry. This is meant to happen—at least, this part is, and everything else will unfold in due course."

The god must have picked up the panic in Ward's eyes.

"I want to get out of here with Camille and our bosses." Ward threaded his fingers through his hair. "This is all so insane."

"By your mortal standards, yes it is. I believe you and Ms. Buhay are here for a good reason. You two have been chosen to adjudicate us in this matter. You're the impartial entities." Mr. King said the magic words, and the golden scale materialized on the desk.

"Are you ready for payment?"

The god presented a jade bracelet with gold accents along with a live golden corn snake. The reptile moved with its gilded scales, hissing along Mr. King's wrist. Its eyes were tiny onyxes watching Ward as he slipped the bracelet onto the right plate.

"She doesn't bite. She's friendly." Mr. King moved closer, and the little snake lifted its head. Its pink tongue slipped out, flickering. "Would you like to handle her?"

Unable to help himself, Ward reached out with his fingers. The little creature nuzzled his knuckle and slithered onto his hand. She flicked her tongue as she explored his palm and then his wrist. Her scales were smooth and cool like burnished metal. Ward had played with corn snakes while visiting his aunt's farm. They were tame and gentle. He snuck them into his room with his aunt's blessing, provided that he returned them to their homes the next morning.

"Where does she go when . . ."

Mr. King arched a dark brow. "Why? Do you want to keep her?"

"I can't." The snake curled itself against the back of his hand. "She's probably worth an amount I can't even begin to calculate."

"You had no qualms with accepting gifts before."

It was true that Ward had accepted all sorts of gifts and favors from Theo. They were the best of chums. There was no better partnership between mortal and immortal.

Receiving presents was natural. Every creature loved presents—from a lowly spider receiving a droplet of water to drink, to a hygienically challenged Ward imprisoned against his will. It was also a fact that he had no issues with the golden necklace that Mr. King slipped him so that the bargain could be completed.

Yet, now, the thought of accepting the beautiful snake elicited a violent surge of disgust. Ward shook his head to dislodge the strange emotion.

Mr. King shrugged and took the snake back. He tucked her into his jacket pocket and fished out an ancient prayer wheel. "Because of you, I've decided to keep her."

Ward breathed a sigh of relief as he added the prayer wheel, and the scale balanced. He handed the god the ring and braced himself for the intense emotions it would provoke. He closed one eye and left one open to see Mr. King push the ring across the desk toward him.

The god leaned back in his chair and crossed his arms. "I'm not going to test-drive this thing in public unless you want me to."

All this ring needed was Ward's touch. He peeled off the gloves and, again, poked it with his pinkie. The magical worm oozed out and slithered across the smooth tabletop. It disintegrated into letters. *Kadesh and the Canterbury Tales.*

Ward took out his planner and wrote it down. It followed the other format—some sort of event and a noted literary work. Camille would research and provide him with the details, which she theorized was the combination of the vault.

"This must be your clue. I can't read it."

"I do wonder why that is." Ward closed the planner and shoved it back into the drawer. "It circles back to your point that you need us as the judge and, possibly, the jury."

Mr. King popped the gold ring into his pocket without wearing it.

"Have you seen Camille recently?"

"Define recently."

"After the headdress incident."

Mr. King leaned back in his chair. "Why? The letters back and forth aren't enough of an indication?"

Ward hated asking him for anything, and yet, here he was close to begging for any scrap or hint of how Camille was doing from another source. Nothing else would ease his guilty conscience. He yearned for a speck of hope.

"She's doing well. She's determined to escape this place. Ms. Buhay is very capable. I admire her intellect and resilience. Frankly, you two need each other to get out of here." He raised his brows. "Is there something else you were waiting for? If you think she's still upset with you, I can correct that perception. She's not."

"But how?"

"The woman I have spoken to on multiple occasions isn't vindictive or manipulative. I'm sure you agree with me. This place and some individuals in here tend to fuck with your brain. If you let any of this screw with what you know about her and your relationship, you're at best a fool and, at worst, an asshole. Which are you then, Mr. Dunbar?"

"A bit of both. She wrote that she was still upset. Very much so."

"And you always believe everything you read?"

"Why would she lie to me?"

Mr. King tapped his lips. "*She* wouldn't."

"Theo wouldn't do that. He's done nothing but help me."

"Of course, of course." The god jumped to his feet and braced his hands against the edge of the desk. He took his time searching for something inside his pockets. "I hope you're ready for what I'm about to give you."

Ward blanched. Even the thought of a gift made him nauseated. "I don't want it, whatever it is."

Mr. King placed an obsidian skeleton key on the table. Tiny wisps emanated from the complicated set of wards.

Ward's curiosity mixed with revulsion. He turned his head away.

"This is a gift freely given."

"I don't want it," Ward repeated. "I can't take it."

The god pushed the key toward him. "*Night for day, day for night.*"

Familiar words. They penetrated through the potent

aversion. Camille had said these words to him when they were together for six months. It was after their finals, and they were recovering from all the study sessions by spending a weekend away in Toronto. They stayed at a boutique hotel in the Entertainment District and ate their way across the city. She was ecstatic that they were together and so far from everything else. This was when she told him that she worried that they were so different.

"Yes, we are. It's not a bad thing. It'll make life more interesting," he'd told her. "Think of twenty-four hours and how that measure of time is blessed with two different phases to mark its passage. Two contrasting halves making a whole."

She ran her fingertips across his lips. "Night for day, day for night."

Camille had wanted him to do this.

Ward gritted his teeth, fighting through the sea of repugnance as he reached for the key. Bile rose in his throat the instant he wrapped his fingers around the shank. He drowned in the ensuing wave of nausea. He gripped the side of the desk and vomited, heaving until his stomach was empty.

Cleanup on aisle one.

"What you did was unexpected, brave, and difficult, Mr. Dunbar. You won't regret it. I do warn you, though, that saying anything about this to anyone will endanger both of your lives." He made a zipping motion across his lips before making a quick exit.

After Ward cleaned up his mess, he hid the key in a different drawer in the desk.

To say he didn't feel good about Mr. King's gift was an

understatement. His whole body rebelled against it with violence, as evidenced by the filled mop bucket. The uneasiness still rocked his stomach when Theo walked in.

"You need to know how *grateful* Din was for that." The god rolled his eyes to the back of his head and moaned. "Eager, oh so very eager. She has this talented mouth, man. You won't believe everything she let me try with her last night. Thank you!" He clapped.

Ward mustered enough enthusiasm to be happy for him. His heart wasn't in it—it was far too busy trying to understand what had happened with the key and Mr. King's warnings. "That's great."

"She let me do every filthy thing on my bucket list. So satisfying." Theo lowered his sweater to show bright red scratch and bite marks. "Battle scars, baby. It's everywhere. I barely managed to walk straight this morning too."

"I'm happy for you."

Theo glanced around at the empty glass display cases. "Shit. Did you sell it already? Did you get a clue?"

"I did. Don't know what it means yet though. It'll be up to Camille to figure everything out."

"So, your ex, is she that good in bed? I mean, she looks like she is." Theo placed his arm around Ward's shoulders. "Tell me. I gotta know. I mean, I spilled. It's your turn."

"Uh . . ." Ward didn't answer. This part of Theo's personality was always here, yet now, he found it abrasive. "She's good. She won't appreciate me discussing anything about that."

"Your loyalty is misplaced. I get that she was your ex and you wanted to get back together. It's not going to work though.

She's moved on. She's making plans for after. Did you know that she has an ex back in Manhattan? He's the one she wants to be with." Theo widened his eyes and pressed a hand against his chest. "Dude, I'm not shitting you. It's some hustler restaurateur. She mentioned he was Filipino, so her family loved that even more. They met each other when her parents visited the city last fall, and get this, she met his parents earlier in the summer."

Camille had never said anything about this. Then again, Ward never asked. The cognitive dissonance building inside his brain made him feel queasy again. "No, we're going to be together. We decided this after we met back up in London."

Theo fished through his pockets. "I have receipts. You know I'll never lie to you, bro."

"I'm not . . . all of this is too much. I can't believe she had someone."

"How long were you two broken up for? Years, right? I mean, by mortal measures, that's a long-ass time. Your ex is hot. It's unrealistic to think no one's sniffing around her when she's single. It's always a matter of when." The god took out a velvet pouch. "Bear with me. The past is tricky to conjure. Here's what I mean."

Theo opened the small sack and sprinkled sand into the air until a clear pane of translucent glass appeared, the size of legal paper. The windowpane flickered after he muttered some ancient incantation. An image appeared of Camille laughing and in the embrace of a handsome, dark-haired Filipino American with perfect teeth. He kissed her temple as he wrapped his arms around her waist while they both cooked soufflé pancakes at the stove. Images of her introducing him to her parents flashed before him, and when it panned to more intimate scenes, Ward turned away.

He was attempting to decipher lies from the truth while trying not to fly into a jealous rage. Mr. King's description of Camille's current state matched his hopes and what he wanted to see, while Theo showed him the version of her that moved on and never wanted him back in her life in the first place.

His brain hurt from the amount of thinking he had to do today. A pressing matter popped up every five seconds, and the queue of unanswered questions was longer than those he'd seen at the mouse-owned theme parks. He wanted to nap but he couldn't because there was still a guest milling about the house.

"If it's any consolation, you're better looking." Theo tapped the hovering pane of magical glass and it shattered into sparkling dust. "Women like her move on quickly. They have to. Looks don't last forever unless you're one of us. Once everything goes kaput, her options are limited. It's always about someone younger and firmer, you know?"

"Camille isn't like that—"

The god shook his head. "She moved on. You have to. I'm speaking as a friend here. You can't keep moping or dwelling on this. Cut your losses and stop being her bitch. Work with her to get out of here, but she doesn't give a shit about you."

Ward closed his eyes and took a deep breath.

"After you're out, I can show you all the hot women out there. All access. Now that you know this world is a lot bigger than you thought it was, the possibilities are endless." Theo pointed to the open windows, where a sunny London existed. "You and I can get all the chicks out there . . ."

Ward wasn't sure if Theo's enthusiasm in trying to console him had Theo forgetting about his relationship with Din. Meanwhile, the image of Camille with the other man burned into his memory. Raw jealousy was replaced by sheer disappointment—that he hadn't been enough for her.

If any of this were true.

He didn't know if he could trust anyone anymore, even himself.

27

Camille

. . . . .

DAY THIRTEEN

. . . . .

MR. SAMSON AND I stood by the counter.

He had managed to make it out of his office to see the over-whelming influx of spirits. "I don't understand this, Ms Bu-hay. In all my time here, it has never been this busy. Three ghosts a day at best. This is untenable."

The ghosts kept coming. They resembled translucent, in-candescent koi swimming in an overcrowded small pond. The overlap of spiritual bodies almost made them partially solid. The mirrors and glass surfaces of the shop's trinkets frosted from their packed presence.

"They said it's because they believe everything is ending. Is there any way we can limit the amount that enters the shop?" I kept track of them in the aisles and crowded around the main doors. "Be careful not to touch them. They're very cold, and you can get hypothermia from exposure."

"We can tell them we're not acquiring at the moment. The shop is close to full inventory-wise. It has always been driven by acquisitions. You processed the only purchase we had in years. There is a finite amount of space here. In the near future, the scales won't work anymore if we continue at this rate."

"Can we break the point of transactions? I mean, if they don't work, nothing can happen." I scrambled to get the scales from the counter.

Mr. Samson placed a hand on my shoulder. "Don't be rash. There might be consequences that we can't fathom. Breaking it will cut off any legitimate chance they have of passing on. It'd be cruel to deny them that."

He was right.

The ghost crowd rumbled with a restlessness that set me on edge. I wouldn't be able to protect myself, let alone the both of us, if they mobbed the counter again. I had to use my leverage.

"Everyone!" I raised my voice and hoisted the scales with my hands. "If you all don't behave, I won't hesitate to break this. Need I remind all of you that this is your ticket out? Without it, you'll be stuck here."

They hushed.

"Behave and form a line. We can take, at best, ten tonight. Tomorrow, the first ten of you will be served. The rest will need to keep trying in groups of ten. I will not have what happened last night repeated. Do I make myself clear?" I smacked the countertop with my open palm for emphasis.

The ghosts lined up quickly, and the rest left when the ten spots were filled.

"Well done, Ms. Buhay. Are you sure you weren't an elementary school teacher before specializing in antiquities?" Mr. Samson turned to me and gave me a grin of approval.

I returned the sentiment. "I don't have the patience needed for that vocation."

"Have you ever thought about having children?" he asked, with a dreamy quality to his voice. His remote gaze was one I'd seen often now—it was of peace, as if he were lost in his good memories. "A lifetime ago, I wanted two. One of each with her."

With the crowd dispersed, my shoulders settled back down to their normal position.

"Who? The goddess you spoke about?" I teased.

"No, no. It's the love of my life. The one I lost before all this. My memories are faded. So many things about this place I'm unsure of. It changes *you*. I can't even tell you anything about her, but I know she existed as sure as I still breathe."

I patted his hand. "Two kids would have run you ragged."

"I wasn't always as old as I am now, Ms. Buhay." He lifted his chin. "I was very handsome once, and fit. I was once called a 'snack.'"

Snack. Weird. That was a modern term. If he had been here for decades, he might have entered the shop in the sixties or later. How did time unwind in here? Until we could leave, I wouldn't know its progression—whether a moment in here meant years out there, or if years in here passed a mere minute in real time out there.

"Do you know how time works in here? Do you remember when you first entered the shop?"

He creased his brow. "I don't, and for that matter, I don't even remember when you came in here."

"Oh, that was in . . ." The date was clear in my head. Was. Trying to remember now broke my brain. The harder I tried to narrow it down, the more it fell apart. The concept of numbers as dates escaped me, yet with the Underwood typewriter on a nearby shelf, I managed to land on the early nineteen hundreds. Time flowed strangely in this place.

"I'm surprised it hasn't happened earlier. No point in writing it down. No firm dates stay in this place, or ways to mark time. It's like they don't want you to know how long you've been here." He pointed to the windows. "That also has never changed for me. The outside world feels as static as it does in here."

His hands were shaking, and he seemed exhausted. "Do you want to go back to your office?" I asked.

"Yes, please."

I escorted him to his door and hoped to see him again the next night. My gut told me that he didn't have much time left. The man had aged decades before my very eyes. Ward and I better figure out this mess, because if Mr. Samson died before we got out, I'd feel responsible for his death.

I PROCESSED THE ten ghosts by the time Theo made his appearance. I hated him but needed him to pass notes. He had no other purpose in my life. The headdress was the best thing that had happened to Ward and me, the killing me part notwithstanding.

"I take it that Ward has the last clue?" I asked him with a neutral expression.

He threw the note toward me. It sprouted paper wings, flapping across the distance before landing flat on the counter. I opened it and read it.

Theo hopped onto the counter, and the smug sneer on his

face creeped me out. "So, you're technically single now, right? I mean, you were exes before."

"How's Din, by the way?" I didn't even bother glancing up from reading.

"She's out with her girlfriends again, doing all the girly shit. You know, getting out from underfoot of menfolk."

"Huh. So you're still together?"

"Yeah, why?" His voice hitched. "What have you heard? Has she been in here without me?"

The paranoia almost made me cackle. Din clearly got what she wanted from him in some way and had lost interest. They were an odd pairing to begin with. His goddess girlfriend never showed any kind of affection toward him, nor was there any indication on his end that he saw her as anything more than a piece of ass. Seeing two people together all the time meant anything from a relationship to a friendship to a forced association.

"No, nothing like that. I haven't seen her in a while. Just curious is all."

"We're still together. I'm killing that rumor now." Theo frowned. "Keep talking about this curiosity though. Maybe you've reconsidered my proposal. Din also thinks you're scorching. It'd be a win-win sitch."

Creepy asshole. "Yeah, still not interested. Sorry."

"Gods have lots of upsides. Why do you think there are so many bargains between us and mortals?" He pointed to the windows, where night blanketed London under the streetlamps. "You don't know the true extent of my powers. I can get you out of here."

Bullshit. Though this was a better bargain than his insistence that I join his threesome. He'd keep offering me everything under the sun until I gave in. He'd needle me with persistence, escalating into aggression and then violence. The worst part was that his presence came under the pretext that he was doing me a kindness. Until Ward and I solved the last puzzle, I needed Theo to deliver our messages.

"I want to write Ward back today. I'll need to check my books for a bit. Can you stick around until I'm done?"

"Yeah, no problem. Be quick though. This place isn't my style."

I hurried upstairs to my flat without looking back.

With the previous clue as a guideline, I managed to narrow down the numbers quickly. *Kadesh and the Canterbury Tales*. The years 1274 and 1392. I jotted this down along with a few sweet words. I didn't want to be transparent about my emotions, but I worried about Ward.

I hadn't spoken to him in a long time, and the time apart would destroy him. He'd assume I was still angry with him and who knew what else. The man was guided by his heart. He tended to see people for the best version of themselves— their potential, their good nature, and their vulnerability. He did this not to exploit their weaknesses and manipulate them. Ward wanted to help whomever he came across. I admired him for it, and when coupled with his capacity for kindness, he had the ability to change people's lives for the better.

On the other hand, Theo was a lost cause if I ever met one. This misfit god was doing his best to screw with Ward in every way. The letters were one of the many tools he used to weasel into my ex's good graces.

I folded the note and rushed downstairs. The sooner I handed my note to the creep, the faster he'd leave.

"Hey, so you got your own digs up there? Can I see?" Theo rubbed his hands together.

I handed him the note. "I don't think that's allowed. This place has its own security system. The clue is ready for Ward. Thank you."

He waved the piece of paper in his fingers, toying with it. "You know, I've never really charged you for delivery fees."

"It's out of the kindness of your heart," I replied with a rare smile to cover up the fact I didn't like what this asshole was insinuating.

"I mean, yeah, I'm a stand-up guy. Ward vouches for me." He tossed the paper heart in the air, and with a wriggle of his fingers, it floated in a zigzag pattern. "You two don't know what's involved in traveling between the two places. This isn't an easy walk to the corner store."

"You and the other gods seem to swing by often enough without any problems."

"It's still tricky. It involves inter-dimensional travel. You see, this place and where Ward is right now aren't exactly in London. These places exist outside of time and space. So not a simple cab ride from one to the other, know what I mean?"

It explained some of the unanswered questions I had about this place.

He changed the paper heart's trajectory so that it flew above our heads. "Camille, you have to learn more about gratitude. That in some cases, words aren't enough. You don't want to be a selfish bitch, do you?"

I didn't give this lowly god the satisfaction of any reaction.

"My generosity is finite." He lowered his middle finger. The folded note veered from its high orbit to dive down, hovering dangerously close above the lime-green flame of the black candle. "Tell me, what are you willing to do to get out of here?"

Ward needed that last bit of information. If everything went according to plan, he'd have all the numbers for the vault's combination. I wouldn't be able to help him beyond what came next. If this was the last Ward would hear from me, so be it. Anything to get this fool to play errand boy.

"Deliver that note and find out. I'm sure Ward's waiting for it. Your friend wants to get out of here as much as I do. You wouldn't want to disappoint him. This is group work. If we don't figure this out, your war stays undecided."

Theo scrunched his face. "War is overrated. It'll destroy everything or not. It's been going on for so damned long that I don't even care anymore. Petty shit back and forth."

"Din cares, though, doesn't she? I'm sure she'd want your side to win." I continued to prod, hoping that he would capitulate. When in doubt, stroke a man's ego. Hadn't failed me so far. "She'd be impressed with your role as the hero in all this when everything works out in your favor. As you said, it's been going on for a long time. The guy that wins it for the team will be praised to kingdom come."

"I never thought of it that way." He rubbed the cleft in his chin. "I like the sound of this."

"So take the note to Ward and win it for the team. Time's running out." I made a shooing motion. "He's the last one left to figure out his end of things."

Theo snapped his fingers. "Right."

The paper heart flew into his pocket. He ducked his head and left.

The abrupt exit unnerved me. He was invested in getting what he wanted out of me and then was gone. If he had gotten a call or something during our discussion, I might understand why. This didn't make any sense. Theo was nothing but a calculating, opportunistic jerk.

Had I said something I shouldn't have?

Shit, I had. I mentioned that Ward was the last left to figure things out—implying that I'd already finished up my end and made a decision.

28

Ward

THE KEY IN Ward's hand was warm as if it were alive. It pulsed with quiet energy.

However, his thoughts were consumed by questioning what was true and what was false, where his loyalties lay, and his current and future status with Camille. The anxiety, obsession, angst, and overall drama associated with romantic love proved the idiom "madly in love" was indeed accurate. No one would put themselves through this kind of arduous torture unless they were afflicted. It wasn't a surprise that sleep wasn't possible for Ward when his brain buzzed with too many terrible thoughts. Repeated mental flagellation had that effect.

Meanwhile, the key continued to degrade. The particles coming off it were far more prominent now, appearing like tiny wisps of smoke. It wasn't a coincidence that Madam Selene told him she was dying. Time was running out. Ward needed to get his head out of his own ass and get moving.

He picked up the key and scanned the empty shop, searching for a physical lock or keyhole. The glass displays had their own mechanisms for access. Even all the drawers on the desk were unlocked.

The lock or keyhole could be invisible. The vault could be anywhere. Every wall was occupied except for one—it was the one between the glass cases. The smooth golden surface glimmered from the lights. Tiny specks swirled within its honey-gold surface.

After finding the middle of the wall, Ward took the key and pressed it in the center. The key sank in, stopping short of the shaft. He turned it, hoping something else would happen. The clinking, shifting sound of grinding metal gears echoed in the shop. The wall shook, vibrating, as tiles shifted, rearranging and moving while a large round shape emerged from its depths.

The vault.

By all appearances, it resembled a golden bank vault with a four-pronged, crankshaft handle.

Cue the applause, because he deserved a badge of merit.

Ward covered his mouth and studied the handle, spinning it to see if it would give. It was locked in place. There wasn't anywhere to input the numbers. He'd hoped for a keypad or even an oversized combination lock that accommodated four digits. Nothing.

"You did it. It looks exactly as I remembered." Madam Selene stood beside him. "Will it disappear this time, I wonder? How did you do this?" She brushed the stray strands off her forehead. Her hair was almost completely white now. It had been dark with silver streaks when they met.

"I used a skeleton key." He patted down the area around the crankshaft handle. "We have to figure out where to use these numbers. It's part of the combination to unlock it."

She pressed her ear against the wall while tapping the heavy door.

"What are you . . . ?"

"I'm trying to see if there is something on the other side."

He frowned. The serious expression on her face and the deep crease between her brows advised him to keep his mouth shut. Never interrupt a woman intent on doing something that wasn't life-threatening.

Madam Selene stood up and stretched her back. "The first thing I want to do once I leave this place is get an acupuncture appointment and a deep tissue massage afterward."

"Any idea how to open the vault?"

"No. I do suspect that you'll need to solve something else, Mr. Dunbar, or wait until you have all the information you need. You're still missing two numbers, am I correct?"

He nodded. Camille had the information he got last night. Theo should be bringing him the last two numbers today. He had been very reliable as a messenger. He had always been a stand-up bloke. After everything Theo had done for Ward, questioning the god now was selfish of him. Or was it?

"Well, the solution might present itself then and not a moment before." She yanked on the wheel. "Open this, and freedom is on the other side."

"Allow me to buy you a few drinks post-lockup."

Her dry laughter had a rusty quality. "Perhaps, Mr. Dunbar. I'd need something strong."

"Macallan whiskey or Kentucky bourbon?"

"Nikka whiskey from the barrel. I'll accept nothing less. I remember having half a bottle once in my youth. I think I can still manage to hold my alcohol." She turned toward the windows. "I want to be out there. Feel the sun on my face. See other people. To remember what it's like to be with other humans again. No offense to you, Mr. Dunbar."

"I remember you mentioning you weren't sure if you were alone all these years."

She closed her eyes and rubbed her temples. "I'm still uncertain. Something about this place lies and manipulates your mind. You start to question everything forward and backward. It gaslights you into redefining your version of reality."

Her shoulders slumped and she swayed on her feet. He walked to her side. "Are you tired? Do you want to rest?"

"Yes. Exhausted. Walk me back, if you please, Mr. Dunbar."

He escorted her to her office, where she thanked him before disappearing inside.

THEO'S NAME WAS in the appointment book. Ward checked the clock again. His friend was late. The god should be showing up. Theo had never skipped an appointment before. None of them had. If the name was in the book, these gods made an appearance.

There were two hours left before the end of his shift.

To be fair, out of all the gods, Theo seemed to be the one highly likely to have a punctuality problem.

Ward paced back and forth, parallel to the vault's heavy door. He spent most of the day poking and prodding every inch of the contraption, and it produced no results.

Everything up to this point was conjecture. He and Camille

kept making guesses until something happened to prove them right or wrong. This was a true experiment in its constant testing of hypotheses, methods, and changing conclusions. Given the two's experience in escape rooms, they had as good a chance as any of succeeding.

With Ward assuming that she was still holding on to her anger, he missed Camille's humor and her wordplay. She had left little puzzles for both of them, born from inside jokes in her previous messages. Ever since his bargain with Theo, the letters had changed in tone.

The door chime snapped him out of his thoughts.

Theo.

"Sorry I'm late." The god walked in with his head down, buried in a bright orange baseball cap, and hands stuffed in his hoodie pocket. "We need to talk."

"Sure. What about?"

Theo kept the brim of his hat low to cover his eyes. He handed Ward Camille's folded note. One of the corners was singed. "I had to do something yesterday that I didn't want to do. I was compelled. Gotta say that first before I even start."

The sinking feeling in Ward's stomach continued to wreak havoc on his system.

"You know we're in this war and which side I'm on. Anytime we learn what the enemy is doing, we have to report it. If we go against this, it's treason." The god shuffled his sneakers across the smooth floor. "Your girl did something that the faction's considered a betrayal to us."

"What did she do?"

"I can't say. I know now she'll be dealing with the full brunt of the Western Faction soon. I'm sorry, Ward. I tried to get leniency and talk them out of it."

They were going to kill her.

Ward grabbed Theo's shoulders. "You can't let them do this. Can you stop them? Tell me what I can do. Another bargain?"

"She made her choice. Can't take it back. There's nothing you or I can do." The god let out a long sigh.

"Bullshit. There's always something."

"No. Not this time. I'm sorry, man. It's such a waste. She's so beautiful."

Ward crumpled to the floor and covered his face with his hands. His throat was closing as his breath rushed out in gasps. His reason for living was going to be taken from him.

Theo crouched down and slapped his cheeks lightly. "Get it together. There's still hope."

"What?"

The god pointed to the vault door. "You made this happen! If you can open it, maybe you can do something in time. Open the door and save your girl if you can get it open quickly. We can do this."

"I don't know how to open it." Ward fumbled with Camille's note, trying to open it fast without ripping it. After scanning it for the last two sets of numbers, he scrambled to his feet to get the previous note. "I think I have the combination. I don't know how to open it. There isn't anything here that I can . . ."

"You said you wanted to save her. This is the only way I know how." Theo smacked his fist against the vault door. "Get up and get shit done. This is go time."

Ward tucked both numbers into his pant pocket and again searched for any mechanism to input them. Because there wasn't a keypad or combination lock, the input system could be anything, like the way the key fit into an invisible keyhole.

He said the numbers aloud. Nothing happened. Thinking it might be in another language, Ward tried everything he knew—Latin, French, Spanish, and Italian. No response. If Camille were here, she'd be spitballing ideas; she would be throwing everything at the puzzles. She and Ward approached them differently, and this was why they worked so well together.

What would she say?

Work backward to see the method. Every puzzle master had a flair, a telltale signature detectable in any given room. This set of patterns mimicked the way someone wrote their name. It dictated the nature of the clues and their solutions.

The vault appeared when Ward placed the key after he had run out of places to try. He had all four numbers for the combination yet nowhere to input them. The door didn't respond to auditory feedback. The next strategy should be tactile.

Ward streaked his fingertip across a clear spot over the wheel. He wrote the numbers down first in Arabic and then Roman numerals. The vault didn't budge.

Camille would be thorough enough to try Morse code.

He tapped the surface four times.

"Look." Theo pointed to a small engraving above the spot Ward had touched. "You see that?"

There it was. A tiny inscription of the number four. Ward repeated the gesture eight times and was rewarded with another digit. For the zero, he used a horizontal streak of his finger, and he continued his series of taps until the entire set of numbers was inscribed on the vault door.

Theo clapped his hands. "It's gotta open now. It has to. Turn the wheel, baby. I think you've done it. Let's see what's inside."

Ward double-checked the numbers, then checked them again to be sure.

For Camille's sake, it had better open.

He reached for the wheel and cranked it.

It gave.

29

Camille

MR. KING'S WARNING about the skeleton key rang in my head. The Western Faction would kill me if they knew I had taken the opposite side. My careless mistake with Theo might cost me my life.

I thought about missing my shift and staying in the flat upstairs. The consequences for violating my work agreement might result in the same predicament. Every single scenario I concocted had Theo always running to his faction with new information. Under the creepy frat boy veneer was a devious mind.

If only Mr. Samson were here. I wanted to ask him about the security in the shop—if it would prevent any harm from coming to us. He spoke about having protections in place, but how far did they extend when it came to its workers?

"It will be fine. Everything will be fine," I repeated to myself as I closed the apartment door and made my way down to the main floor.

I wouldn't die here, not when we were so close to leaving. Ward had everything he needed to open the vault. The final door of this magical escape room prison. He would find it in time and save us all.

The unwavering belief I had in him was intrinsic. When we met, I recognized his potential to achieve great things on his own. He needed to believe it himself. He was far stronger than he thought he was.

The last morning we spent together in bed at my hotel seemed a lifetime ago. I took for granted being able to have him within an arm's reach, the scent of his clean cologne, the way the sunlight hit his golden hair and the fine stubble on his jaw, and the way he laughed, eyes crinkling at the corners. The deep sound resonated from his chest and heart.

I loved this man. All of his strengths, his flaws, his quirks, every fiber of him. It wasn't infatuation anymore or complete head-over-feet lust. It was this profound connection I wanted to celebrate by spending the rest of my existence with him.

Each morning, I awoke with the hope I'd see him again. I wanted to relive those days when we didn't need to talk. We spent the day in each other's arms and company, side by side. The funny part was that he didn't annoy me. My father pointed this out. "You're one who always thinks there's an expiration date when spending time with people. This one is different, Anak. In a really good way."

And Ward was. I'd give anything to see him again if that were possible.

I passed by Mr. Samson's office door and peeked down the hallway into the shop. He wasn't here. He needed to rest more than anything. The cost of venturing out drained him. If we had access to any medical services, I'd want him checked out. Being in here for this long was killing him.

The luxury of time wasn't on our side.

I marched into the shop and took my place behind the counter. The number of new acquisitions spilled from overflowing shelves onto the floor in some places. Ghosts kept coming in hopes of passing on.

However, today, no spirits. This wasn't a good sign. The fine hairs on my arms prickled with a growing, unshakable sense of foreboding. It was all confirmed by the black candle to my left, which had burned down to its last inch. It marked time better than any of the working clocks in this place.

Had it been summer or fall when Ward and I got our job interviews? A brain fog crept in every time I tried to decipher how long we had been trapped in here, and this sense of forgetfulness permeated everything, from distant to recent memories—anything related to timekeeping.

The front doors opened to reveal Eryna. She wore a black leather belted jumpsuit. Her long hair was swept up into a smooth ponytail. Her ruby-painted lips curved into a wicked grin, not the kind that denoted happiness.

"Good evening, Eryna. How can I help you?"

"You've already decided not to." She laughed. "Oh, Camille, why did you make the wrong choice?"

I gripped the edge of the counter. My hope of coming out of this alive was dashed. "I doubt it would make much of a difference in your war."

"You've cut down the chances of our victory. Mortals shouldn't have been a part of all this. All you do is meddle, with your short, meaningless lives." She held up both her index fingers, and two sharp rapiers appeared in her hands. "You will ask for death after I'm done with you."

The new blades didn't set off any of the shop's alarms. It made sense since there were battle-axes and various swords on display in the shop—none of which I was able to use with any kind of competence. While I didn't want to die, it seemed inevitable at this point.

This place gave the illusion of control. I'd been trapped here against my will and had never been told the reason why. We were treated like laboratory mice, and once our purpose was realized, we'd be killed. Fighting this goddess was pointless. The outcome would be the same.

"Before you kill me, can you tell me what Ward and I stumbled into? What is this situation, and why are we here?" I asked. "Tell me about the experiment."

"And this is what you would consider your 'last meal'? I can never understand how mortals yearn for one last revelation in their final moments. It's fumbling for something, anything to appease your tiny minds." The tips of her sharp blades caught the light.

She spun them with effortless competency. I had to make peace with my death tonight.

I tapped my left foot to try to settle my nerves. "This mortal wants to know why. Isn't it a fundamental desire to question one's purpose or existence? Why shouldn't I want to know?"

"I suppose that it's a reasonable ask. This is the final version of the experiment—the 'civilized' way of settling immortal affairs." She made the air quotes while still gripping her knives. "This happened two times before with unsatisfactory results. We had problems agreeing on how to run it. You being here and the way it is now is a compromise between both parties."

Twice. Was Mr. Samson in the first attempt or the second? Maybe both. "What went wrong with the other two tries?"

"The first was a waste. Nothing happened. The second created far too much conflict. And now, this go-around is again disappointing." She walked toward the counter and cupped my chin. "Killing you is a pity. You're such a pretty and clever little thing. I can find more exciting uses for you. Both you and Edward." She licked her upper lip.

I dared not move. If I weren't facing death, I'd have laughed at how horny these gods were. Recorded myths got that right. "If you see him after this, please tell him that I love him."

"I'll vow to relay the message. Now, step out from behind the counter and let's get this done. I won't leave this place without having taken a life. My faction has decreed it so, and I must obey."

I closed my eyes and tried to will a sense of calm into my body. My execution was set. Any minor infraction here might have resulted in my death. At least I was damned for making a choice. If it was the right one, I wouldn't be able to see for myself.

In my last moments, I reveled in my sweetest memories of my family and of Ward.

The whirring sound of the rapiers in the air contrasted against the sound of their impact when they struck their target. I clutched my abdomen expecting pain, blood, something. My hands were dry. I opened my eyes to see someone standing in front of me. The tips of the daggers protruded from his kidneys.

"No!" I cried out, and caught Mr. Samson's slumping body.

"Not the life I expected to take." Eryna shrugged and snapped her fingers. The daggers dislodged from his body with a squelching sound as they returned to their master. "The blood price is paid."

I laid him down carefully, placing his head on my lap. "Why did you do this? Why would you even . . ."

His light blue eyes were wide open, and his breath came in shallow gasps. "I had to. It's what a true gentleman must do, Ms. Buhay."

My heart constricted as I dashed away the tears from my cheeks. "You shouldn't have. This was all my fault. I chose a side. You're not even involved in any of this."

"But I am." He reached up to touch my cheek. "For the longest time, I can't explain why I felt this connection to you. You reminded me of someone. I didn't remember who because this place robs you of your past, present . . . and future. Someone I loved dearly."

"Yes, it distorts time in a way I can't explain. I'm so sorry for this."

"You made your choice and I made mine. No regrets. Always live with that in mind." He coughed. His fingers grazed my lips. "You really do remind me of the one I loved most in this world. I haven't seen her in so long. She was my sun."

"You'll be with her soon. I'm sure she's waiting."

"Is she? Then death will be a release. Don't cry for me. I've been here for far too long. I'm happy that I'm leaving this place as a hero."

He was—he was mine.

"Thank you, for what you've done for me. For saving me,

for being a friend, for making my time here as good as it was under the circumstances. I'm glad I wasn't alone." I hiccuped as sobs escaped my throat once more. "You've been so kind to me."

He closed his eyes as a rattle shook his chest.

His last words were "Night for day, day for night."

30

Ward

. . . . .

DAY FOURTEEN

. . . . .

THE LOUD CLANK signaled the unlocking of the vault.

Huzzah. The end was nigh.

Ward yanked the wheel forward to pull the door open.

The intense light inside made it impossible to tell what he would be walking into.

"Go in and get it," Theo yelled, retreating to keep his distance. "I got your back!"

Ward stepped inside.

THE VAULT'S INTERIOR was approximately eight by eight feet. Black tiled marble covered every surface. A levitating oval disk hovered overhead, providing the sole source of light in the room, illuminating a pedestal with a wooden box. The sound of his breaths and steps echoed in the space.

Even from a distance, the different colors of the object indicated it was one of those complex puzzle boxes he'd played with before. Camille had superior dexterity and would be the one eager to wrestle a mechanical challenge. His confidence dipped at the prospect of solving this by himself.

Ward picked up the note resting on top of the item.

"Solve Marcus Licinius Crassus's box in the time given, then you may proceed."

The name rang a bell. Wealthy Roman general.

A translucent hourglass materialized behind the pedestal. The grains of white powdery sand had already begun to fall. The clock was ticking.

Ward pulled the wooden box from the pedestal and sat down on the floor. It contained interlocking panels, each in different shades of stain. Seven accent pieces in total. He tried to slide each of them to see if it worked like a Rubik's cube. No give.

"Figure this shit out and save your girl," he muttered to himself. "Find latches, anything that moves."

He ran his short fingernails along each tiny crack to test them, all the while remembering every single puzzle he and Camille had dealt with in their escape room dates.

Their first excursion was an idea, a dare from Camille's cousin Rina. "You two are so damned different. I mean, yeah, you look amazing as a couple, but your vibes are incompatible. Let's see if you can survive and succeed in an escape room together." Rina then handpicked an especially brutal escape room with a low success rate. This was her firewalk test for him, for them.

At first, they argued, wasting ten minutes until their communication styles synced up. Camille was far more cerebral than he was. She did her best work independently, resorting to verbal communication only when necessary. On the other hand, he was a constant oral stream of consciousness. He had to verbalize his thought process to crack the code, as he was doing now. Once they understood each other, the rest was effortless. They found out another truth that day—they loved puzzles and the thrill of solving them together.

"Seven panels. Seven . . . What did I see that was seven?" Ward rubbed one of the darker-colored panels, and when he tilted the box, his finger left a mark on the edge.

He examined the pad of his thumb and the fine layer of chestnut-brown powder that dusted it. Those panels were concealing something. He rotated the puzzle to the last panel he had touched, rubbing hard to see what it would uncover. A golden symbol—two tiny squiggles parallel to each other.

Ward squinted to see if there was anything more. "What the hell is this? It's definitely not quotation marks. Symbol or language related? Which is it . . . The others should show if there is a pattern or message."

The remaining six were a circle, a circle with a small square, a circle with a small oval, a rotated *e* with the ends pointing down, a rounded band, and a rectangle.

"What the hell do they mean? Think, think, think. Not in any language, or even some sort of standard universal meaning. They have to represent what I've already seen. Circle, opening, not the letter *o*. What if this is a form of language and I don't even recognize it? Damn it."

He slumped forward and groaned.

"Camille would tell me to focus and simplify. The shapes themselves are already reduced to linear representations of . . . what?" he screamed in frustration.

A third of the hourglass had run out. With each grain

trickling down, more beads of sweat formed on his brow. Tick-tock. The running commentary was becoming more frantic than the calls of a World Cup match.

He returned to the first symbol—the one that resembled a pair of single quotation marks. "Pair, pear, two things, what might be two things. Fuck. Earrings! These were Electra's earrings that I sold to Eryna. They had to be. I sold six items in the shop and linked each symbol with one, so this box must be the seventh. What's the next step? What do I do with the panel now?"

The verbal diarrhea meant his brain was emptied through his lips with the force of a broken dam. The direct highway to his mouth left nothing upstairs. If this was how the world worked, silence and peace would have state funerals.

"Electra," he declared, and pressed the right panel.

Nothing.

"If it's not that, what else can it be? Is there another pattern to the pieces in the shop? Each one contains a distillation of pure human emotion. Theo was zapped with lust when he touched Hunac Ceel's necklace. This has to be it." Ward rotated the puzzle to the corresponding symbol and pressed it. "Lust."

He was rewarded with an instantaneous warmth under his fingertips as the panel sank down. He pumped his fist in the air and whooped. "The others, what were they? Din took the necklace without wearing it, and Mr. King also avoided wearing the ring.

"Seven emotions. Seven deadly sins. Lust is one of them. Wrath, pride, greed, sloth, gluttony, and . . . shit! What's the last one?" He winced and pressed his steepled fingers against the bridge of his nose. "And how do I pair the rest?

"Get rid of the most obvious ones first. Electra's story involved patricide and revenge. Out of all the sins, hers had to be wrath." Ward pressed down the symbol and declared the parallel sin. It worked.

Five more panels left to go. "Pride. Which one of you is it? Eryna bought the earrings and the crown. What did she say about Amanishakheto's crown? Something about wanting to ride into battle with the Nubian queen. Worth a shot."

He tried it and it worked.

Four more.

"Mr. King bought the headdress, the jade necklace, and the ring. The necklace is done, but the other two . . . One belonged to his old girlfriend, some courtier. Lust is taken, and I don't have enough information to even guess what this ties to. The gold ring was owned by Erysichthon of Thessaly, who cut down trees to hold a feast and was cursed with hunger. Gluttony!" He knocked out another successful panel.

"And this box is owned by Crassus. Rich-ass Roman general." He flipped the box, searching for the panel with the rectangle symbol. "Greed!

"This leaves the ruby necklace Din got, and the headdress. One of them had to be sloth, but which one? I might attempt it by process of elimination, but if I make a mistake, will the game be over? Might as well try, Camille would say." The symbol for the headdress was the rotated *e*. He pressed it down. "Sloth."

The panel responded. One left. Camille would be so proud.

Yes, she would be. Though the never-ending soundtrack might not be as well received.

He checked the hourglass and it was over half-full—plenty of time left for the last panel. It had to be enough time to figure out the last sin.

"Every time I count them, I always come up one short. What is the last one that I keep missing? Camille is the lapsed Catholic. She would have known it by heart."

His family went to church once a year at Easter, basically to remind themselves that they were part of the Anglican flock. His parents donated to the church's charities but weren't overtly religious themselves. They were never big on prayer, only saying grace over Thanksgiving dinner. If he were to be classified under any denomination, he would be agnostic. Either way, Sunday school wasn't going to save his hide this time.

Ward rattled off the six, hoping, hoping to come up with the last one. "Switch it up. Dead end." He tapped the floor to the drum line of Queen's "We Will Rock You," using his fingers and palms to maintain a steady rhythm. "Erzsébet Báthory's necklace. What did the card say? Blood countess. Too bad I don't have Camille's library for access or even the internet on my phone. I don't know her biography to even begin to make guesses about the last sin I can't remember.

"Emotions, emotions. Back to emotions. What are the basic ones? Happiness, sadness, anger, fear, disgust. Thank God you watched that movie with your niece. None of this works. It can't be an offshoot of one? Like happiness can be satisfaction and sadness, depression. Fear, paranoia. Disgust, broccoli, green . . . green . . . shit. Jealousy? Is that it? It sounds like the last sin, but that's not the formal name of it."

He yanked the box toward him and fumbled for the final panel, smashing his thumbs down on it. "Envy!"

The last panel lowered. The box glowed in his hands, pulsing with a bright light as a chorus of chimes played an unfamiliar tune. Behind the pedestal, the vision of the hourglass vanished. The audible click of the box unlocking snapped his attention back to the object on his lap.

"What do we have here?" He flipped the lid open to see . . . another box.

This one was larger than a die and smaller than a standard Rubik's cube. The iridescent black stone highlighted the fact the entire surface area was decorated with carvings. He had no idea what any of the symbols meant nor the influence on the design. This might be a vessel for something more, but somehow, he didn't think it was his responsibility to open it.

Indeed, this was the ultimate prize—such a small trinket to justify this entire setup. It could contain anything from a nuclear bomb to the cure for all diseases. What else could immortals want as an ultimate prize?

"Decades of imprisonment for some of us. All for this." Ward left the puzzle box on the pedestal and clutched the small black box in his right palm. "How are you supposed to end this god war?"

He stepped into the blazing light and out of the vault. "Hey, I got it! Not sure what this is or what I'm supposed to do with it—" His words trailed off the instant he felt cold steel against his Adam's apple.

Theo pressed a short hunting knife to his throat. "Hand it over. This isn't a fucking joke. Give me what you found in the vault."

"I don't understand. Theo, what the hell is going on?"

"You're going to give me the fucking thing you found in there. I am so sick and tired of kissing your ungrateful, self-absorbed ass." The god pressed the blade harder, drawing blood from the shallow cut. "No more listening to you fucking whine about your hot ex. The stupid bitch shouldn't have turned me down. The only thing I hate more than women like her is golden fuckboys like you. Living your short life with everything handed to you. Never had to struggle, or listen to people tell you no."

The vitriol in his voice was combustible. Ward kept still, hoping Theo wouldn't cut him even deeper than he had already. This wasn't the same immortal Ward had built a friendship with—the kind, awkward god who was hopelessly in love with the girl of his dreams.

No, Theo saw the relationship as transactional, and Ward had proven Camille correct.

She never trusted him. Ward now knew why.

Being the last one to know was never the best position—he came in dead last and therefore had to be the fool left holding the bag.

"If I give it to you, can you ensure Camille's safety?" Ward asked.

He laughed. "You're not in a position to negotiate. She's probably dead anyway, and you'll be too. I never understood why we should bring mortals into this. They're useless. This shitty game is going to end today. I doubt you'll be alive to see it."

31

Camille

· · · · ·

DAY FOURTEEN

· · · · ·

MR. SAMSON'S LAST words were "Night for day, day for night."

Ward. Was he Ward? This didn't make any sense. This man was in his late seventies and had been imprisoned here for decades. How was this possible? They didn't even look that much alike. Or did they?

Mr. Samson had blue eyes, the same as Ward, and his height and build were similar. His voice was . . . I tried to remember, to compare, to see if I'd missed anything.

My great-grandfather was in his nineties when he died three years ago. The pictures of Lolo Gonzalo and Lola Bebang at their wedding in the fifties showed him in his prime. He stood straight as he stared at the lens, eyes bright with a shy smile that hid his uneven teeth. Fifty years later, my mother took a photograph of her grandfather holding me in his arms as a baby. Lines of wear creased his forehead and his jawline, and he had lost all of his hair. His shoulders curled inward as he stood. He was more gaunt in his advanced age. If I placed the two versions of him side by side, it'd be difficult to say it was the same person without the grin.

The scars. There was a small, crescent-shaped scar on Ward's right elbow. He got it when his brothers shoved him off the hayloft of his aunt's barn. His elbow caught pipes hidden underneath the piles of hay. Ward had another mark near his right ankle—a tiny patch of skin that hadn't quite healed from a barbecue burn in college. I accidentally dropped ribs straight from the grill, and they nicked him because he was sitting beside me.

I pushed up Mr. Samson's sleeve and checked his left elbow, searching for the half-circle wound. I found it quickly. God, it was him, or might be. I had to check his ankle to be sure. I laid his body down and arranged it in a respectable fashion before checking his ankle. The mark was faded, but there.

I didn't understand this. He was Ward, but he would have recognized me. Then again, Mr. Samson did say his memories were foggy the longer he was in this prison.

Ward had been here the entire time—an older version of him. Was his boss a version of me? Then we had both been trapped for far longer than we ever imagined. Almost an entire lifetime. My mind raced with every possible scenario that explained all of this. I clutched the sides of my head to anchor myself from the rising sensation of dizziness.

The front door's bell rang. I scrambled backward and hit the counter. If Eryna returned or anyone else was hostile, I didn't have the energy or the heart to fight back. I relaxed when a member of the Eastern Faction walked in.

"I'm checking in on you to see—" Mr. King winced as he took in Mr. Samson's dead body. "Damn, I'm sorry. I'm too late."

"He died saving me."

"Admirable. I admit that I hadn't seen him in a while. I wasn't sure if he was still alive."

I scrambled to my feet by scaling the side of the counter. "He has slowed down. He told me he was dying before all this."

"I apologize if I sound callous. The man looks ancient. I'm surprised he lasted this long." Mr. King leaned down to assess the wounds. "Eryna's work. Twin rapiers. Quick death."

"You warned me about all this. How much did you know about what was going to happen?"

He covered his mouth with his hand and lowered his head.

I wasn't demanding his accountability so much as I was trying to make sense of what had just happened and what I discovered. An alternate version of Ward lived in this shop for decades, and he never saw the outside world from where he was taken again. Death in captivity.

"I knew they would go after you. I gave my warning before you made and solidified your choice, as I did with the head-dress."

This was his way. Mr. King offered choices and transparency about the consequences. I never blamed him for any decisions I made. Mr. Samson's death was on me. "What do you know about Mr. Samson?"

"He was here before you. He was here for every iteration of this experiment. I can't say anything else other than those two facts. Even then, my memories change. This place tends to eat away at your sanity when you stay here for too long. The tolerance for gods is far shorter than you think."

It explained how brief their visits were. "You do know he was Ward. The old man you see before you is and was the same man that runs the other shop."

Mr. King raked his fingers through his short dark hair. "I don't see it. This isn't me being obtuse or insensitive. I truly don't see the resemblance."

"They are the same person. I checked." I told him about the scars, the gaps in Mr. Samson's memories, and his final words.

"The harder I try to understand this, the more my thoughts get muddled. It might be that you're close to unraveling the truth, Ms. Buhay. We gods might know more of the rules, but we are as much a participant in this as you are—the difference being we can come and go as we please. Be fortunate that you don't know what's happening in immortal affairs."

"If Ward and I were here from the very beginning, how and when is this possible?"

"Mortals believe the world revolves around their existence. You believe time conforms to your history and progresses at its own pace. What if time isn't linear? What if it's far more chaotic than you ever imagined?" He snapped his fingers, and Mr. Samson's body was wrapped and laid in a closed coffin along with an arrangement of white roses. The bloodstain on the floor was gone as if a murder never occurred. The way this world so easily wiped away unpleasant events made me uncomfortable.

I walked to the coffin and placed my hand on the polished cherrywood lid. "This version of Ward was very lonely, with ghosts to keep him company. He didn't deserve this. How is this not cruel?"

"Cruelty is subjective. I can tell you about my comrades who were captured by the other side and tortured for centuries. In a way, you are fortunate to have such short lives. There is a limit to the amount of joy and suffering you can experience. Our ability to feel emotions has been dulled over our long existence both in range and duration. I digress—we still remember what it's like to feel pain. I don't think that ever goes away."

The regret in his voice was palpable. I hadn't even thought it was possible to feel pity for a god. "Then, in a way, you lived as he did. Lonely. With all of your power, I thought being a god would be a good thing."

"Like everything else, it's not as it seems. You develop the tendency to not get attached to anything because of the helplessness you feel when watching them grow old and die." He touched one of the pristine white roses. "Imagine feeling your loss over and over again, hoping you'd be numb to it. Of course, it doesn't work that way. Inside every god is still an essence of humanity. We can't eradicate it, no matter how hard we try."

Mr. King shook his head, and his demeanor changed to the one I was accustomed to—the lighter, somewhat philosophical version of himself. "If all goes well, you'll leave this place with altered memories. You won't even remember this, because in your version of history, when you step back into it, it never happened."

"But I want to remember. Every experience is valuable." I

patted the polished wood. "He mattered to me. He was real. I don't want to forget him and this place."

Mr. Samson was Ward, the older version of the man I loved. I cared about him and he cared for me too, in his own way, going as far as to make the ultimate sacrifice. He wasn't disposable. None of us were.

"I would negotiate that for when or if you leave this place. You still intend to walk out of here with Mr. Dunbar?"

Ward. "He's in trouble. You have to go check in on him. I have this feeling he's going—"

"He'll be fine. Trust me."

"Eryna tried to kill me. I can't imagine her standing by and not punishing him as well. She's been itching for blood from the beginning. How can you be so sure?"

Mr. King beamed. "Everything will work out. Have a little faith, Ms. Buhay. We'll all know our fates soon. In the best-case scenario, you and Mr. Dunbar will walk out of here and resume your lives together without the scars of what happened. No consequences or trauma. You'll be together, am I right?"

"Yes, I want to be with him. If anything, this experience has reminded me how much I want him in my life." I leaned forward to touch one of the silken rose petals. "The idea of growing old together is really appealing."

"This is because you haven't seen the older version of yourself." He covered a chuckle with a cough.

"What? What is the older version of me like?"

Ward had mentioned he didn't get along well with his boss. Had the older version of me turned into a salty, raging bitch? As curious as I was, I didn't know if I wanted to meet her. Part of me feared I wouldn't like what I saw. This would be me living alone for decades—every weakness and flaw exacerbated without anyone tempering them. The years had been kind to Mr. Samson, turning him into a soft romantic. I doubted I'd get the same flattering filter.

"You are far more unforgiving than reality. Where you see her failings, someone else can see her strength and her convictions. Madam Selene turned out all right. She's a survivor."

"Then she's still alive. What will happen to her when this experiment is over?"

"Don't know. All we can do is wait and see. I'm as much in the dark as you are in this. The war can't go on any longer. I can't speak for my faction, but any resolution would be welcomed." He smoothed down a wrinkle in his sleeve. "I don't want to do this anymore. I'm not Eryna, who gets off on conflict. All of this is exhausting. I want to move on."

"To what?"

"I don't know. I never had the luxury to think about it. If the war ends today, then everything changes. If my side wins, we want certain things in place. If they win, they have their own grand plans, which include total annihilation. There's a valid reason why it's dragged on for this long."

Then I might have chosen the right side—the one against the destruction of everything. "You weren't allowed to tell me that before I made my decision, were you?"

"No. Destruction is often taken by mortals as a dire consequence. To us, it doesn't have that terrible connotation."

"Because you survive everything. Immortal cockroaches in a nuclear war."

He nodded. "Accurate. All of these complicated rules are

meant to create an even playing field. It had been run twice before because there were flaws. I don't think they'll run it again. This is the last try at mediation."

"I guess it doesn't matter now." I pointed to the stubby black candle and the smoking, bare wick. "Time's up."

32

Ward

DAY FOURTEEN

"GIVE ME THE prize." Theo's voice rattled his teeth. "You owe me this."

Din walked through the front doors. Ward almost exhaled in relief. She paused to take in the scene, then she clapped.

He was fucked.

"Hi, babe. Can you come here for a moment?" Theo gestured to her with his free arm. "I need you to help me out with this."

She approached them with an unnatural gait. Her bright ice-blue eyes twinkled to match her eerie grin. Her eyes had changed since he'd known her. It must be a goddess trait.

"He needs to give you something he found in the vault. It has to come from his own free will, and this is how we'll win this war for your mother." Theo tightened his grip on the knife. "Then she can bless our union and leave us the fuck alone."

Din's vigorous nods prompted a chuckle from my captor.

"Give it to her. Tell her that you're doing so out of your own free will. Let's get this over with."

"And if I don't?" Ward asked.

"Camille's already dead. You still have other people you care about. Din and I will kill every single one of your family. And if that doesn't do it, I can figure out a way to reanimate your girl-friend's corpse so she can feel death a few more times just for fun. I've got even more dark ideas if that doesn't compel you."

The threats were quite valid. These immortals were far more dangerous than anything he could imagine. Ward would certainly die if he refused to give up the box. Other lives hinged on his decision.

It wasn't a choice he wanted to make.

In any other situation, he would be overanalyzing all the consequences of any major decision, gathering all the information within his reach, and asking for friends' opinions. Anything to shush his brain for having made the wrong choice. This wasn't a case of indecisiveness. Camille called it FOMO prevention. "You are so scared of having regrets. You'll do whatever it takes so that when you've committed, your mind is at peace." It made sense with most things, especially this.

His decision would affect the immortal war, and in turn, humanity.

"He's thinking too much, isn't he?" Theo punched Ward's kidneys.

Ward grunted as pain radiated from his lower back.

Din cupped his chin, tilting it up so Ward met her eyes. Her perfect brows arched as if she were asking him a question. She reached upward to squeeze his cheeks before patting them. The action was comforting, and odd, given his circumstances. Camille used the same gesture when she told him he was being insufferably adorable.

Theo smacked his shoulder. "Babe, do I need to cut an ear off to get this prick to do something?"

She placed a hand on his elbow to steady his knife arm and shook her head. She stepped back, cupped her hands together and held them out to Ward.

"If all else fails, go with your gut," Camille would say. At this point, he assumed she was dead and nothing, not even an Easter resurrection, was going to bring her back to him. In his mind, all hope was lost and the forces of darkness were winning. He did what any prey would do when backed into a corner—he surrendered.

Ward fished for the cube in his pocket and placed it in her hands. "I'm giving you this of my free will."

The small black box shimmered. Every symbol on the surface lit up until it became a blaze. The light swallowed everything in the room until it was replaced by an explosion of shooting stars.

Game. Set. Match.

WARD DUNBAR AWOKE in a white room, and he wasn't alone.

His elbow bumped into something that groaned. He turned to his right to see the most beautiful face in the world.

"Camille, God, are we dead?" He reached out and touched her brow, down her cheeks, and then her full lips. Slight dark smudges settled under her brown eyes. The stress of the time they spent here had taken its toll.

She nipped at his fingers with her teeth and laughed. "Doesn't seem like it."

He pulled her toward him, devouring her mouth as she settled her hips above him, straddling his waist. She pressed her hands against his chest and blurted out in between kisses, "I missed you. I thought I'd never see you again."

"Same. I thought you were dead." He cradled her in his arms with no intention of ever letting her go again.

"Does this mean it's all over? That we can go free?"

She rested her head against his shoulder. "Don't know. I'm happy that we're together now and that you're alive." She tugged at his hand before threading her fingers through his. "I love you and I want to make this work. That is . . . if you still want to be with me?"

This was the question he had always wanted to hear. It made the torture of this entire ordeal worth it. All of it. He was a simple being who had been handed the very key to his happiness. No creature was happier—not even a clowder of cats in a field of catnip could equal his joy.

"Are you kidding me?" He squeezed her hand. "Of course. I thought you'd still be angry with me because of what I asked Theo to do."

"I understand why you did it. I was angry at the time, but I let it go. When we broke up and I was living in New York alone, I learned that I've lost too much time to it. It took losing you to understand the parts of me that were destructive. This brings me to your boss. What do you think of her?"

"What? What does she have to do with this?"

"Please indulge me. I'll explain everything later, I promise."

"She was a tough woman. Survivor. She embodied iron will, was unforgiving, and I admired the hell out of her despite her flaws."

Camille pushed herself up to rest her chin on her hands. "Was she hot?"

Ward made a gurgling noise.

"I want to know if you were attracted to her."

"No? She was ancient. I mean, she was attractive for her age. I don't know where you're going with this and I'm not sure I want to know."

"I'm asking because she is me. She is an older version of me that spent decades in here alone."

Yes, as farfetched as the idea was, it was plausible. In this world, anything could and did happen. The two women didn't resemble each other or share any obvious mannerisms—it was their common worldview. Madam Selene was adamant about her disdain for gods, often citing how they belonged to the upper class and held all the power. When Camille spoke about race and economics, she had the same passion.

Of course, for him, it became so much more obvious after the revelation.

"I guess I can see it. Wait, does this mean that you were with the older version of me? God, what was he like?"

Her face softened into a dreamy expression. "Hopeless romantic. Gallant. Sweet."

"Did you have a crush on your boss? Is this why you asked me . . ."

"I liked him a lot. He got under my skin even faster than you did, if that was possible. He was handsome and charming. The more I think about it, the more I see so much of you in him." She brought his fingertips to her lips and then kissed them. "You're going to be hot and wonderful when you get old."

He brushed his lips across her brow. "I guess that's a good thing."

"What's going to happen now?"

"With this warped escape room or with us?"

"With us."

"Going to book a hotel for a week. We'll order in and we don't have to get out of bed if we don't want to. I'm going to do my damnedest to make up for the lost time. Clothing optional." He ran his fingers along the curve of her spine. She shivered. "We can figure out if we want to stay here or go work somewhere else. Might be fun to see if we can establish ourselves in another new city."

She traced lazy circles on his chest. "I'd rather think about the week in bed, to be honest. If anything, this experience taught me how much I crave physical contact. I need to reacquaint myself with every inch of you."

He hardened.

She grounded her hips against his.

"Don't start something you know I can't stop." He half begged her. "I'm not sure how much longer we'll be in here or together."

"I hate it when you're the logical one. So this war, it's been decided then? Which side wins? Mr. King tells me that if the Western Faction wins, they are considering the destruction of everything. I chose the East without knowing anything about which side stands for what. They weren't allowed to tell us anything. How did you decide?"

He told her the truth and how he solved the box in the vault. "Theo is as bad as you said. I mistook his ulterior motives for kindness. I don't even think he can stand being around me."

"He kept trying to rope me into a ménage à trois with his girlfriend. I swear he probably doesn't know what I look like. He only stared at my tits. He's one of those transactional types. Tell me about the bargain."

He told her everything—all the details of his interactions with Theo and his observations of the gods and their war. After that, she caught him up on her side. She respected Mr. King and when she explained why, he found himself reassessing his own harsh judgments of the god.

"You picked the West and I picked the East. Then it's a stalemate again." Camille furrowed her brow. "I'm not sure then if we'll be able to leave. Both of us were supposed to pick the same side."

His heart sank. "They never told you who was in charge, did they? I've gotten hints about a higher power, never anything explicit."

"Who governs the gods then? There's so much we don't know. They only tell us on a need-to-know basis, and even then, I feel like we've been kept in the dark about everything."

"Impartiality. We're the lab rats. They want their results untainted. As for who's in charge, I can only guess. Creation myths usually start with big elements before giving birth to the gods. Things like water or fire, even trees. I guess it would be something like that?"

"Atoms or energy. There aren't goddesses for those around, are there?"

"Not that I can recall."

They both jolted at the sound of something being scraped open. At the far end of the room was a dark hallway that hadn't been there before. Ward scrambled to his feet and helped Camille up. It was the first time he noticed the bloodstains on her blouse and skirt. Mr. Samson's death must have been far more traumatizing than what she disclosed.

"So we're being herded there?" She straightened her blouse's hem and sleeves. "I'm not sure how to feel about this."

Ward took her hand in his. "Whatever happens, as long as we're together, we'll be okay."

She rested her head against his shoulder.

"It can't be as bad as what we've already been through."

"All right. I'll try and channel your positivity and optimism. Right now, I don't have any." She stopped and cupped his face. "I love you. Now, then, forever. I want to grow old with you. This is what I'm walking away with from here."

"I love you too. I want to spend the rest of my days knowing I'm waking up beside you every morning." He kissed her and held her tight.

"Okay. I guess I'm ready."

Ward steadied her as they made their way to the dark hallway.

His optimism was genuine because it had to be. He was reunited with his beloved and was in the process of riding off into the sunset with her. The trolls and ogres were dead or in another kingdom far away.

Surely, after all that they had endured, future torment wasn't scheduled. How this would all end was anyone's guess.

33

Camille

. . . . .

DAY FOURTEEN

. . . . .

THE WARMTH OF Ward's hand in mine gave me the strength to keep moving forward. I had wanted nothing more than to collapse in a helpless heap the moment Mr. Samson died.

Something inside me broke at the thought that he died here after decades of being trapped. He should have been out in the world, strolling around London, flirting and charming all the ladies.

What happened to him was my worst nightmare.

After my breakup with Ward, I was alone in Manhattan and I had never felt more isolated. I pushed people away and never socialized, burying myself in work to stave off the pain. In the back of my mind was the worry that I'd die in my apartment without anyone knowing—to be found a week later by the landlord.

This job opportunity found me at the right time when I yearned to change my life.

I had never asked Ward how he found this job. Though

now, with everything that had happened, I suspected it had found him.

The dark corridor was short and led into an endless white chamber. A group had already gathered, forming some sort of council. All four gods were present. Mr. King stood by himself, while Eryna, Din, and Theo clustered together.

Eryna narrowed her eyes when we made our entrance.

A popping noise echoed behind us as the hallway vanished. There were two figures behind the gods. Two women, both East Asian. One had her dark hair pulled tight into a severe bun and wore a crisp black pantsuit. The shade of black almost made it appear that she was wearing a spatial void. The other woman wore a loose-flowing caftan in the same shade of white as the endless room. Silver streaks decorated her long, dark, unbound hair. Her striking face appeared old and young at the same time.

"Welcome, Edward and Camille. I am Time. My pronouns are they and them. And they . . ." The white-robed being paused to point at the serious one in the pantsuit. "Are Chaos. Same pronouns. We are gathered today to discuss the results of the experiment." They clapped their hands and gestured for us to come forward. Their voice had a choral quality like Din's. "Since we are all here now, we can proceed."

Ward and I found ourselves seated beside each other on a bench where the jury would sit. The layout mimicked a courtroom. Mr. King occupied one table while Eryna, Theo, and Din sat at the other. The two strangers presiding over us stood behind twin pedestals.

Chaos tapped the edge of their lectern. Their voice was singular and neither feminine nor masculine. "This hearing is to settle the war of the gods. The Eastern and Western Factions need to settle their dispute, and it ends today, with this ruling."

"First, attendance." Time's demeanor reminded me of a cheerful kindergarten teacher right down to their mannerisms. "Western Faction. Eryna."

The haughty goddess raised her hand.

"Theo."

Theo shot Ward a withering glare before lifting his open palm.

"And Din?" Time pursed her lips. "No, is this right? The numbers aren't adding up. Each faction should have two members. The Eastern Faction is missing a member."

Eryna stepped back to study Theo's girlfriend. Din ducked her head and rubbed her upper lip. Theo scratched his head and moved away when Eryna approached the younger goddess, grabbing her chin and squeezing. "My daughter is supposed to be on a covert assignment. This . . . this is not her!"

Din laughed, exposing very sharp, pointed teeth. She jumped back and shook her head, sprouting two furry ears. She transformed into a golden, anthropomorphic fox and rushed to stand by Mr. King's side.

"You little shit!" Eryna screeched as she tried to get to the Eastern Faction's table. An invisible barrier prevented her from leaving her own table. Instead, she turned her wrath to Theo. She backhanded him with her knuckles, drawing blood at the corners of his lips. "You fool. How can you be so easily deceived? Were you so desperate to get laid that you can't even tell who you're fucking?"

Theo winced and wiped his mouth with the back of his hand. "She told me that you wanted us to win. I did what I could, and when I brought her with me, you were good with having one extra member on our side."

"Because you said it was her! I'm too busy fighting this goddamned war to manage every single little thing." Eryna pressed her nails to her temples. "I told them I wanted someone else, and they saddled me with *you*. Of all the incompetent, spineless . . ."

Ward whispered in my ear, "I can't believe I'm feeling pity for him right now."

"Did you know Eryna and Din were related?"

"No. And the fox situation sort of makes sense. Theo said that Din recently started paying attention to him. It can't be a coincidence—"

Chaos smacked the lectern. "Order. No more outbursts. No one will speak unless we ask you to."

Ward's words died in midsentence.

I had found it odd that with all the emphasis on neutrality, Mr. King was on his own. He never objected to the disparity. The lone hint I'd received from him was when he reassured me that Ward would be protected. It was too early to understand what the fox goddess's deception meant, other than her being privy to enemy intelligence.

"All right, let's try this again." Time counted each party twice by pointing before continuing with the proceedings. "Mr. King."

The god raised his hand.

"And . . . not-Din."

The fox goddess waved her paw.

"I suppose everything is equal now. As it should be." Time puffed out their lips. "Attendance is done. The rest is up to you."

Chaos rubbed their palms together. "Then let us begin. We

are here to decide this dispute once and for all. Both the Eastern Faction and the Western Faction have agreed to this experiment and with Time's selection of two mortals for the task. In the first iteration, there were no results. Mr. Dunbar and Ms. Buhay were left to their own devices, and the experiment failed to progress.

"Under mediation, the two sides approved the adjustment of variables to encourage improvement. Mr. Dunbar was given the younger version of himself as a companion, and the same went for Ms. Buhay. There was cooperation and conflict. The second fared better, but still failed."

Was there another version of Ward and me alive somewhere from the second run? We hadn't seen anyone else.

"The last iteration was suggested by Mr. King and approved by both parties. The original Mr. Dunbar and Ms. Buhay would be reversely paired with their younger counterparts. Eryna has also proposed her own amendment—that two members of each faction would be able to participate. As the Eastern Faction representative, Mr. King agreed to the amendment. The experiment was restarted again, and this time, we have a definitive outcome."

Eryna raised her hand.

Chaos acknowledged her.

"I object," the goddess protested. "I said two members. That impostor played our side and violated the rules—making it seem like there are three members of the Western Faction."

Time held out their hands. "Oh, let me answer this one." When they received Chaos's approval, they continued, "At all times, there were a maximum of two members of the opposing sides in each venue. No rules were broken. And might I add this. Eryna, you endorsed the imbalance when you were notified, am I correct?"

Eryna narrowed her eyes and kept her mouth shut.

"Then I take that as confirmation. Anyway, proceed, Chaos. Let's get this over with." Time made an impatient rolling gesture.

Chaos cleared their throat. "Now we come to the choices. These are the arbitrary and final choices the mortals have made. These votes are final and irrevocable. Ms. Buhay, please rise and state your decision."

I obeyed and stood. Ward kept his grip on my hand. "I chose to give the key to Mr. King."

"The Eastern Faction has gained the first tally. And now for the second, please rise, Mr. Dunbar, and state your decision."

Ward took his place beside me. He declared in a clear voice. "I gave the box to . . . not-Din, whatever the name of the goddess is who is sitting beside Mr. King."

Theo shot him a killer glare from across the room. The weasel had the nerve to blame us after everything he'd done. Karma would be swift. I was certain Eryna was itching to get her hands on the fool who cost them the war.

I squeezed Ward's hand.

"Then we have two Eastern Faction votes. This dispute has been decided in favor of the Eastern Faction. The God War is over. After a brief recess, we will move into arbitration for both sides. There is much to discuss about how to proceed after this." Chaos closed their eyes and vanished.

The benches, pedestals, the gods, all disappeared, leaving Ward and me alone with Time.

"So all this unpleasantness is over. Isn't it a relief?" They fluffed their hair and did a twirl. Their robes fluttered and shimmered with a new array of rainbow dust. "Did that answer your questions about everything?"

Ward and I exchanged glances.

"Sort of?" he replied. "Honestly, I still have far too many left to ask."

"Are they important questions though? Or are they ones that are really indulgent? You know what I mean, Edward. I'm sure you've been often told that there's a time and place for everything."

Ward blushed to the tips of his ears.

I dared not laugh.

Time might appear to be a hippie Asian auntie, but nothing seemed to escape them. What we were seeing was a specially crafted veneer. They manifested themselves into any shape or form, yet they chose this.

"The good news is that you are free to leave. We're not keeping you here any longer than necessary. However, before you do, I want to speak to you both individually." They walked toward us and drew us into a huddle. "You two have been very good about all this, and frankly, you've solved a massive headache that Chaos and I have been dealing with for far too long. Family disputes are the worst."

"Is this an exit interview?" I asked them. "Or something along those lines?"

They bopped me on the tip of my nose with a playful poke. "No, no, no. You always think about work, Camille. Lighten up. Life is so much better when you have balance." They turned to Ward and ruffled his hair. "I can guarantee that

Edward here is probably thinking it's a chance for wish fulfil-ment. His guess is closer than yours."

I asked with caution, "You're granting us a wish before we leave?"

"Yes and no. I guess we'll see how our little meetings go. There's a few things I want to clear up. It's your turn to indulge me, and what you get in return will be worth it." Time grinned. Their cheeks glowed pink.

A wish. Too good to be true, even for a cynic like me. It had to have strings and caveats. This was one of the two forces governing all of existence. Anything was possible.

My mind raced and spun at a dizzying rate. If Ward weren't here with me, my sanity would have left me a long time ago. We, the lab rats, were getting rewarded with a gift—one whose worth and scope we barely comprehended. Unreal.

"Am I going first or is she?" Ward asked Time.

"Oh, dear boy, you do know whom you're talking to." Time let out a childish giggle. "The same time, of course. The way you mortals perceive me is reductive. We can fix that. Might as well start now."

34

Ward

NO MORTALS ON record had ever been in the presence of the primordial entities of Chaos and Time. Ward and Camille set a precedent in what were considered strange times. These two lowly mortals were now being rewarded for solving a Gordian knot of all dilemmas. The world as it was would change after this momentous decision, and no one knew how yet—including Chaos and Time.

One second Ward had Camille's hand in his, and the next, he found himself weightless, suspended in space with the vastness of the stars and the universe around him. He reached up to cover his nose and worried about suffocation. Time flew before him in a silver jumpsuit. They twirled in an infinity loop pattern, laughing before settling across from him.

"Don't worry so much about science, Edward. You're safe here because you're with me." They stretched out their arms and assumed a lotus position. "Don't worry. Camille is safe. She and I are talking right now."

His heart rate slowed and so did the rise and fall of his chest. "Thank you for letting me know."

"I chose you two for a reason. I wanted to appease my curiosity about patterns and possibilities. Do you remember when you found out about this job in London? Tell me what you were thinking."

"I was searching for change," Ward replied. "This was the best opportunity for me to try something new and, maybe, move on."

Time tapped their chin. "Did you move on though? You still loved her, and if anything, you're following the same patterns. Don't you think it's interesting that if you hadn't gotten sucked into the experiment, you two would have ended up breaking up again?"

"Perhaps. Camille and I never had a chance to address it before all this, and our experience in this place wasn't conducive to any long or meaningful conversation. The time apart did change us, and to me, we're in a better place now."

"I'm fascinated by the idea of mortals making the same choices again and again despite changing all the conditions. Chaos wanted to end the war, and while I wanted it as well . . . this is what fascinates me. Would you and Camille have ended up on the same path had I not intervened?"

"Maybe. It's possible." He shrugged. "Can't know unless there's another timeline where we didn't end up here."

"That is where I'll be dropping you two off. Back before any of this. Wipe everything clean and let you resume your lives as they were."

He winced. He'd lose the precious progress that he and Camille had made during this unconventional experiment—

for, in its strange, twisted way, it had brought Camille and him closer. They wanted and agreed to move forward together.

"You said you would grant us a wish earlier. Can you give us our memories of this place? We can't go back to the outside world the same people as we were."

"Not possible."

"I don't understand. You're all-powerful. Shouldn't this be some very minor task?"

Time scrunched their nose and made a face. "Can't. It's not that I don't want to. Your mortal minds are very . . ." They made a pinching gesture.

"So our minds will break if we keep our memories?"

"Yes. Very much so. You're all very squishy and fragile. I mean, you think I'm linear." They laughed, devolving into wheezes, as they clutched their stomach. Time held out their hand as he waited for their giggling fit to subside. "Okay. So yes, I will entertain requests that I *can* grant. I'm surprised you didn't ask for something mortal-y like riches, fame, or immortality."

"I don't care about those things. I love Camille and want to be with her. What use is any of that to me if we're apart?"

"Such a romantic. You would die for her, and in a way, you did. I don't doubt how far you'd go for her. This is what makes mortality unpredictable. All the impulsiveness with all the consequences. Gods can act the same way, yet they don't have the same stakes. There isn't much they can lose unless they decide to do that collectively. It's what Chaos is doing now with them. Sorting out all their quibbles and squabbles."

"Back to the memories, is there any way for us to leave this place with the progress we've made?"

"What do you mean? Please explain."

Ward took a deep breath to collect his thoughts. Because of how limited their interactions had been, he and Camille managed maximum efficiency in communication. Scarcity created a way to cut through all the noise. The letters reminded him to stop and think before saying anything. His tendency to blurt out all his emotions was his way of processing them. The need to put them down on paper made him aware of his flaws in action. Everything he'd written to Camille was precise instead of vomiting emotions. She never had this issue. She was far more logical than him.

He explained to Time in the best way he could—concise, almost to a fault. Camille would've been proud.

"Oh, I guess I understand." They frowned. "Even if I'm rooting for both of you, I don't know how this will work the way you want going forward. Memories are off-limits. Anything you've experienced here including this conversation needs to be erased for your sanity."

"Even if you changed it so that we remember only our interactions. Will this work?"

Time pressed their fingertips to their temples. "No. Everything is connected, Edward. Knowledge of something leads to another. Even if I were to leave one kernel here and there, we still end up liquefying your mortal brain. You'll drive yourself insane trying to fill in the pieces that you're missing. Human curiosity is a wonder to behold and can be deadly, as proven in many cases in your history."

"Then what are my options? I can't leave here the same person as I came in. I just can't." He balled his fists.

"I don't know how mortal minds work. It's still a mystery. I mean, yes, I know what makes your little brains explode, but all the nuances and how you perceive the world are so fascinating. Don't even get me started about love and how that works with you all." Time traced little ethereal hearts made of stardust with their fingertips. "You treat love like it can die. Love is an emotion, a bond. Is it alive though? What do you think?"

Time acted like a sociologist and anthropologist from another planet. Their obsession with humanity was almost adorable. It was comforting to have one of the two greatest forces in the universe invested in what happened to him.

"I think it's alive, almost sentient. What I feel for Camille is what kept me moving forward toward survival. You mentioned before that knowledge is interconnected. I'd like to think that emotions are as well. My love for her gives me so much happiness, and yes, there's also passion and fun. It's a far more complicated concept. It'd be foolish to describe it as a simple emotion."

Time laughed. "Ah, Edward. I feel like we can sit here and chat until the stars burn out. As fun as that would be for me, it won't help you though. You still have this problem, and Chaos doesn't want me to keep you two for too long. You've been detained for too long as is."

He wasn't going to give up. "Wait, is it possible to keep our emotions? I want Camille and me to feel as we do now when we leave this place."

"Wouldn't it also screw up your memories? Emotions are tied to them, aren't they?"

"They can be, but emotions can exist outside of memories.

It's the sentient quality I mentioned earlier. I'm thinking that maybe if we keep how we feel, it's the best way to retain our growth in our relationship."

"You're very possessive about this. Not so much of her, but of this. It's interesting. Edward, you're one intriguing mortal. I wish we had more time together, and if Chaos approves, I might steal you away for a bit for another chat."

"Does this mean that what I said is possible?"

Time leaned forward and cupped his cheeks. Their touch was neither warm nor cold, yet the sensation was comforting. "Yes. I've thought about it and figured it out eventually. It's possible. You can get your wish."

"Thank you." Ward almost cried with relief. "I love her. I want to be with her, and she feels the same way. This will help us going forward."

"Aww, true love. Some gods are obsessed with this. Something about feeling something they can't anymore. I work in a different way. I observe everything. I'm not interested in *feeling* what I'm seeing. I want to know why and how. It's all about the questions, and you don't want to know how many I have." They winked at him before pulling away. "I'm wrapping up with Camille now, and she has her own unusual request. Ah, gone are the days when mortals ask for uncomplicated things. Ah well, what can we do?"

"What did she ask for?"

"Something very different. She is as passionate about her cause as you are about yours. I have to say that both of you are making me think harder than I have in a while. I suppose if all goes well, you two will be together and living out the rest of your lives with less excitement?"

"That's the plan. Though I do worry about repercussions from the gods."

Theo, to be exact. Ward feared that even a lowly god could wreak havoc on his life and those he loved. The power dynamics were unequal and not tipped in his favor.

"Oh, their memories will be wiped too. At least, that's the agreement right now. The Eastern Faction won the war, and they have the right to change things up. Mr. King and not-Din might ask to keep their memories. Who knows? Not my headache, that's all for Chaos to handle. Even if, let's say, the Western Faction won, you and Camille wouldn't be harmed. You're under my protection."

"Thank you."

"All right then. Ready to rejoin the world you left?"

The rest of his life needed to unfold. This wild, magical, dangerous place was plucked out of his most outlandish fantasies—gods, ghosts, magic, and dangerous immortal bargains. The dreamer in him was satiated and now turned its attention to a wonderful life with Camille.

His adventures would be with her, as they should be.

No more ambrosia, mermaids, or unicorns. Of course, he hadn't seen the last two but was more certain now that they existed or could exist. This was the realm of magic and gods after all.

"Yes, Camille is waiting for me."

"Then hold on to her and don't let her go. Night for day, day for night." Time pressed their fingertips together and winked.

35

Camille

· · · · ·

DAY FIFTEEN?

· · · · ·

I PUSHED DOWN the rising panic when Ward vanished again.

"You'll see him soon. Stay calm. You didn't lose him. You'll see him again." I repeated this to myself over and over until calmness took root.

"I hope this is more relaxing for you." Time addressed me from across the table. "This should be familiar."

I glanced around me. The air was salty, almost stinging my eyes. The brilliant sun was setting over the boardwalk café we were sitting in. Ocean City, Maryland. This was the yearly summer vacation spot for my family where we'd hit the beach and eat a pile of steamed, seasoned crabs with little wooden mallets over a table covered with newspapers. The smell of them nearby perked up my dormant appetite.

"I appreciate this, thank you."

Time stirred their Bloody Mary with a straw. They pulled out the stick of celery and nibbled on the tips. The salted rim of the cocktail rubbed off on the green stalk, leaving a trail of powdery brown and black. "Do you want anything? The bar is open."

"Uh . . . a bourbon sour, please."

I wasn't sure if there would be a server bringing the drink or if this was in a magical realm akin to virtual reality. As Time munched on their celery stalk, a tumbler filled with ice topped with white foam materialized in front of me.

I took a sip. Booker's bourbon, and at the perfect chilly temp.

"So." Time set down their cocktail. "We're here because I have questions. Burning questions."

"About . . . ?"

"Humanity, love, emotions, everything. You know that I chose you two out of all the mortals in the world. Can you guess why?"

I imagined it was an "eyes closed and throw at a dartboard" scenario. Ward and I weren't anything different or special when compared to everyone else. Nothing about us was remarkable or even peculiar. "I honestly can't think of a reason."

"I was intrigued by your previous relationship's dynamics. It's the idea that you two are so different, yet you were together and happy. I suppose it's my own fascination with how mortal attraction and relationships work. It's all a mystery to me."

This all-powerful being viewed Ward and me as some sort of slice of reality television. Unreal. "You must have seen everything though? You're Time. Nothing is a surprise anymore."

"But it can be! That's why I love observing mortals. Gods are boring. They don't have range." They cupped their hand to the side of their mouth. "Don't tell them that. I know they'd be offended. They're still a touchy lot. Overemotional, and it's ironic how they have the inability to *feel*. They keep doing the same things over and over again. Look at the war. They don't have the ability to change. You mortals do."

"Do we? Some of us keep to our destructive patterns."

"In general. It's all about scope. You have that. The potential for change is greater. Take, for example, you and Edward. You've changed during this experiment. Edward is adamant about this. He calls it growth."

Ward would. He believed in the redemption of others far more than I did. He was the first person who had the capacity to look back on this experience and call it transformative. Ever an optimist and generous with how he perceived everyone, almost to a fault.

"He's much more magnanimous than I am."

"Oh, Camille, you're so harsh on yourself. You need to be a bit more kind." Time paused to refill their drink. "So, have you given it much thought? What are you going to ask me for your wish?"

"Are there any limits to what I can ask for?"

"There are. Edward has run into one. We're trying to sort it out right now. Even though I'm omnipotent, there are constraints even I must follow. Think it over. Don't take too long, because you two are itching to get out of here."

I'd been thinking about this since she mentioned it to us. I braced myself for what I was about to ask. "I want Mr. Samson and Ward's boss to leave this place when we do. Mr. Samson died, and if anyone can bring him back to life, I thought it'd be you."

"Wait, wait. You're asking me to resurrect your old boss. Why?"

"Because he should have gotten a chance to taste freedom before he died. He's been alone in here for so long. I know you had different versions of us in other iterations, but it doesn't make me feel any better that he died lonely."

"But he doesn't exist in your version of reality. You and Edward are going to walk out of here together to resume your lives. This is a phantom version of him. He wasn't meant to leave—that honor belongs to you, the younger selves."

"He wasn't disposable." A sob caught in my throat. Mr. Samson had as much a right to live and be free as Ward and I did. This wasn't a case of being satisfied because my own ass was saved.

"You loved him, didn't you?"

I lowered my eyes. "Yes. Not in a romantic way. He was wonderful to be around. I've always had difficulty forming attachments with people. Maybe it's because it was another version of Ward that made it easier."

"And this is guilt?" Time narrowed their eyes. "I'm unfamiliar with emotions. I'm incapable of having them. I can only guess what you may be feeling."

It might have been. It was deeper than that. Mr. Samson unlocked something inside me. After seeing him die, I was reminded of the life I thought I was destined to have—one of loneliness and regret, devoid of any lasting joy, and in so much pain that I needed to work myself to death. Yes, I might very well be projecting.

"This isn't about reviving an idea. Mr. Samson was a real person to me. His existence had meaning. He should be allowed to finish the rest of his life out there." My voice trembled. "He should have a few years left, at the very least. It's not like I'm asking you to rewind too much time. I want him to be able to have a little bit of happiness before he dies a natural death. He should see the world again and remember his experience outside as his final memories. The same applies to Ward's boss. They deserve this chance."

"I didn't consider that more than one version of you and Edward could leave. This is going to be complicated. After all, Mr. Samson is Edward. He'd have the same family and connections. Those shared memories will cause him trouble if he ever returns to seek out those ties. I had every intention of erasing your memories from this place. Mr. Samson and Madam Selene's memories will be a much harder task. They've been here for longer, and that would be problematic."

"In that there won't be much left after they've been wiped clean?"

"Yes. This is a definite quandary. Edward has also given me a tricky situation to deal with. Oh, you mortals doing your best to get me to come up with creative solutions."

Time pursed their lips. They had a way about them that sent all the mixed signals—approachable, sometimes even flaky, yet powerful enough to incinerate me on the spot. The odd combination kept me from being too open or critical.

"What if you gave them new ones? New memories, I mean. Will this work?" I asked.

"Well . . ." They bit their lower lip. "It can. I have no idea what kinds of memories these will be. I can't even fathom what the content would be. I'm not a creator. Technically, I can set this up, but I'd run into the same problems of what to replace it with. The level of detail needed is beyond my capabilities."

Possible, but difficult. I could work with this. "How? Do

you need someone to give a narrative like how a writer crafts stories? Is it a matter of micro-details versus a general overview?"

"I suppose a general overview could work. As you mortals age, your memories degrade anyway. They become softer and more about emotions than facts. My issue is that I can't shape your lives for you. A mortal life is composed of a multitude of decisions. It's very complicated and, yes, messy. Deliciously so." They steepled their fingers and giggled. They definitely liked mess, and who knew how many hours they wasted marathoning reality television?

"What if I did it? What if I laid out what happened in their lives in the past fifty years?"

"And you can come up with this in a short amount of time? I can't break the rules for you when Edward is already done and waiting. In this respect, it might not be fair, but it's equal. My generosity has its boundaries."

"Can I have a pen and paper? I'll need to write it down. I think better this way."

A notebook and a black ballpoint pen bleeped into existence next to my almost-empty tumbler of bourbon. I scratched down the details of two lives with ruthless efficiency. Years of dreaming and wishing about what the future would be like between Ward and me had been a useful outlet.

"I hope this works?" I handed Time my drafts.

They scanned the two sheets of paper. Each page detailed enough milestones within the fifty-year span. I had made sure to add in grounding touches that someone wouldn't be able to check up on. I had to straddle the line between being specific enough and not supplying so much that it became detrimental.

Time scrunched their nose. "I suppose this can work. No,

I have to say it will work. We have to be optimists, Camille. It's important to see that things can work out." They folded the papers in half and set them aside. "Since all this is figured out, I want to get back to one last thing before I let you go."

"One last thing?"

"As I said earlier, mortal life is all about choices. You and Edward had made the choice to get back together before being snatched away for the experiment. Do you think you two will stay together or break up again? Are you bound to make the same mistakes over and over until you both get tired of the result?"

I never gave it much thought. Ward and I loved each other, and for a while, it was enough—until it wasn't. Trying again this time was my idea. We were in a city far from everything we knew. No one interfered here, especially not his family. They were lovely people and very supportive—so much so that they'd kill any ambition Ward cultivated. He was at his best when he had a challenge. We wouldn't have reached this point of the experiment otherwise.

"We are going to make it work this time. I'm more hopeful than I've ever been."

"Good! He is too. He loves you very much. I suppose it's time for me to grant you your wish. Remember that you won't remember a thing from here. You and Edward will be placed back before all this happened. No magic, no gods, no ghosts, nothing. You won't even miss me." Time winked. "Maybe a little?"

"A little," I conceded. "This is all too much. I want a more normal life with a dash more fun. Together with Ward, every-thing is possible."

"Yes, even more fun than that. Don't be cheap. You two earned a lifetime of joy. I'm rooting for you two kids. Go make me proud." Time grinned and waved their hand. "Make the most of those short years. What I mean is have all the babies. You and Edward would make the most adorable children."

And with that, Time became the auntie I hadn't met yet.

36

Ward

WARD CLUTCHED THE planner he had bought for Camille and waited for her outside the antique shop. He was vibrating with emotions like a shaken soda can. He felt like he hadn't seen her in years, yet they had been together, at the coffee shop, then in her hotel room yesterday. Every atom in his body oscillated in anticipation of seeing her combined with the fear of losing her. The maelstrom of warring emotions spilled over, making him jittery.

He was the human equivalent of a bottle rocket ready to explode.

Camille pulled her rolling luggage behind her. He'd never seen a more beautiful sight. Darkness crept at the edge of his vision until he almost passed out. Every sensation screamed from his pores.

"Ward!" She dropped the handle and ran toward him, into his open arms.

She bathed his face with kisses. Her voice was breathless. "Why do I feel like it's been too long since I last saw you?"

"I feel the same way. There's so much I want to . . ." He cupped her face and kissed her with all the pent-up passion shrieking through his system. She moaned and then pulled away, breathless. "Can't . . . do this here, though I want to."

They pressed their foreheads together. She braced her hands against his chest. His heartbeat thundered under her fingertips. "Why don't we go back to my hotel room, stay in for a week, and order in? Is this crazy, because all I want to do is fuck you until we're both Jell-O."

Camille laughed. The clear, husky sound was the sexiest thing he'd ever heard. "Then why don't we grab a black cab? There's nothing I want more than being naked with you for an entire week."

He pulled her in front of him to conceal his arousal as he flagged one down.

THEY KISSED IN the elevator with their hands in places that he was certain would make the security room blush. He barely had the motor skills to slide the key card in the lock. Camille had her hand down his pants and was kissing his neck.

"Woman, unless you want me to take you in the hallway, give me some grace and let me get it in the slot."

She squeezed him. "That's the whole point, isn't it? Sliding it in."

He groaned. "You're pushing me to the edge. I'm not going to—"

"You won't." Camille used her free hand to jam the key card in and open the door. "Besides, I need you inside me. Don't make me beg."

Ward almost tossed her luggage inside as they tumbled through the doorway. The heavy door locked behind them.

What happened next was making up for the prolonged absence. Physical relief in the form of multiple orgasms was what they wanted, and afterward, love rose to the surface—far more clear than it had been since it appeared the first time.

THEY ORDERED A giant sushi platter after three more rounds of stimulating physical intercourse. Once their brains returned to full function, they fell into a pattern of domesticated bliss.

Camille created a cozy nest on the bed. She tied up her hair in a loose bun and was browsing the menu of a nearby vegetarian curry spot on her laptop.

"So, I've been thinking." He picked out all the toro nigiri, her favorites, and put them on her plate. "We don't have to be in London per se. I'm going to expand my job search further into Europe if you're open to it. I contacted a local headhunter. I'm sure she can line up a few interviews in the coming weeks."

"I've also submitted for a few positions around the city. Too bad our initial job prospects didn't pan out." She sipped champagne from a nearby flute. They had ordered the bottle between rounds one and two. "London should be doable if we can find a flat here to rent with our combined incomes. No need for a car yet, we can take transit until we figure out if we need one. As for the work visas, we can handle that."

"We're doing this then? Permanent move together?"

She grinned. "Hell yes. We're both ready for this. I want to be with you, and I'm not running away this time." Camille lowered her eyes. "Our time apart. I was miserable and got into an unhealthy cycle of overworking. I did everything I could to get rid of the pain of losing you. I know I'm stubborn and can be difficult. I . . ."

He took her hands in his and squeezed them. "You're the most incredible person I've ever met. You're driven and you shouldn't fucking apologize for that. I always feel like the luckiest bastard that you've chosen me. It's going to be a challenge to keep up with you, but I'm up to it."

"I never thought that you weren't good enough. I'm sorry if that's what you thought."

"I did at one point. When we broke up, I felt my world crash. I drifted through everything, going through the motions. I left Chicago because it was easier for me. Everywhere I looked, I saw you and where you should be. It hurt too much to stay. I went to LA thinking it would fill the void you left. It hasn't. I'm sorry that I didn't take the more difficult road, that I took the easy way out when it was available. I don't want to do that anymore—not for myself, for you, or for us."

Camille leaned in and kissed him. "I love you. It's going to work this time."

"Optimism from you? I thought that was my job."

"You're not monopolizing internal growth here. I can be chipper. It doesn't feel natural now, but the more I do it, the better I'll feel." She stretched like a cat, naked and languid in her movements. "I'm prescribing myself more fun in the future, which is where you fit in. You're kind of important in that formula."

"How so?" He dragged a fingertip along her bare thigh. "What does this future full of fun mean exactly?"

She playfully swatted his hand away. "I can't think when you do that. More trips, less work. Better balance with life. See more of the world. I want to dislodge this horrible feeling of being trapped. I can't explain it. It's like . . . what we have here isn't related. We chose this. I guess it's like having this gushing geyser of feels. I have so much of it. Is this weird?"

"No. I'm going to say the same thing. It's all genuine. It's how I feel about you, but dialed up to the extreme."

"Yes, that's it. I can't ignore anything I'm feeling right now about you and about us. I'd like to think of it as some sort of emotional revelation. Sometimes, we think too much and ignore what our heart is saying."

"And hello to the sexy philosopher I know well." She purred and moved her laptop to the nightstand. "And what is your heart whispering to you now?"

"That I want to spend the rest of my life with you, that even then, it wouldn't be long enough. That being apart hurt like hell and I never want to do that again. That I'm thinking a week might not be long enough to get our urges out. That growing old with you will be a grand adventure."

She blushed at his confession and kissed his cheek. She tipped his chin and studied his face. "I think you'll be hotter when you get old. A veritable silver fox. Aging like a well-researched dividend fund."

"I guess it's better than shitty cryptocurrency."

Camille smacked his arm with a pillow. "Anything is better than that."

"Eat up." He pushed the plate of toro nigiri toward her. "I need you to recover your stamina."

Ward grabbed his own loaded plate and popped a spicy

spider roll into his mouth. She crinkled her nose at him and blew a kiss before attacking her sushi.

"You're staring again. Do I have rice on my face or something?" She poked his shoulder.

"Nope. Don't mind me, I'm just sitting here grateful for all this."

"Ah, is that what that is then?"

"Yeah. I'm lucky. I get a new start in this city with my career and you're with me. Everything's fantastic. Should I start worrying that something will crop up to sidetrack it all?"

"I'm the pessimist, not you. We're both on the same page now. There isn't anything left unsaid. We've always operated on love. This time, we have everything else going for us and we're planning ahead. It's no longer that thing we won't talk about. Before, I think we avoided it because we thought it would break us up, and yeah, it kind of did."

"And where do you want to go from here?"

"After a week here, we can think about the adulting stuff. It's not going anywhere." Camille placed her empty plate on the floor. "Live in the moment and not let it pass you by. New personal motto in addition to the fun."

"Any more new, exciting changes I should know about?"

She licked her lips. "Well, for starters . . ."

"Thank goodness I'm recharged then." He pushed his empty plate toward the nightstand before leaning back against the bed's upholstered headrest.

Camille straddled his hips. She ran her fingers across his lips. "So we're clear. This time, I won't say no if you ask."

Before they broke up, Ward had intended to propose. She found out about it ahead of time and confessed that she wouldn't go through with it because of the massive issues she saw them having. He was going to use his mother's ring, and knowing this now, it would have been a bad idea. Camille would want to go shopping with him to pick something out for herself.

"There's a jewelry store down the street. Maybe after we're done here, you can see if there's anything sparkly there that you want on your finger." He brushed a loose strand of dark hair away from her eyes. "Camille Maria Teresa Buhay, will you marry me?"

"Yes!" she squealed before kissing him.

Epilogue

~⚜~

Camille

. . . . .

A week and a half later

. . . . .

WE SAID IT would take a week, and it took us a week and a half before emerging from Ward's hotel room. We had both forgotten what civilization was like.

"Ugh, clothes." Ward made a face as he watched me pull a short jersey dress over my head. "Naked is better."

I slipped into black heels. "It was fun while it lasted. Where is the place you booked brunch?"

He told me about the hotel's penthouse café on the way out of the suite. "Better to rejoin humanity one small step at a time," he reasoned.

Ward's golden hair caught the sunlight streaming in from the glass walls along the corridor leading to the restaurant's lobby. A short stubble shadowed his jaw and chin. I had asked him to keep it. It was ever so useful in certain erotic situations. This man was gorgeous and he was all *mine*.

The busy café was crowded. All of the tables were full, and the few that weren't sported cards labeled RESERVED. Thank goodness I made a reservation last night. We were ushered to our spot beside an elderly couple. The man was dashing, with snowy white hair, and his partner, a very stylish Asian auntie. I acknowledged them with a nod as Ward and I took our seats.

"You need to lay off the sweets," she chided as her partner lifted a sugary sprinkled palmier to his mouth. "I swear, your sweet tooth is notorious."

He picked up her hand and kissed it. "Isn't that why you love me? Because I'm so sweet?"

The lady giggled and blushed.

They were too cute. I signaled Ward with my eyes. He made a small nod of approval before skimming the menu and asking aloud, "What should I get? The lobster eggs Benedict or the traditional English breakfast?"

"You're American, aren't you?" the gentleman asked him. "If you are, go with the eggs Benny."

Ward introduced us to them. "Ah, thank you. I'm Ward, and this is my soon-to-be-wife, Camille."

The stranger grinned. Genuine pleasure sparkled in his blue eyes. "Samson Smith, and this is my wife, Selene."

Selene and I nodded toward each other and exchanged hellos.

"Congrats on the impending nuptials. What brings you two to London? Vacation?" She scooted closer.

I replied, "Work. We're both moving here and hope to build our careers and the rest of our lives in Europe."

"We're here on vacation. Selene insists that I follow through with my promise to travel around the world. We've made our way across Asia and the Americas already. Europe is the latest continent we're exploring, and we're starting here." Samson turned to Ward. "Make sure that when you make a promise to her, you make good on it. Doesn't matter if it's big or small."

Selene gazed at her husband with starlight in her eyes. "We've been married for forty years. He tends to brag to anyone who will listen."

"It's very sweet." I took Ward's hand in mine across the table. "You two are inspiring."

Samson laughed and then turned to his wife. "Now we are. We had our rough patches. Marriage is never boring for us. She is my light. I can't imagine my life without her."

"It's how I feel about Camille." Ward gave me a grin that wobbled my knees. "I love her, and thinking about having decades with her is the best feeling."

A handsome Asian man in his late thirties or early forties walked toward our tables. He wore a black suit with a bright red silk dress shirt. He stopped by the married couple. "Mr. and Mrs. Smith, your limo is waiting for the airport. I've already had your luggage transferred."

Samson folded his napkin and placed it on the table. "Thank you, Mr. King."

Mr. King offered his arm to Selene and helped her to her feet.

"It was wonderful to meet you both." I waved goodbye.

After a brief set of farewells, the three walked away toward the exit.

"Do you want that?" Ward tipped his head toward them. "The whole 'travel around the world in our twilight years'?"

The idea that we would entertain a similar lengthy trip later in life was wonderful. Experiencing everything for the first time with him would be delightful. It'd be the best reward after decades of marriage. My parents went back to the Philippines and did an Asian tour for their thirtieth anniversary. They came back refreshed and giggling like teenagers.

"Yes! Look at them. Those are goals." I settled the lavender cloth napkin over my lap. "They are so damned adorable that my teeth hurt."

"Then it's done, it's a promise."

A brave and very frivolous idea crept into my brain. I called it inspiration. "So, how about we take a trip to Paris for a week? I mean, we'll start our jobs right after. It'll give us time to set up interviews for when we get back. I've never been to Paris and I want to see the city."

Ward's sudden flash of confusion was replaced by a wide smile. "You're serious about this. What about the whole 'getting our careers on track ASAP'?"

I didn't blame him for his skepticism. I was a renowned workaholic after all. But we were both in between jobs, and this was the perfect time to do this.

"We'll do that eventually. I'm not saying I'm giving it up. I think that this detour feels right," I reasoned. "It'll be a week. We can walk Montmartre and visit the Musée d'Orsay. If we plan it right, we can even go to Monet's house and garden in Giverny. We'll get to see all the art. Can you imagine standing for hours admiring Monet's waterlilies at the Musée de l'Orangerie in person? Think of the art, Ward."

"You're supposed to say, 'Think of the children.'" He leaned back and chuckled.

"Fine. Our future children. Sure, why not?"

A server approached our table. "You can order anything

you wish. Mr. Dunbar and Ms. Buhay, your table has been paid for as well as your hotel reservation."

No one else we knew had that kind of cash on hand, unless . . . I turned to Ward. "Is this from your family?"

"Oh no, it's from Mr. King. I believe he stopped by your table earlier. The generous gentleman paid for your bill in full. Please enjoy your meal." The server made a slight bow before making his retreat.

"Do you know Mr. King?"

"No, never met the man."

"Me neither."

Ward patted my arm. "Sometimes these things happen. He might be making up for something. Acts of kindness are a thing. People, in general, are inherently good."

"All right then. Might as well order the sevruga caviar I've been eyeing on the menu."

Life was good, and I was going to enjoy every damned minute of it.

Acknowledgments

Fantasy has always been a love of mine, and when my incredible editor, Cindy Hwang, was open to my fantasy pitch, I was thrilled to pivot into a genre I've always wanted to write. I can't thank her enough for her support and my incredible team (Angela Kim, Tara O'Connor, Anika Bates, Samantha Felty, Megan Elmore, Angelina Krahn, Jennifer Sale, Hannah Gramson, Adam Auerbach, and Katie Anderson).

Jenny Bent is my longtime agent and champion advocate. I'm so lucky to work with her and the fabulous team at TBA. To Mary Pender, my film agent, I still remember the walk through Little Italy. Thank you for being so awesome.

To my family, whose support made it possible for me to write and weave words with my keyboard. You provide me fuel through yummy foods as rewards, and your love sustains me.

To my wonderful coven of friends: Helen Hoang, Suzanne Park, Mike Lasagna, Annette Christie, Sonia Hartl, Kellye Garrett, Sam Bohrman, Farah Heron, RM Romero, Judy Lin, Nafiza Azad, Victoria Chiu, Jamie Pacton, and Bethany Robison.

Your camaraderie, texts, and bright presence in my life make it fuller. I appreciate every morsel of interaction because modern technology makes it possible to connect the long distances between us.

A special shout-out to Andria Bancheri-Lewis, Hannah Pyo, and Rina Tjoa, for being extra special beta readers and reading an early copy of this novel. These three are amazing escape room enthusiasts and the perfect audience for Camille and Ward's story.

I must thank two special local friends who helped make my novels possible. To Catherine, the owner of Firefly & Fox Books, whose support and presence in the county is much appreciated, and Joy of Joy's Bakery, whose cheddar scones are absolutely divine and spectacular.

Author photo by Shelley Smith

ROSELLE LIM is a Filipino Chinese writer living on the north shore of Lake Erie. She loves to write about food and magic. When she isn't writing, she is sewing, sketching, or pursuing the next craft project.

VISIT ROSELLE LIM ONLINE

RoselleLim.com

🐦 RoselleWriter